WHAT DOES THE DAWN BREAK?

Walden Shock

© Mark D. Robbins

Cover Design/Art

© Jack Wylder

Hydrogen Rodeo LLC

P.O. Box 1369

Kingsland, Texas 78639

https://**H2rodeo.com**

Acknowledgements

There are so many that have helped on this project but as the book itself hints, it is better to not be named. It has come to that.

My family, of course, I owe them everything.

My friends who listened patiently while I poured out nonsensical things. I really appreciate your patience.

My initial readers helping me to refine the story: JB, BF, DR. Thank you so very much for taking the time. Your input was golden.

The United States of America. The place where our rights are recognized as coming from God. I am so blessed to have been born here.

Introduction

The energy has shifted. The robots and artificial intelligence that are coming our way are no longer the things of science fiction pulp. Robot home vacuums, robot lawn maintainers, and police drones are opposite ends of the same thing. The new world is coming. And quickly. How is our humanity going to be integrated in the world when the Singularity arrives?

Our Eminent Destiny ^{TM} in a new age has rarely been envisioned as the warm, inviting place that has forever been planned for us.

NOW it has!

Voyage of Discovery

By Veronica Soyars

To you, America – vast above all
—

One, amongst the many who have
answered your call.

Your spell I came to see, to hear,
to understand

What lured…as to the promised
land.

Each and every one of your
assorted band.

Like me, they came from near and far,

Came and found beauty that time could not mar.

Came and found freedom and liberty for all.

But to each, and uniquely his own,

Came and found America was, above all, home.

1.

I'd put the five gallon plastic bucket up against the tin-covered blind as quietly as I could. It was, after all, a half hour before you could discern anything with a good scope, which was forty minutes late for my normal morning hunt. Leaning down to enter through the low door, my head lamp cleared the 2x4 when I heard the scream, and then saw stars. Lots of them. Feeling myself falling, I instinctively reached around to my left side shoulder holster to protect my Encore handgun's scope. In a second I was face down in the leaves and debris covering the carpet at the bottom of the blind. It is easy to get disoriented in a starry blackness.

There are times when a cry you hear outside your body actually did come from within. I was sure it wasn't me until I realized it was once I hit the floor. I'd gotten to my blind late after putting out the other hunters, who needed some hand-holding to get organized. I'd rushed through feeding what I called my "trophy feed" where I walked dried corn in rays out from the blind for 300 yards, up next to trees, and down narrow senderos. If you looked at the blind from above, there were five long rays of corn waiting for a trophy whitetail to intersect the deliciousness. The morning was crisp enough in the Texas Hill Country so there was no way a hungry, cold deer would pass it without taking a nibble. Fed this way, you had the capability of dozens of deer eating peacefully and not fighting over the food. That's why I called it deer shopping instead of hunting.

The combination of the tin rattling at the strike of my head, and the too loud cry of pain, led to some of the deer blowing an alarm and, I knew, scampering off. They didn't repeatedly blow, which was a good sign. It was a good sign, too, that they'd already found the corn before I got to the blind, but a wary, mature buck, the only kind that lived through November in this area, might not show himself now that I'd banged the drum announcing my presence.

I crawled into the blind after wiping off the hard, long dead oak leaves pressed into my face. Reaching behind me, I closed the door and stayed on my knees for some minutes to catch my breath and rock back and forth, holding the wet place on the top of my head. It was going to be a good one. The exposed finger tips of the shooting glove on my right hand felt around the dent in my bald head and I figured it wouldn't need stitches, more of a mash up than a cut, but it was going to be an interesting scab for sure. Yet another character scar on the shiny pate.

After a couple of minutes, I'd carefully worked myself into the old, swiveling, office chair. The bleeding seemed to have stopped, and I was almost set. It was still dark and the gray of the coming dawn had not started leaking over Donner Mountain.

Mountain … that set some to laughing at naming a tall hill like that.

I tested the swivel of the chair a little, to make sure that I wasn't going to be surprised by a squeak, giving away my presence if I did decide to shoot and needed to reposition a bit. My Thompson-Center Encore handgun was in my lap. I was sure glad I had it in that shoulder holster under my left arm or I probably would have banged it's scope on my trip to the ground. Probably. Surely. I hadn't been able to keep my face out of the dirt! I loaded one of the 7mm-08 Remington handloads that I'd brought.

This was supposed to be the day. New load, a good trophy feed out on the hillside, and early enough in the season where there was a good chance a quality buck could cross my sights. Now my head banging, tin rattling arrival had alerted every deer in the area that I was here, and the fact that I did hit the ground hard gave me a little pause about whether the scope might have been affected, even if it was protected under my arm. My neck sure was. I was not going to be taking any iffy long shots today unless I got to prove it up close first. Of course, that was a pretty hard strike to my brain and my judgment might also be dimmed. Surely.

I took up my waiting routine. With the Encore on my lap I closed my eyes, steadied my breathing, and counted my breaths until I got to 50, then I'd open my eyes and check the light. With nothing to concentrate on but your breath and your ears you gathered up what you could hear from your surroundings. As soon as photons began bouncing over the hill, I'd start scanning the corn rays for prey. It was the fifth pass, when I could actually start making out some landscape. I pulled up my scope to test; it was still too early. By the eighth breath pass, I was glassing with my binoculars.

It wasn't really a surprise that there were a dozen does and spikes over the hillside, head down on the corn. This area of Texas is where there are deer like rabbits, and not much bigger either. Because they could each find their place on some corn line, there wasn't any fighting, just heavy feeding to start the day off.

The closest three does and two yearlings were following the corn up to the blind slowly, and they were already within the 50 yard line. The fat dry doe might be freezer meat today, but I wasn't going to shoot unless I heard one of the other hunters shoot. I'd been hunting on this family place for decades, and had carved the hunting senderos out by hand. I knew it so well, I could normally feed out the corn lines with no light, if there was some moon. I'd walked over every rock and by every tree hundreds of times. I knew exactly where placing a few kernels of corn would make a shot, or hide one. Even the threat of a stick in the eye was almost nil, because I walked every sendero before the season trimming any twig that might make a bullet fly off.

When I put new people out they always asked me what I thought would be the best blind. Because, for sure, I would know a deer's mind when there were five hunters out surrounded by bright yellow, delicious rays of corn. As sure as the sun was coming up, the fact that I was sitting in the "Hot Spot" blind would be a point of gentle contention if I was the only one to bring back some venison. Even though, the "Flat Patch" and the "Sanctuary" had been seeing Axis deer and I thought they'd have a better experience there.

This is such a great ranch in the Hill Country: three running creeks, hilly terrain to separate the hunters from each other, and high-fenced ranches down the road where the fancy stock escaped with some regularity. Axis deer are now a regular feature of our region and our hunts, and they don't have a regulated season. They are part of the environment now and much better eating than the whitetails. We didn't lease the place because we didn't need the money and we only took friends, or friends of friends, hunting. Letting some newbie come out and shoot their first deer, a big Axis buck with 4 foot tall antlers, generates a smile and a story that lasts a lifetime. I live for those days.

Today, I was hoping to see something like that myself, but it was a pretty rough start. The odds had slid, and not in my favor. Because the does were getting close enough now to see into the blind, I just scanned without moving my head unless they were all head down on the corn. Looking across the hillside, easily shootable now with the sun brightening the top of the hill, it was getting to be hard to count all the deer. My father-in-law had once said he counted over fifty deer at the "Flat Patch" one morning. Most people scoffed but I've seen those kind of days. Deer shopping.

Looking into the sendero of one of my favorite shots, I saw the ass end of what might be a large Axis deer. A reddish hue of the fur, barely visible at 175 yards in the dim light, was the hint. If you want to be successful, you have to be prepared, so I thought I'd start moving my Encore onto the ledge of the blind and scope it some. You have to be ready to take advantage of opportunity. Having a doe so close to the blind meant I was moving into position like molasses and whenever they looked up I froze until they looked away.

This major hurdle, setting the forend of the handgun on the ledge of the window without banging it, now completed, allowed me to relax a little. Nothing disturbed. Move in behind the scope and -

"Bong!"

My phone sounded the Liberty Bell.

I froze in place as every eye on the hillside looked in my direction.

Oh sure! I'd forgotten to silence my phone. That just reinforces that there are lingering effects from a Jack Daniel's night, and following that with a 2x4 a-lerting, ensures a detrimental impact on a person's brain. This was all so ... fiddle!

Wow ... I actually used the word my Dad

had substituted for the F word. It made me proud that it had come to my mind. For a second. At least I didn't punctuate the phone tone with even more loud verbalized frustration, conscious or no.

The hunting situation had taken a seriously negative turn. All of the more mature deer were leaving in a hurry with their whitetails flagging in the air. The younger ones had run off a few yards and were all looking directly at me across their backs wondering if that bell really did require them to leave breakfast. Of course, the potential target was nowhere to be seen now.

Still as a statue from the level of the edge of the blind window and above, I reached over and silenced my phone. Looking at the text message completely froze me.

unknown 06:42: "Port A swan, what's up?"

I completely forgot what I was doing and grabbed the phone. All but the most ignorant soon-to-be venison headed out when they saw my head move.

"Port A swan" was a term I hadn't heard in … what … forty years? I just sat there staring at the phone in my hand completely forgetting about why I was sitting in this tin box in a chill

Texas dawn.

Holy Moses! The memories engulfed me like an August dust storm. There were good and there was bad. There was so much. So very much. Could it really be forty years since my best friend and I had communicated? The heat and grit of it made me catch my breath.

In our youth we'd been inseparable. 'JJ' was known by all as a reference to Jack and Jeremy. Every day we were into adventures of one kind or another, from the time we were in fifth grade until I decided it was too dangerous our first year of college to hang with Jeremy. The nickname he always preferred was 'Jem', like a rare and beautiful gem, he thought, but I always called him Jam, because he had a talent for finding them. Of course, I'd always been right there offering support instead of looking at the issue at hand with a little common sense. I guess more accurately then, we had a talent for finding ourselves in jam. This is the reason why I know, without a doubt, that good sense is *not* nearly so common.

As young boys with BB guns we'd played mountain man out in the vacant lots and fields and those images littered my memories. Hunting any type of bird and grilling them over a small fire, or boiling them in an old can we'd found that would still hold water from our canteen, without any seasoning, was routine. It was a schedule we kept for many years, enhanced by the knowledge we got in Boy Scouts, which led to better stews with wild onions and bitter sorrel.

His 'Jam' nickname originated from his idea to shoot dove off a neighbor lady's bird feeder. We were excellent at stalking and harvesting her feeder. The part we never perfected was running over to gather up our limit when she wasn't looking. That went on for years. Imagine how it would proceed today! I'm betting there's plenty that would be happy to have minors in prison for shooting doves off a neighbor's bird feeder. For most people today, it seems more punish-worthy than jumping the border. One is likely a felony.

So we had adventures. When we got our driver's licenses we had more and of a type with a quantum more jam. Sneaking girls out of their houses at 1 a.m., in Texas, can be life threatening. Especially back then, when one face is black. Drag racing at Green Valley out in Bexar county was a howling good time. We rode jackpot rodeos as a traveling team when we both sucked. Why? No sense, especially the common. There was much, so deep and warm, so many memories that I wanted to call him back immediately.

And then I started thinking about why we hadn't communicated through all those years. Jam was driving late one night and all of a sudden I realized he wasn't going to stop as we came up to a four lane road. It was screams of *"Stop!"* outside the body, as images of fresh, bloody sausage filled my mind as we shot through the intersection. It being 2 A.M., there wasn't much traffic in Alamo Heights, but especially on Vandiver. The adrenaline high was amazing. Better than straddling a bucking bull. This was real, and very serious; a life threatening risk and we'd lived.

I was screaming at him about how stupid it was but we were both laughing the relief of those missed by a bullet. After another beer, a toke on a joint, then he let another stop sign flash by on a busier road. This time we ran right in front of a car close enough that I could see the lady's expression. We weren't 20 feet from her and she didn't even have time to apply her brakes, but her eyes transformed into pie plates.

This time I started yelling at him about how he didn't have the right to expend my life on some stupid, childish, ignorant, maximum risk of death stunt. He laughed the entire time until I started punching him on his right shoulder to try and get him to at least recognize my view.

By the third punch, a real one, he'd stopped the car, and on my opening the door, his boot helped me onto North Saint Mary's Street. Not the place to be at zero dark thirty back then.

Cursing him as I got up, I turned and got half the "N" word out before I caught the flinch in his eyes. The tires were squealing down the road as I finished speaking. We never really spoke again.

We'd see each other from time to time and just nod. At parties, we might exchange some small talk. The thread of our relationship had been totally burned, in my mind, because I demanded the right to direct how my life got used up. It's nobody's but mine to spend it as I see fit, and the fact that he didn't understand that was an endpoint. Looking back now it's weird to think that 30 seconds of yelling had such a devastating effect ... almost. I was proud of myself for rejecting someone that thought they could borrow my life with no ability to make good on the loan. It was a lesson I learned even though it left an empty place for years.

The best part about that kind of incident is that it breaks through *The First*. Once you pass the first, you become better at handling incidents and being aware of something like it starting your way. Hopefully, you then have

18

enough common sense to not become enmeshed in something like that again.

So here it was, the memory of the "Port A swan" thrown up. How many times had that story been told? How many times can you test the boundaries of common sense and survive? I know I've surpassed several people's quotas.

The swan was born on a road trip we took to Port Aransas one summer. We were invited to share a condo with a friend and her father, whom we liked (it was mutual I think), and were going to stay for a week. Her father went fishing all day long trusting his daughter with us. Common sense? I think we were seventeen. The age at which you really start to learn about holding your liquor ... not. The old man was always so exhausted from fishing he'd turn in early. We'd tell him we were going down to the pier to fish at night.

"Ok," he'd say, "just watch out." Then he'd roll over into a coma till 5 A.M. when the fishing started again.

We didn't turn in early. It was always easy for her to smile at some customer at the liquor store and get us a pint of something new. It wasn't even a challenge. One night we'd been drinking tequila and were walking down Horace Caldwell pier and had reached the end.

"I think it'd be fun to swim back in." the

tequila said.

"*No*, dumbass!" Jam said.

"That's crazy! You're so drunk!" Sandy reiterated, accenting it with a slap to the back of my head.

The tequila had been shamed into admitting that it probably was a crazy idea. We started heading back in but the tequila kept arguing with himself until he just ran and jumped over the railing doing a perfect swan dive into the surf. Like this morning, there is a moment before the stars where you realize something ain't right. That millisecond before you realize what's going on can be full of lots of words in your head, like,'I should have paid attention to how far back we'd walked'. A hard jam onto the tequila head, and stars, then being shaken by the waves. At my first conscious breath of sea water, I stood up! *Holy crap*! How stupid is that?

Jam and Sandy ran down the pier and helped me out of the water. I was stumbling back to shore when they grabbed me.

"Holy crap," Jam said, "even your hard head can get broke!"

With a friend under each arm I was helped back to the beach. I just laid where they dropped me. They were on each side of me, head to head, passing the tequila across me until it was gone. I'd had enough for sure and they knew it. We laughed long past the end of the tequila. My consciousness was filled with giving thanks that I could feel the sand under my ass, wiggle my toes, and all I had was a sore neck.

That story was a common request at parties. It is a funny story but it would have been totally different if I had ended up in traction forever. When you're young, alcohol stories can be funny. If you live. If you're whole afterward. As you age, the stories lose their sparkle until they are only dark. The odds are troublesome. Many friends did not pass through their swan dives.

unknown 06:56: "whatchadoing?"

Jack 06:57: "sitting in a blind"

unknown 06:57: "so you're still dangerous?"

Are sixty year olds ever dangerous? I guess there might be a few, but that is a select population. We are at the top part of the ladder that's for sure. I should be asking him that! The flush of wanting was still there so I decided to be nice.

Jack 07:04: "duh. You?"

unknown 07:04: "I need you to see something"

I looked up from my phone distraction to see that nine deer, yearlings and doe, were already back on the corn. I always told people that a serious hunter watching out in the woods sent *hunter energy* out that the deer could sense. I hadn't been paying attention. A story my father-in-law told was about a still drunk Houston hunter, known for his snoring and his pony tail, who fell asleep in the blind. A deer was so intrigued by that loud pony tail that it walked up, grabbed a hold of it, and wouldn't let go even though he was yelling! He ended up shooting the roof off the blind! Since I had been totally distracted, not sending any hunter energy, this bunch of doe had came right back in.

I started being slow and careful of my movements again.

Jack 07:10: "what"

unknown 07:11: "a 'community' near Sanderson"

A community. Of course that brought thoughts rushing. Drunks, or pot heads, always run their mouth about how they would change things. Endless hours of loud nothingness that never goes anywhere. We'd had those types of discussions.

"When they make me King I'd ... ," Jam would say. When he puffed up and strutted around the fire, I could believe in the black king, too. That really made his eyes sparkle.

It got to where that was the announcement of the game's restart.

"If you were King" always led to strange and crazy ideas being discussed. Over time, we'd actually started calling it *our community* because it had been built on layers and gallons and pounds of previous enhanced discussion. Once we had something agreed, it became an acknowledged part of the community, not susceptible to change until there was a vote. This sounded like it might be more than crazy talk.

Jack 07:12: "community?"

unknown 07:12: "you WILL love it. We need you NOW!"

Jack 07:16: "I'm busy with hunters"

unknown 07:16: "we'll have fun. It'll be GREAT!"

Jack 07:17: "ok. Where?"

I really did just leap at it.

unknown 07:18: "Between Fort Stockton and Sanderson, GPS attached"

He'd sent a Google Earth tab. It looked like some big mesa country out in the middle of nowhere. Nothing at all community-looking, but his invitation already had me.

unknown 07:25: "I haven't had a drink or anything in 12 years"

Now that one really had me. I still drank,

not like in the old days, swear, but the thought of Jam not drinking was almost unbelievable. I had to see this.

Jack 07:27: "I can be there Tuesday maybe"

unknown 07:27: "Text me when you hit Fort Stockton. I'll meet you on the road and bring you in."

Jack 07:29: "ok Later"

I put the phone down quietly, to check all the deer that were now back on the corn. The closest one was about 80 yards away so I brought up my binoculars and started glassing the hillside. My mind was racing so my concentration was a little fractured. He doesn't drink any more?

After I'd checked out three of the corn rays, the deer all suddenly started looking off to the west. This was a pretty sure sign a herd of feral hogs, axis deer, or the Big One was about to make an appearance. Some of the doe were nervously stamping their front feet on the ground but they didn't blow. Slowly turning I saw what the issue was. I could see young Angora goats up in trees before the main herd crossed the rise. Oh yeah, that Jack Daniels brain rushing to get to the blind left a gate open and the goats got loose. This hunt is over.

As I watched the goats come up the hill with their own type of bleet and blow, the deer all wandered off. I'm pretty sure I know why. The goats blow so often that it makes the deer think there's an issue, they sound somewhat like a deer blowing, so deer can't ever relax around them. Certainly the goats don't scare them.

So this was the end of this hunt, watching the goats trot up the hill. I knew exactly what to expect. All of them would come up to the corn and vacuum it up in minutes. There were about 150 of them walking in mostly single file. On the way, if a goat took a bite of weed or even cedar, every goat after it would have to taste it, too. It would tend to evaporate as they passed.

When the main herd had passed onto the top of the hill, those in the trees started trying to come down and I heard one cry as it hit the ground. They weren't often hurt, but it happened. Goats are one of the types of animals that can be very fragile. Hair goat, Angora, ranchers always say they are born then go around looking for a place to die.

And they're hard to fence in. It was always easy for someone to get your goat. My uncle used to say if you took three goats and welded each one into a 55-gallon drum and opened the barrels the next day, the first would have screw worms, the second would be dead, and the third one would be gone! That's a true story there, ya know?

They were making their way up the hill when the lead goat stopped in its tracks and all the others started circling around. I had a good idea of what was happening because I'd seen it before. There was a snake on the ground and they were about to stomp it.

As I watched, the older goats began the dance by taking a high hop, holding all four of their feet together, and coming right down on the snake. Those sharp hooves in such a compact area with a gravity assist were deadly. As soon as they hit the ground they sprung off. One after the other, the snake dance would continue until the reptile was lifeless. They knew that if it was moving it wasn't dead. As soon as it quit moving, and it had been inspected by the important leaders, they came on up to the blind and started working the corn.

I've never interrupted them when they were

mashing a snake into the dirt, but I always wondered if their aim was good and where the first shot went. By the time I got to it, the snake always looked like it had been run through a commercial meat tenderizer. If you know animals at all, you know they can put the bite or kick exactly where they want it, so I always wondered if they bounced off the snake's head on the first round.

What a strange day. Old snakes now sober, real snakes, and the introduction of a chance to visit old dreams. It helped take my mind off the throbbing in my head.

After holstering my Encore, I unloaded myself from the blind. Being careful to duck completely this time, I headed back to the cabin to wait for the other hunters to call me to fetch 'em in. I had plenty of memories to replay. There was some pondering that needed to be done, too.

2.

When I woke on Monday morning it felt like a different kind of day. The air felt fresher and lighter in my lungs, the light clearer. None of the hunters at the ranch had bagged anything, or even seen anything like I had, but this day was fresh and bright and pretty cold for early November Hill Country. No disappointment for being skunked, my head mash had crusted over and quit throbbing, and I was looking forward to this new adventure.

When I had my first cup of coffee as the sun rose, it was a very still 38 degrees. Now two hours later, it was already over 50. Without checking the weather radar site, it was obvious to me that the day might warm up to the mid 60's. The thought of heading out to West Texas was starting to excite me almost as much as the thought of seeing my old friend, Jam, again. A spirit that was really close, then not, brands a place on your heart.

Everybody knows about meeting up with a long lost friend and it being like no time at all had passed. I was hoping for that with all my heart. I'd spent some time in a bourbon nap last night pondering where this was leading, but hadn't settled on anything. I was as excited as Christmas and at the same time dreading it like a root canal.

Amanda, my lovely wife, rushed by, grabbed a cup of coffee, kissed me and headed out the door.

"Late for a hair appointment!" she shouted over her shoulder as she headed to the garage. "Then some errands, back by noon."

I'd made up my mind I would go, I think, but still hadn't told Mandy. There were things to consider. I didn't have any hunters coming out to the ranch until Friday and I should keep them informed if there were a change in plans. The obvious burst upon me. It was likely that mule deer season in Pecos county might have a few days left in it.

Jack 09:45: "dude ... there any hunting out there?"

Jeremy 09:47: "Oh yeah, big muleys fed fat, hogs"

Jeremy 09:47: "I can tie one to a tree if you're too old to shoot

straight"

Jack 09:53: "cute. Can I bring my wife, daughter and her husband? All shooters."

Jeremy 09:55: "Sure. Setting up two rooms right now."

Jack 09:59: "thanks looking forward to it"

Jack 10:02: "I'll text you when we get away tomorrow"

Jeremy 10:03: "and when you get to Fort Stockton"

Jack 10:07: "sure thing"

This was great. Being able to bundle a hunt for my family at the same time really wrapped the decision in bows. Of course I didn't ask him how much it would cost if we shot a nice muley. I guess I was maybe trusting an old friendship that hadn't had any life for decades. It just felt right, but if there was a fee, I could afford a couple of nice ones. The check for a decent buck started going up fast from $1500 now a days. I set about organizing the group by texting *the* daughter.

Jack 10:15: "Hey sugar, can y'all make a quick trip to Fort Stockton for a muley hunt"

Aisley 10:17: "Sure, Dad, Bear is working at home all week, too. When?"

Jack 10:19: "Let's get off tomorrow early-ish. At least one night, not three?"

Aisley 10:20: "Packing NOW. Bringing 7-08, Bear's .300"

Jack 10:21: "works good"

Holy Moses. Guns. Duh. This was going to be painful sharing this with Mandy. I know she'll want to go but I'd had a custom rifle made for her and just got it back last week. My failure to load some ammo and sight in her rifle was why she wasn't out to the ranch with us last weekend. She was not about to hunt until her new gun was ready. And it was all my fault it wasn't ready. Some gift!

It was a beautiful piece of work she was waiting on. The rifle was a Ruger No. 1,[2] in stainless steel .308, lighter than her .308 Browning. I'd converted it to .338 Federal because she wanted to try something with more smackdown. Again stainless, with the heaviest barrel. This made it a pound or so heavier than her Browning. It also had a 24 inch barrel which she insisted on because, even though it was heavier, she said she didn't need to carry it if she could just reach out and touch them long distance. They'll be in heaven before the carcass hits the ground with this combo.

The forend and stock were clear mesquite. The stock was carved with basket-weave across the grip, and laced with climbing roses that really bloomed out as it went around to the butt of the stock. The forend was the same. I was especially happy with the outcome as we hadn't overdone it but the design was full and elegant, the buds and blooming roses almost alive. Holding the rifle was pleasurable as you felt the rose buds under your grip.

That heavy stainless barrel was truly a wonder now. I have a buddy that's installed a new 5-axis CNC robot milling machine [6] and so us two gun lovers aimed to test it. Thoroughly. I'd decided that instead of getting something like the typical fluted or helical fluted barrel, we'd take some weight off of it with some serious CNC milling exercise. We cut the climbing rose up the barrel and the relief was amazing. Closing my eyes I could feel the leaves and flowers climbing to the muzzle where they started a blooming encirclement. We'd burned up some tools perfecting it on stainless bar stock. Cleaning it might become an issue but it was worth it. Nobody had a rifle as unique or beautiful as my wife's. A rifle she couldn't shoot because I didn't have any ammo for her! Me again!

The thing that might save me was another friend who had a .338 Federal who'd moved on to some techy gun. We'd fired a couple of his spare rounds through the new rifle initially. That's what led me to getting Mandy's barrel ported to take some of the buck off it. That'd only left him 7 rounds in his supply. I was determined to beg for his remainders for this trip.

I was practicing in my mind how I was going to announce this opportunity when Mandy picked up the phone before I even heard it ring.

"Yes, sugar." she said in that sweet West Texas lilt. "I've got a moment, talk fast."

"Mandy, baby, I got an offer to go muley hunting out by Stockton tomorrow" but I didn't get to finish.

"Did you know about this yesterday?" she said with the lilt now sternly wilted.

"I had a hint but hadn't decided." I said but she was done listening.

"Hang on," she whispered in almost a hiss as I could hear her telling her compadres that she had to go outside.

"I HAVE THINGS HAPPENING THIS WEEK AND YOU'RE NOT CONSIDERING ME AGAIN!" she laid on me.

I have to say that I get this with some regularity because:
1) I'm insensitive to her life,
2) I'm unaware of how I affect other people, and
3)...?
I always forget number three. I'm definitely in a familiar place. There have been so many others. I guess it's good I have a poor memory or I might be depressed at my failures to account to my lady.

"Sugar, please, I hadn't decided until just a while ago." I pleaded. I was putting my best honey on the

36

line and hoping.

"How long are we going to be gone?" she said. Softening!

"For sure one night, not more than three." I replied trying to make sure I was sounding whipped.

"'Aisley and Bear are invited, too, and I texted them already." I blurted out without thinking. As soon as the words crossed my lips I knew I'd kicked the hive again.

"Oh, so I'm the last on your list? That's par!" she said just before the line went dead.

This hadn't gone as good as I'd hoped, but it could have been worse. There had definitely been some softening. *Muley* probably did it. I sometimes don't have a strategic sense. I don't really think I'm a narcissist but sometimes she paints me with it and it feels like it might be sticking.

Then a very pleasant text.

Amanda 10:40: "I'm shooting your .260"

That was a breath of fresh air. I don't even have to get into discussing her rifle. I'll just take it and hope that Lloyd still has those cartridges. You can't find .338 Federal at every Walmart.

Amanda 10:57: "bowing out hosting Wed morning Ladies Bible class, BLAMING YOUR INCONSIDERATE NATURE"

Amanda 10:57: "NOT ... psych!"

Of course, I'd forgotten about that, too. Water under the bridge now. It does appear I leave a rough wake.

"I have set the Lord always before me, because he is at my right hand, I shall not be shaken."

Psalms 16:8

38

Always before me. Always before me would keep me out of disasters.

Monday night went fine after the steak dinner with which I bribed her forgiveness. I was up early Tuesday fixing breakfast to polish the apology some more.

I was starting to get really excited about this. Both the .260 and the .338 were safely in the back of the new Ford Excursion 4X4 which was my latest cowboy limo. West Texas tan, of course, covered with ASAT camo, of course. It had a bumper guard that looked as if it was made out of supersized twisted barbed wire, but heavy steel, that could certainly bounce an elephant off the road without getting dented. This was going to be a cherry busting trip for the truck, too.

This vehicle was one of the first 10 in Texas that had the new robot driver. My car salesman in-law got me this one, an expensive special order, sort of a beta pre-release version, but I hadn't really learned to trust it yet. Ford had introduced the headless [3] driver for Uber in Pennsylvania weeks ago. It had been weeks and no reports of trouble from up north but who can believe that. I let it drive around Boerne in the evening but I never could really relax. I was thinking that maybe a long distance trip would let me learn to trust it. Plus, Bear had been aching to monitor the Controller Area Network on this self-driver. Aisley, too.

Mandy and I had packed overnight bags with just two changes. We decided we'd wear our light camo on the trip out and just pack some heavier for whatever. Even if we ended up going out to eat we wouldn't feel out of place in camo in Stockton.

Mandy was up as the sausage started flavoring the air, and I even got a kiss for breakfast. Lloyd dropped 5 cartridges off before 8:30 and we were on the road after tossing some drinks in the cooler. When we arrived at the kid's, they hadn't returned from dropping the grandkids off at Bear's Mom's house, so we let ourselves in. I organized their gun cases by the door, and a closed bag, but I learned long ago not to put anything in the car until it had been properly blessed by the lady of the house. They'd done a good job of packing light, too.

"Hi y'all." Aisley said as she burst through the door spreading hugs and kisses. Bear shook my hand and kissed Mandy on the cheek.

"Y'all look so cute. Matching camo!" Aisley giggled.

"Saving space. Camo only." Mandy said.

"I like that. I'm going to wear mine, too. I got new pinks!" said Aisley as she headed to the back. That made me think that we might feel a little uncomfortable in Stockton with somebody wearing pink camo but when she came out, like always, it looked very very nice on her. Tailored?

Bear returned from a back room with a handful of wires and a computer pad saying, "I'd like to hook up a monitor. Check the current version, and capture some event logs as we drive. Ok?"

Bear had been aching to monitor the Controller Area Network on this self-driver. Aisley, too. I had been pretending to understand what they were saying but declining their assault on my new ride, until now.

"Sure, dude." I smiled at him. I always like watching those two tackle a technical issue. Deep they was.

"Don't worry y'all," Aisley said, "he's been working with Ford all night to get organized on this. First name basis with level 3 support." She had her Masters from Texas A&M in "Constraint Programming", or something. Raising the kids had removed her from the commercial world for a while but she was really an unpaid but respected and serious assistant to Bear. They worked together better than a matched pair trained to harness. The image that said it all was the one I had on my desk. Aisley had infant Sadie against her breast and they were in the dark, the two geeks bent over a computer screen, lit like gnomes counting their gold.

It was just after 11 when we hit the road. It looked like we might not get to hunt tonight unless we made good time. You can't just show up to an old friend's place and head straight to the blinds without spending some time saying howdy. Definite maybe, though. In any case, Mandy and I started the trip in the front and listened to the music she had on her phone via the Bluetooth. Bear had run a line into the back and he and Aisley were bent over the screen talking a language that neither of us understood. It was easy to ignore.

I couldn't keep my hands from off the steering as we opened up the robot onto the 80 mph speed limit on Interstate 10 outside Junction. It's not that it was incapable or anything I could detect, but when you're traveling at almost 120 feet per second, it's hard to trust an electron steering you past a fully loaded fracking semi. Eventually, the kids decided that they wanted to supervise the robot because my inability to keep my hands off the wheel was skewing their logs. We exchanged places. Aisley rode shotgun with the laptop open towards Bear capturing, then analyzing the event stream, while we leaned on each other in the back. Like lots of old(er) people, the monotony of West Texas after we hit Sonora, but mainly the techno babble, sent us right off to sleep.

"Stockton's coming up y'all." said Aisley.

"You're kidding." mumbled Amanda. As she uncoiled from our pile I could tell she had a kink in her neck.

"You OK, sugar?" I questioned. From the look on her face it was going to take a little while.

"I'm going to text Jam and tell him we're here." I said. Aisley turned quickly back and looked at me, then her Mom. Their eyes said something that no man can read.

Jack 16:42: "We're entering Stockton"

Jeremy 16:43: "meet you at the gate in 20"

It was a fast twenty minutes to the ranch, flying low by autopilot down an almost deserted road. One thing about Pecos County roads, with all the oil and gas taxes, even the smallest, most deserted roads could be

43

professional drag race tracks. Perfectly flat, pretty perfectly straight. By now, half of us were completely comfortable with the electron mite pilot speeding us down the road.

By the time the E-pilot warned us that it was taking a left, we'd already seen the bright red GMC one-ton dually sitting by the side of the road. As we pulled up to it, Jam got out, looked to the driver and was obviously a little surprised. We pulled to a stop and I got out.

"Hello there, brother." he said. He shook my hand and pulled me in for a shoulder bump and pat on the back.

"Howdy, Jam." I said, struggling for what to say. I could feel the emotion starting to wash over me and didn't want to let it show.

"It is soooo good to see you," I said at last. "Thank you for inviting us out."

We stared into each others eyes for a few long seconds then that smile that I remembered broke loose and he walked over to the truck.

"Hey y'all," Jam said, "I'm Jeremy but he calls me Jam. You can too. Anybody with him is with me." He beamed as they introduced themselves.

"Aisley. What a beautiful name and young lady. Obviously you got the genes from Mom here. Lucky thang," he said laughing out loud while patting me on the back.

"Bear? Nice to meet you."

"Aiden Barrett Cohen," said Bear smiling, "but 'Bear' will make me turn around."

"Ok now, I don't want to bust your chops too much," Jam said, "but two good lookin' sisters riding with these guys ... I know they got excellent taste, but ... how many fingers am I holding up?" He showed two.

"Heard that before," said Aisley. "My eyes are just fine, thanks."

"Ok, then," Jam said laughing, "I want y'all to get an early chance at a nice buck I seen. I was going to tie it up so your Dad had a chance to bag it, but when I heard y'all were coming I figured one of you might be a shooter so I let it go."

"If we hurry, I have three blinds nearby that I can drop you in," Jam said as he looked around the truck.

Amanda said she didn't want to go because of the kink in her neck and, of course, *her* rifle wasn't ready. The icy stare wasn't missed by anyone

Bear said he was too wrung out from robot watching, so it was just me and Aisley. We unloaded our guns into Jam's truck, unpacked our heavy insulated camo coveralls and got in while he gave directions to Bear about where they were going.

We drove down the road a mile passing what looked all the world like a Comanche camp on the right with a Trading Post off behind it. Bear pulled my truck in there and it was obvious that each tipi, based on first impressions, had to be thirty feet across at the base. The smoke flaps were glassed in windows. Feathers danced from the pole extensions at their peaks.

"Has your Dad told you any stories about us?" said Jam.

"Oh yeah, yeah. I can't repeat them in certain crowds," said Aisley with a smile looking over to him.

"So I guess he did tell you some truth," he laughed.

I didn't realize till this very minute how much I'd missed that laugh.

"And bring the fattened calf and kill it, and let us eat and celebrate."
Luke 15:23

Another couple miles down the road there was a green swath thirty yards wide curving back into the mesas. There was no gate, or road, or fenced field or anything that was obvious to explain the green in the middle of the surrounding brown of the desert. There were deer and rabbits all over it. As we came abreast of it, Jam stayed on the horn until the deer, whitetail and muley, were piling over each other getting away. Muleys were hopping up the mesa, whitetails flagging their retreat across the draw at speed.

"Putting them on y'alls blinds," he said. Another chuckle.

"I want to sit with Dad I think," said Aisley.

"Not a problem, plenty of room. I'll put y'all in the Hot Spot. Three seater," Jam smiled at her.

At that, Aisley and I smiled at each other. Of course there is a Hot Spot wherever you go!

Jam pulled off the road a couple miles away, he held our rifles as we climbed through the fence, and then pointed at a rock outcrop 300 yards away.

"Head to that outcrop and you'll see a box blind off to the right another 100 yards on a rise. It's later than I like so move quick and quiet. I'll be waiting for you here with the emergency blinkers on so you don't get lost. Got a flash light?"

I showed him my headlamp, switched it on, off, and stuffed it back in my pocket.

Aisley and I were stepping it out to the blind. By the time we got settled there was one thumb of sun left. Half an hour of good light. We glassed across every bush and rock, then we started waiting. Aisley reached out and took my hand. We hadn't been hunting like this in the same blind since she was little. The stories we had about times when she had to sit on my lap to shoot out of the blinds were many. Every few minutes we'd start glassing again, and when she grabbed my hand again, without a word, it made me shake inside. Without saying anything I knew she knew because of the corner of her mouth.

What a day.

We saw a few whitetails but no muleys. Heard a few shots in the near-ish distance maybe. As in any desert, when the sun started getting low, the chill factor immediately went up. We stayed until our scopes could not differentiate at 200 and then we headed back. Aisley was right in my foot steps as I made my way. Turning at the outcropping we could see the truck blinking along the roadside. I was glad it was there as I realized I would have headed back the wrong way.

Jam met us at the fence and we unloaded and handed the rifles to him.

"See anything?" he said as he checked the safety on my rifle.

"Whitetails only," Aisley answered, "but it was really nice."

We stowed the rifles in the overhead racks,

hopped in the truck, and he handed us both a cold soda.

"This stuff happens," he said, "and I can't ever believe it when it does."

He pushed his phone at us showing a video of a muley buck, huge at 26" wide at least, standing in blinking yellow lights. It couldn't have been ten feet in front of the truck, bobbing it's head along with the blinking hazard lights.

"Did that happen tonight?" I said, shaking my head.

"The only thing I can figure is you need to bathe more," Jam said, "uh huh."

Aisley caught his smiling eyes with a glance, nodding her head in agreement.

On the little trip back to the Comanche camp we passed the swath, now on the right, and the headlights lit up scores of eyes of every height. It was alive with creatures again.

Pulling in we could see the ten tipis[5], the nearest with my truck parked in front of it. They were so big that they made my truck look small. I had been right when I thought the smoke flaps were windows. Out of the top of the nearest two tipis there was smoke wafting out of the peaks. Farther off to the right was the Trading Post, obvious because of the sign hanging on the porch. Except for us, the place seemed deserted.

Jam pulled in and stopped.

"Got some stew for you, it's my specialty… Chorizo rabbit stew," [4] he said smiling at us in turn. I know he didn't think that would shock me but the look at Aisley confirmed we were good.

"Jack, I'm really glad y'all are here. Like I said, I want to draft you for something important, but I don't want to talk about it when you're tired. I'd like to pick you up early, have a hunt, and then show you all something." He looked at us both closely, and said, "Something special."

We looked at each other, his knowing smile, and then we both shrugged.

"Do y'all want to hunt in the morning?" he asked

"I'm in," I said as I walked to the door of the tipi, "I'd like to meet that one you showed us. I'll check with Mandy."

It was a regular size door recessed into the building just enough to give height to place the door. I hadn't noticed till now that the foundation it grew out of was limestone quarry blocks which made the start of the tipi two feet off the ground. It was obviously a building, made of gunite or something, painted and shaped so it looked like the traditional tent of the Native American nomads. It even had the sags between the poles. Opening the door and stepping in was not at all what I expected.

It was 30 feet or more in diameter, with a fire in the center like you might find at a ski resort, with steel chimney reaching through the peak. The floor, what you could see of it, was etched and stained concrete with the rest covered with deer and cattle hides. Very rustic and warm. There was a large pot over the fire hanging on one of the hooks from the chimney. The aroma of a well cooked meal filled the space and my nostrils. Bear and Mandy were sitting together to one side with plates on their laps and what I supposed was rabbit quarters in their fingers.

"Wow!" I said checking the pot. "Jam wants to know if we want to hunt tomorrow. Whatcha think?" I questioned as I started looking around. Half way up there was a light canvas screen reaching down to the base, tied about the poles, hiding a string of LED lights which gave a diffuse background light. The main direct lighting was a couple of LED spots shining down from the peak. Looking up through the smoke flap window was sky showing the last light of the day on high wispy clouds.

They both looked at me and nodded yes with their mouths full.

I stepped back outside and Jam and Aisley were giggling. They gave me a look when I came out so I know it was something I did. *Long* ago I hope.

"They're in," I said, "What time?"

"The blinds I want to put you in means we have to cover a few miles. To make sure everybody gets set 45 minutes before the sun I'd like to start off at 4:45. Ok?" he said. He'd addressed that like somebody that puts out hunters all the time and knows how long it takes. To the second.

"No problem," I said and Aisley smiled at me and went in.

"Thank you, Jam."

"Thank you, Jack," he said smiling. He waved me off with two fingers, and immediately went to his truck and drove off. As his lights panned across the campsite they painted the Trading Post and another metal building, maybe an RV garage, hiding behind it. He hit the road and took off. Just as his taillights vanished over a rise, the blaring horn announced him readying our blinds for the coming hunt.

The beer was cold. The stew was spicy and good. Some of the stories were good, but especially the one about the big muley waiting on us. The beds were great. When the lights went off the stars and moon shone into the building through the smoke flap window. The peaks of the poles, dividing the sky over our heads, reached a dozen feet over the tipi and the feathers were outlined by stars as they waltzed in the breeze.

It didn't take minutes for me to drift off. I was young again, and we were planning a hunt, and sharing all the laughter we'd shared as kids.

3.

I've always been a fairly light sleeper, even after too much vitamin "B"(eer), but this morning was interesting. The LED light strings behind the tipi liner were slowly coming on as I rolled over and opened an eye. Mandy can be seriously disturbed by stray photons escaping into a room from behind blackout drapes, but she was still purring. This was a surprise. She's sent me to check the back porch lights on a full moon night more than once only to discover those darn moon photons were ricocheting around the curtains. Good sleep, like this, is rare for her in a new bed.

Checking my phone on the floor, turning off the alarm minutes before it was to go off, I repositioned to look out the sky window, and then she moved.

"Oh, sugar, did you leave the lights on?" she said as she nudged me. "I can't believe I slept so good."

"Nope, I guess this is Jam's way of waking us up. I just canceled my alarm. Time to rise and shine."

I swung my feet onto the cowhide on the

floor, expecting to feel the cold of the concrete through it. There was no chill at all. Tapping my foot over onto the bare concrete, its warmth confirmed it to be a radiant heated floor.

"The floor's heated," I mused. "It is just one surprise after another."

Digging around in the pile of camo on the floor, I started getting organized. Instead of pulling on cold clothes, like most hunting mornings at the hunting shack, the floor had kept everything pleasantly warm. Pulling on my pants, I was walking to the head, when there was a light knock on the door.

"Y'all up?" leaked through the door from Jam.

"Yessir," I replied.

"Come on up to the Trading Post when you're ready. Got some tacos working. We got half an hour."

I knew that he was passing the same message on to the kids as I went into the bathroom. The facility was right next to the door and took up very little space in the interior. In fact, it protruded into the interior just as far as the door passageway, which was four feet max. Inside, it was like a cruise ship head, having the toilet right in the middle of the shower, underneath the sloping tipi wall. One side had the sink and the other had a hand rail which I really appreciated. Having to admit that getting up is getting hard is the first sign. Sitting on the toilet was obviously the preferred method, because at my 6'2" height, the slanted tipi wall was on my nose. That surely explained the spray nozzle for the shower, too, as you certainly couldn't spin around in this closet. Showering while sitting on the toilet? Ok, whatever.

Having my face this close to the wall, it was obvious that it was probably gunite, and smoothed by hand. I made a mental note to myself to check the edges at the supporting posts to see if I could discern more of the construction techniques.

"Hey!" Mandy shouted with some urgency.

"Okay, baby, one minute," I mumbled as I handled the paperwork.

Flushing, washing, and stepping out I was almost pushed to the floor as she went in. Vitamin B, for sure.

She was already in her camos and only needed to put on her boots. As I finished dressing, she started to uncase her rifle.

"Oh ... uh ... we can get your baby sighted in when we get back. I'll sit out this time so you can use my .260," I offered with as much whipped puppy as I could muster.

"You don't need to," she said abruptly.

"Jeremy sighted it in for me yesterday while you and Aisley were out." Then she turned to give me that sly smile she wears when she's verbally abusing me and loving it.

She reached into her phone holster, withdrew it, stroked the front screen a few times then showed me a closeup of a target with two touching bullet holes a little more than an inch above the bullseye, certainly .338, and one at four o'clock, three inches off the bullseye.

"I thought I heard a few shots, but you only had five," I noted with some trepidation.

"We used four," she said replacing her phone. "I'll *only* need one." Then she was waving her hands at me to hurry up. She slung her rifle over her shoulder. Good Lord, it looked good on her. Both of them were serious pieces of art.

"Jam was great. Laser bore sight, then shot the first one at twenty five yards, spent thirty seconds checking the ballistics charts, then adjusted. The next shot at 100 was the low right. Adjusted it right away, and the next was on. The fourth shot was mine, and it blew his mind that I printed on top of his," she bragged with that twinkle in her eye.

"I'm heading up, slow poke," she said turning to the bed and retrieving her Lady

Smith. Inserting the snub-nosed magnum in her shoulder holster under her camo, she stepped off. She's always been that way. That lady never goes out in the woods without her baby under her arm. She shoots it as good as anything, too.

I rushed to get my gear on, putting my knife on my belt, loading my pocket with extra cartridges, head lamp and pocket flashlight. A quick look at the sky light again to validate I didn't need my rain poncho. Getting my rifle out and slinging it across my shoulder, I almost headed out the door. Remembering then, to pocket my little .22 Smith and Wesson Escort in case I needed to issue a coup de grace, I was out the door, too.

Closing the door behind me, I saw Aisley and Bear were stepping onto the porch at the Trading Post. Aisley in her all pink camo was impossible to miss. Porch flowers. They looked back as they heard my door close and Aisley waved me off as they entered the Post.

I was a bare minute behind them when I entered, but they'd already managed to get tacos onto their plates and the steam coming off the cups for sure meant coffee.

"Mornin', Jack, come on and grab some," Jam said. "We'll be heading out in a few. While y'all eat I'd like to go over the rules."

Jeremy reviewed the gun safety rules, ranch rules, and the plans for blind placement.

"I'm looking for y'all to take off a whitetail doe this morning, and I'm betting that's going to be Amanda."

"Please, just call me Mandy, everybody does," she interrupted.

"Ok, Mandy, I'm going to put you in a box canyon that has three arms running off from the blind. It's almost always productive, so take a big fat doe if you have the chance. And everybody ... there's some big muley bucks out here, a couple even bigger than the one I showed you yesterday. You can each have one if you have the opportunity. so don't take a doe if you see something coming in," he said with the smile of encouragement I always gave my hunters. You want people to be shooters.

"Everybody is going to be miles apart, so I'm not worried about you shooting each other, but please, don't leave the blind," Jam said. His demeanor as he said this was much firmer. "If you shoot a deer, just mark it and stay in the blind. Hogs, javelina or something else might show up, but if you can't stand it and just have to look at your kill, don't wander off. We don't want to be looking for you in the sticks after you get snake bit tracking a wounded deer."

We all looked at each other on that one. I

hadn't thought about snakes at all but of course they would be out if the day warmed up like it was supposed to.

The thought of snakes put a crimp on the early morning conversation because we all spent the next few minutes packing taco and washing it down with coffee. Jam made himself a taco, a cup of coffee with too much sugar, and started wolfing his down, too.

At the first taco intermission, Jam said, "Dude, that gun of Mandy's is a rare piece of work. Never seen anything like it. You design it?"

"Sort of," I said nodding, "scoped out things on the net and just put it all together. A buddy of mine did the work after we got it designed. Miracle of science wouldn't you say?"

Jam looked at me with taco in his mouth, shook his head slowly no-yes-no and smiled. "Miracle of science? Better than a four door pickup truck? I'm betting you been into too many magazines!" he said as he looked down to his food, then glanced momentarily back up with that smile.

That was a line, and a smile, that brought back memories by the score. Many times I'd experienced them. When we were running buddies in the teen years we lived to hunt and shoot. Guns were it. Like most teenage boys with a passion, we could argue for hours about the next new thing, and shooting and hunting *always* has the next new thing. His Winchester Model 70 in .30-06 Springfield versus my Remington Model 700 BDL in .270 Winchester. Guns and calibers almost older than us put together. Two fine tools, cartridges built on the same brass, the working end of the barrels separated by thirty one thousandths. It had always come down to shaving hairs.

Just like kids will argue about the power of super heroes they adore, we could spend hours arguing the effect 5 grains of bullet, 20 feet per second, or the effect 3 thousandths of an inch in bullet seating would have on the power and accuracy of our respective guns. One of us, always backed by some magazine article, would argue the new. It would eventually lead us to a loading session and a trip to the ranch with a hundred rounds between us. New bullets, new powders, new loadings don't prove nothing without some serious shooting research.

And shoot we did. There was some steel placed on a hill up from the cabin that we could shoot from the porch: 200,500,900 yards and hanging so you could see the hit easily. It being on a hill meant the person spotting could give excellent guidance about wide shots. On any given day, with spotting assist from the other, we were consistently great.

Taping dimes and quarters to paper targets at 200 after we got "on", we would perforate a handful every trip. We each saved them in our own jars which we'd use for bragging rights. Over the years, it didn't really matter the load, or the gun, or the shooter, they filled at the same rate. The difference between them was another thing measured in thousandths. The following month there would be another magazine and we'd be loud again. Never ending. And it always led to our personal proofs written in smoke!

I was missing that jar instantly. I couldn't even guess which was the last house move I'd unpacked it in, a vague image outside of place, and certainly not where it was now.

"You know you haven't seen anything like that ... ever!" I said.

"Nope, you got my goat there. But, miracle of science?" Jam said with that look, seen many times, that was only eroded a little by age. The twinkle was the same.

"Yep, pure D miracle of science," I said swelling up. I looked around the group to gather up some support. All my group was nodding in my favor.

When he'd finished his breakfast he stood up and headed to the door. "Ok, mount up," Jam said.

We all piled out to his truck. It was then that Mandy and Bear realized what a hunting rig he had. Of course it was raised at least a foot, we'd seen that when we pulled in. What they hadn't seen was the gun racks on the ceiling inside the cab, the deep compartments between the seats filled with binoculars, spotting scopes, and assorted ammo, knives, and other necessaries. The seats covered with tough skins, in camo of course, to protect what I assumed was leather underneath. This tagged it as the truest example of a cowboy Cadillac. Not the best, just another good one.

"Jack, you sit up here with your gun out the window and Mandy you sit behind me with your gun out. Be ready. We might see the one that got away last night!" he said. We took our positions, lowered the windows, and when our rifles were positioned out the window, jacked a shell. Jam helped Aisley and Bear get their rifles put in the overhead racks.

We were off. Even in this elegant cowboy ride, that rifle of Mandy's was clearly standing alone in the field. Miracle of Science! No doubt. Miracle of Science!

"If you see something, don't point y'all,

just say *Stop ... off to the right* or whatever," Jam said. "I'll try to stop us quick without spooking 'em". It was during this instruction that we passed by the green swath on the left. The dark prevented it from delivering the full effect, and he waved all those glowing eyes off saying, "They're in Kings X for now." We hadn't seen any horns, so nobody objected.

In a few short minutes, we were at the Hot Spot again and I was told to get out. He had Bear get his rifle out and move to the front, while Jam walked around to hold my rifle for me as I went through the fence. He reached into his pocket and produced a laser pointer, tracing over the path we'd walked the previous evening.

"There's your path," he said shaking the laser beam all up and down it. "And there's that outcrop, OK?"

"Sure, thank you so much Jam," I said, really feeling it.

"My pleasure, dude. We'll have plenty more," he said smiling, a welcoming and grateful smile, then he turned back to the truck.

Over his shoulder he said, "I'll pick you up first, probably around nine-ish. I won't honk until 9:30."

I watched them disappear down the road, and then turned on my headlamp and started my walk to the blind.

Sitting in the darkness waiting for the dawn is one of my favorites. The night was probably in the mid forties, so it wasn't so bad I needed to wear my wool face mask. There was just the slightest breeze, which I always liked best. You sort of had some idea which way the smart deer were going to be coming, and there was enough of a breeze to keep your scent from hanging around. Or, at least, that was my theory. I hadn't put on any scents this morning, I guess because I wasn't really out here to hunt. I like skunk the best. Birds of a feather Mandy would say.

Sitting in the quiet doing my breathing, it reminded me how different this desert was. Back in the Hill Country, the quiet was alive with armadillos snuffling through the dry oak leaves looking for worms, early woodpeckers beating on the live oaks, and all kinds of little creepy things. As night started leaning to gray, the different birds would start calling their warnings or their invitations. Frequently, on quiet mornings, the heavy wings of a turkey beating the air as it came down from its roost could be heard from hundreds of yards. And deer, finding the corn on the ground silently, allowed you to place them in 3D space by the sounds of them popping kernels as they fed.

The desert was quiet. The only sound was the breeze moving through the widely-spaced bushes. You could tell the difference, between the sound of it being bent around a low cedar fully clothed or a creosote letting it blow through. The feeder was more than a hundred yards away, I was upwind from it, so I didn't really expect to hear anything, unless it was does thumping each other over position on the corn. A dominant doe, defending her spot, can sometimes rear up and crash down on another with her front legs using so much force that it sounds like someone beating a tenor drum.

It was an entertaining morning after the sun finally got above the mesas. The quiet of the night was replaced with, what to me, seemed like an abundance of animals for this dry desert. A porcupine wandered out of the brush first, passing by the corn to check it out. I don't really know if he ate any. At almost the same time, a small family group of javelina came up and there was no doubt they were into the corn. The older ones kept looking up at the porcupine but ignored it otherwise. The young ones, in between corn niblets, would go by it to smell it. It would rattle its quills and puff up, becoming a serious pin cushion. Sniff, rattle, jump, Sniff, rattle, jump. The poor porcupine was too scared to move off, but the youngsters couldn't stay away from that crazy thing.

Eventually some whitetail does came prancing in like they were late to the spread, and the javelina wandered off. I heard a distant shot at 7:23, which certainly could have been Mandy's because it thumped, but maybe Bear's .300. It was pretty far off. The rest of the morning was spent watching deer that didn't need killing. There was one fat, dry doe that wouldn't have made it through the morning if I hadn't heard that shot.

At 8:30, disregarding ranch rules, I started back to the road. I put my facemask on and snuck out of the blind without spooking anything on the feeder. Rifle across my chest at low ready, I decided I'd try stalking back to the road. Three steps. Slowly, very slowly, look all the way around. Five steps. Three breaths. Look all the way around again, checking the same bushes every time. Three steps... three breaths, over and over. It makes for a long slow journey but patience pays. I've had bucks jump up from a bush 30 yards away, that they clearly weren't in when I'd looked over that same bush every time for the last 100 yards. It always made me wonder if they saw me, of course, but they just weren't scared of a very slow moving bush? I'm fairly certain they weren't teleported into that bush when I wasn't looking. PFM:

pure friggin magic.

I didn't see anything but jackrabbits on the way to the road. I leaned my unloaded rifle against a post then walked down a couple, crossed through, and was retrieving it when I heard a truck coming down the road.

"See anything?" Jam said through the open window as the truck pulled to a stop.

"Didn't see anything I needed to clean. Heard a shot about 7:30." I said while getting up and into the truck.

"I was sitting on the porch watching the morning when I heard it, too. I'm thinking Mandy, pretty sure," he said.

We picked up everybody, saving Mandy for last. At each stop we shared the stories of what we'd seen. My porcupine story won that contest. When we got to the last stop, Jam drove off the pavement into a big draw. He pulled up next to the tower blind at the mouth of the three branch box canyon he'd told us about.

As we stopped, we saw her lowering her rifle clipped to a rope. She was 15 feet off the ground.

"It's unloaded, dontcha *know*, because I'm out of ammo," she said implanting a serious gig. By the time she got down we were all surrounding her.

"So?" I said quizzically.

"I saw some muley does and watched them for over an hour, then the whitetails started filtering in. The muleys hopped off up that hill," she said pointing. "Never saw a buck at all. Couple of times I saw them looking around like they were expecting somebody but nothing showed."

"That was you that shot wasn't it?" said Jam.

"She must have missed, or she'd be bragging by now," said Aisley.

"Missed? Shame on you for doubting, Ms. Aisley," Mandy said taking off her outer jacket and walking it over to the truck.

"You might want to follow me in the truck," she said. With that she started walking off to the east.

"Hang on missy," said Jam, "I told you about the snakes. Lemme lend ya a helper."

Jam went back to the truck, digging around under the front seat for a moment, and returned with a Smith and Wesson Governor in stainless steel.

"The first two are loaded with 6 shot, then .45 Colt," he said as he handed it over to Mandy.

"Very nice," she said, "Y'all might want to pack a lunch." She started striding it out.

"Oh Lord," I said, "lead on, we'll follow."

Jam nodded us back into the truck.

Obviously we'd all understood that hint. We were going to ride out to the kill. No sense walking with her amongst snakes if she was going to be bragging every step of the way. No sense getting bit twice.

Mandy was stepping it out, hanging that Governor at her side. It was a pretty good handful for a little lady, but you could tell she wasn't intimidated by it. People that know guns hold them that way. A proper tool.

By the time we were starting to wonder if she was leading us on a goose chase, she pointed. In between a pretty dense creosote bush and a guajillo shrub, was a whitetail doe laid out. We all got out of the truck.

"Ok," I said, "nice one. Drink her dead." At that I got my pocket flask of Knob Hill out and passed it around. Mandy took the first sip. When it got to Jam he passed on it.

"Can't. Got a serious allergy. A sip and sometimes I wake up in bracelets," he said smiling. He was miming handcuffs.

"When did you start that?" he said, nodding towards the flask in Bear's hand.

"There was a German guy that always used to come out to hunt and he said it was a tradition," I said before swigging my shot. I looked around, saw a small cedar a few steps away and went and cut a four inch piece of the tip of a branch off, returned and laid it on the doe's side, the cut end facing back.

"I think that's it. Male or female it lays out different. I think you point the cut end forward if it's a buck," I said as I hit the flask again then passed it.

Jam knelt down and patted the side of the deer's neck. "Thank you Lord for sharing your bounty with us," he said.

The three of us looked at each other, then back to Jam. He looked back to the blind.

"I'm betting that's every bit of 350 yards. Heck of a shot," he said. He touched the red dot at the base of the doe's neck. He pulled it's neck over and the hole on the far side wasn't much different.

"She does that all the time. Not even a record," I said, and nobody said anything. Mandy just smiled at me nodding her head.

"That .338 is not nearly as explosive as the smaller calibers, is it?" Jam said.

Mandy was quick to answer, "That's why I picked this one. Lots of punch but stays together on these smallish deer. Plenty of gun for big stuff though. Doesn't buck like Bear's .300 but oodles of slap down."

I never get tired of her talking about

shooting. I'm just the luckiest guy in the world. Other men go to the range and their wives may accompany them, even shoot some, but Mandy loves to humiliate all comers. As long as there's ammo, a fresh target, and somebody to watch her perform, she's all in. It's hard to believe that I taught her to shoot on a .223 and here we are with her choosing and shooting that .338 Federal. Don't get no better.

We loaded the doe in the back of the truck and headed in. It was 10:30. The day was starting to warm already, the sky was that perfect blue of big skies, and the breeze was laying down.

Mandy's blind was the last one on this string of hunters and I'm guessing it was a good four miles from the camp. We came back to the Trading Post from behind, so the green swath we'd told Bear and Mandy about was missed again.

Jam pulled around to the side of the Trading Post, where there was a covered porch on that end of the RV barn. There were stainless steel counters, a deep sink, hoses, and gambrels enough to have six deer hanging at the same time. There was a walk-in cooler next to the porch, that must have been on the back of a truck at one time. It looked like it could hang twenty deer without crowding. The thermostat by the door showed it was ready, the temperature at 36 degrees.

"Man, Jam, this is quite the setup," I said. We all milled around checking things out. Jam and I moved to the truck and pulled Mandy's doe off.

"I'll clean your deer for you, babe," I said, but the words were hardly out of my mouth.

"We don't have time for that," Jam said. "I'd really like to get started showing you around."

"Oh come on," I pleaded, "you know I'm fast."

"Mandy may know you're fast," he chuckled, " but twenty bucks says I can gut and skin this deer under three minutes."

"How much of that are you willing to take?" said Bear reaching into this wallet.

"I'll take all the folding money y'all want to put up," said Jam swaggering over to the counter and pulling out a nice heavy bladed drop point knife.

"Ok?" said Bear spreading five twenties on the counter.

"Ohhhh, I need that!" said Jam.

I put my twenty on the counter, too. No reason to be greedy when just getting acquainted again. Jam got the doe mounted and hoisted on the gambrel. He scooted an oil changing pan underneath her.

"On your mark," he said.

Siri loaded the stop watch app, then I said, *"Go"* loud enough to rattle the tin on the roof.

He started quick and confident. [1] Starting at the rear legs, parting the hide down the side all the way to the front knee, then the other side. The knife was parting the hide as if it was a laser beam, following his fingers as fast as he moved. Pulling these panels of hide around to the back, then he split the back from tail to head and jerked off those panels. 38 seconds. I was starting to get that feeling. Pulling the front hide from down between the legs, another few seconds. 52 seconds. Opening up the body cavity from between the rear legs, he disemboweled her in another twenty seconds. Didn't nick a gut or leave any debris. Splitting the pelvis, hack sawed the head off, then tree loppers to take off the forelegs.

I called it 2:17.

"Oh my God, I've never seen anything like that!" I said as I patted his back.

"Last time I'm taking bets from you," said Bear. He shrugged shaking his head.

Mandy and Aisley were obviously loving it. "ummmm hmmmm ... It's not faster than you by much!" Mandy said. They were laughing out loud as they headed into the Post.

Jam washed the carcass with the spray nozzle and then he grabbed a box of kosher salt from a cabinet. He liberally coated the carcass by throwing the salt at it until the whole thing glistened with crystals.

"What's that about?" I said.

"Yeah," said Bear, "that's a new one to me, too."

"Sometimes I let them hang for weeks. I like them aged, but this is just an additional precaution," said Jam as he put the salt back.

Bear helped him move the carcass into the cooler, which already had quite a collection of frosted hogs hanging, then we sprayed off the porch, put things away, and headed in.

There was coffee on the stove and a large thermos dispenser on the counter that was completely loaded. The taco leavings were still in the frying pan and the plate of fresh onion, cilantro, and limes was on the counter. Mandy was putting some tortillas on a pan to start warming up the second inning.

"Y'all can start on this again," she said.

After a little bit of discussion about where we were heading with breakfast and checking inventory, Mandy decided that we were having some fresh backstrap and migas. She set Aisley to ripping the tortillas up and breaking eggs. After telling me to sit, she headed out with a knife to harvest some backstrap from her doe.

Jam spoke up, "Once you get your piece off, please salt it again. It's in the cabinet."

Mandy looked around the group with a questioning look. "You'll see, babe," I said. She raised her eyebrows at me then headed out.

We spent the next hour watching the ladies cook as Jam and I reviewed some of our adventures. Everybody, except Bear, had input and questions. There wasn't a single story where one of them couldn't add something I've told them so often. Having Jam sitting there, giving his view of the facts, gave them all a chance to confirm my version of things. Aisley especially, was validating my stories through Jam. (It was almost like she thought I might be just a little BS!) I did most of the talking, maybe because I was scared of any silence. Jam didn't let anything pass that I'd evolved over time to my favor. We laughed so much. We laughed past hurt. It hurt my soul, too, to realize what had been missed. Now it was like we had never been estranged.

"So this is the community you were talking about? I really like it," I said stomping on a pause in the conversation.

"No," he said, "this is NOT the community. This is what birthed it."

Jeremy explained how he'd ended up being

the jefe for this ranch. Just kind of came across it by accident, but was a found place. It was a job he enjoyed, with a family that was trying to make it, ranching sheep mainly. He'd become the indispensable man, while the family was growing up, handling it all. For twelve years he'd been the manager before tragedy struck. The wife and children were going to a high school football game in Ft. Davis. Everybody in Pecos county flies low with fine straight roads, and why make a 90 mile trip any longer than you must? They never discovered whose fault it was. It appeared they'd clipped each other, almost missing and sprinkling turn signal dust on the center of the road. With a closing rate estimated at 200 miles per hour, there were pieces of vehicles spread over acres. Nobody made it.

The owner was the last of his line, too. Apparently he'd sunk into it deep and couldn't pull out. In the space of three years he'd drowned his sorrows and out drunk his liver. The biggest surprise was that he'd left it all to Jam. Everything.

"I couldn't figure it out myself," said Jam shaking his head. "Everybody out here was dumbfounded. About the only black face around was now the owner of one of the bigger ranches. You know everybody thought they could weasel me out of it because they thought I was just some slick nigger; still a city transplant after all those years on the range."

The white men winced and sucked air. The ladies rolled their eyes at each other then shook their heads at Jam.

"How big is it?" asked Aisley.

"Thirty six sections," said Jam.

"Holy shit!" I gasped.

"That's right, *Twenty three thousand acres.* A decent ranch by Texas standards," said Jam.

"So this isn't *the community?*"

"Not at all. This was an experiment in making money without having to drench and shear sheep. It was working, too. Running the numbers it looked like hunting was going to be just as lucrative and more fun. That's when I started putting together this village. It was doing fine during the hunting season. I had a UT student come out with his father one season who had just been back from a study tour of Japan. The kid said they were cowboy crazy. He put up a Japanese web site for me and we were off to the races"

Jam took a deep breath and moved from the bar over to the couch, resting his arm across the top.

"In no time, we were raking it in. To scale it for you, a Japanese businessman will fly halfway around the world, prepay for custom boots and accessories, especially a hat, and pay $5 a shot for .44 mag *All. Day. Long.* Of course, cowboy quick draw is typically .45 Colt or less. *All.Day.Long.* We were smoking thousands of rounds of ammo a day. I had two guys running automated progressive reloaders two days a week, two girls from town as housekeepers, and assigned an Indian maiden, costumed at least, as cook for each tipi. I even had singing cowboys for the campfire at night. Most nights we were roasting whole pigs or several goats. I was hiring a small village to take care of what you see here."

He looked up at the ceiling. "We were all making out, but it was a lot of work, a lot of scheduling, and a lot of dealing with people. Even though I was netting over $3,000 per day, easy, it was wearing us out. It didn't take long before we were only scheduling two weeks a month because the labor pool, even at premium prices, is thin out here in the desert. We pushed some day trips out to Big Bend, because that was a break for us. Choosing between looking at hot desert or hot guns, desert is much calmer. You have to love the wide open spaces to spend time out here. In any case, and always, dealing with people is dealing up problems."

"So ... what's the scoop?" Mandy said.

"I had a major piece of good luck. Frackers came out to look at the place and paid me $100 an acre to lease it. That seven figures pretty much polished off any edge of wanting to work real hard. They don't drill dry holes much any more, either, so the first hole punched in came in big and the first months check was $60,000. Serious mailbox money. There are more on the way."

"Oh man," I said, "that is some story."

He started looking at his boots. "There was a time, Jack can tell you, that I was at the boundaries of sanity. I had my own rendezvous with the whiskey river and it almost took me down. The thing about drugs and alcohol, they make you laugh like a baby, and that's a memory we've all lost. And miss. It doesn't come often enough, but with drugs, and alcohol, you get to that place a lot. A lot. Until you don't and then you're just trying to get back. More will do it, you keep thinking. What I learned, was that the devil don't come at you waving bloody guts. He comes at you small and quiet, like an angel of light, until its almost too late. If you forgot how to pray it can be fatal. If you refuse to pray, you do not have the power to save yourself."

13 For such are false apostles, deceitful workers, transforming

themselves into apostles of Christ. 14 And no wonder! For Satan himself transforms himself into an angel of light.

2 Corinthians 11:13-14

"So this is where I'm at today. I'm filthy rich and wanting to do God's will. We're advancing quickly on a new way of living. I already have a small team of very serious technical students, now residents, but there needs to be a leadership team. Nobody out there will tell me I'm full of shit. They just assume, wrongly, that I'm not. I know Jack will tell it like it is. I need that, too."

Jeremy looked around at the assembled crew, each in turn, then looked at me.

"Please forgive me for my trespasses, Jack," Jam said, "let's live side by side again, and let's try this future unknown together, as the kind of friends we used to be."

"Oh, Jam, I would so love that," I said, as the emotion washed over me in waves. In a single breath, I was overcome and trying to hold back the sobbing, "Please forgive me for my words," I was finally able to get out. Such relief.

He stood up, motioned for me to join him, and we both held on for dear life. "Thank you Jesus," he repeated over and over and it wasn't just words. The waves of emotion affected the very air in the room, energizing everyone. In no time at all, Mandy, then the kids were all part of the hug.

After a few minutes, Jam said, "Ok you guys. Can we pray together?"

We all held hands, and Jam started, "Oh Lord, Papa, thank you for bringing this fine man back into my life with his beautiful family. Fill us with your spirit as we move forward. Help us to always have you in front of us, and know that you are holding our right hand and supporting us. Strengthen us as we move forward, and shelter us under your wings when the storms come, as we know they will. Make us know the way that we should go. God Bless this wonderful family. In Christ's name, Amen."

"That was beautiful Jam," said Bear, "thank you." Everyone joined him in patting Jam on the back.

"I know I'm not alone, but I'm kinda anxious so it's encouraging to have y'all here. I also know that I'm not the only one whose faith has wavered at times. When we started stirring this up, I came across a philosopher, Heidegger[2]. Who, if you can believe the web, was one of the leading philosophers of the 20th century. He seems to be in the top ten no matter where you look. He believed our technology was going to tyrannize us. I think you'll see some stuff coming up that will make you pause on that one."

He looked around at us to gauge our perception, there was slim to none, so he continued.

"The thing is, Paul warned us about people getting sidetracked by those speaking big words, wanting to have pointless arguments, and there's kind of a focus on two of them out here. Heidegger ain't one of them. Philosophers do seem at odds with my spirituality, though, and this thought leader actually became an honest to goodness Nazi. About the only thing I agree with Heidegger on, and understand clearly, was that making philosophy intelligible would likely be it's death. Can't come soon enough for me."

We all smiled at that one. I think we all seemed a little too polite, like he wasn't making any headway with us. Personally, he'd lost me at Heidegger.

"Ok. I guess that's enough of that. Let's go look around and see what you think," he said as he spun in place and started to the front door.

We all followed Jam out the door and off to the other end of the big shed where he'd cleaned Mandy's doe. At first glance it looked like any large RV storage shed you'd see on somebody's property, tall and wide with two huge doors at the opposite end of the cleaning station. In between the two ends,there was a covered porch with fire pit, wet bar, reefers, and neon beer lights that reached around to the cleaning area. As we cleared the porch, he said, "Wait here y'all."

He rolled up the right door and then stood back to the side near us. He turned and smiled.

"You are so going to love this," he said.

"*Martin*!" he yelled at the garage.

A short honk came out like you hear when you remotely lock your car.

"Martin, back out, please."

The sound of a big diesel coming to life came through the open door. At this point, I don't think anybody was particularly surprised. We'd had our robot drive us out, right? My phone could take voice commands pretty good. Remote start, passe.

The surprise came when we got our first view of the vehicle. It was a shiny black, 1 ton dually Chrysler Ram 3500, which had a 4 foot enclosed box extension inserted behind the cab. There was some kind of brush guard or something along the sides. Two in fact. No, as the truck cleared the building there was one on each side of the front, too. In total, it looked like there were six backhoe arms hugging the sides of the truck, two on each side between the back wheels and the cab, positioned side-by-side under the bed extension, and two folded across the front. Instead of buckets, the side articulations had chicken feet and the front two had claws like logging equipment, only finer.

In the long bed there was a 300 gallon water tank, full to the top.

Jam turned around, gave us a hugely open-mouthed smile with his eyes closed like a silent cackle, then opening his eyes, said "Martin, walker mode[3]".

At his command, the diesel reved up, the six legs extended from the side and the vehicle rose up over our heads like a huge bug resting on the four legs, the front two legs just touching the ground resting on it's wrists. Every foot had a fat chicken foot of four toes, three front, one rear, with what looked like old rubber tire tread on them as well as something mimicking the toenail. The underneath of each toenail was comprised of a dozen little tetrahedral spikes protruding downward an inch. The front legs seemed to have only working claws with one large tread-covered pad at the wrist, which was the contact point with the ground.

I'm quite sure that I was frozen and unaware of the others.

"Hey," Jam said, "miracle of science?"

Of course we all nodded.

He turned back to the truck.

"Martin, beg!"

The truck revved and shifted so that it inclined 45 degrees from the horizontal, the rear bumper guard almost touching the ground, then the two front ... legs ... extended to the sky, reaching wide. When it was in position, it idled back, locked in the beg. It was a praying mantis of gargantuan proportions.

"They don't like me doing this one," Jan said, laughing like I remember the crazy man. "They're scared I'll dump the tank ... again!"

Jam turned around and pointed with two fingers at Aisley and Bear, "Why don't we take a couple of rifles just in case."

4.

I'd given up about gettin' going after fifteen minutes, Mandy sooner than that. Jam had "Martin" doing all kinds of tricks so that the kids could study the beast. It had several debugging modes. It could step through actions, pausing after a certain set number of inches, feet, or seconds. Watching it freeze and hold it's position for a second, demonstrated a statue steadiness in every position, however extreme.

The rifles had been loaded into the overhead. Mandy and I had been in the back seat for at least thirty minutes enjoying the ride, while the six-legged truck raised and lowered, spread it's legs, tapped the ground, or did some motion that the kids were eager to see. Finally, even Jam thought we should get on. He'd made the kids promise, on a video that he took with his phone, a pretty stringent ad hoc non-disclosure, that they wouldn't disclose any single thing at all about what was going on here. That gave them the permission they needed to start doing some serious analysis. They were taking close-ups of the joints, videos of the robot motion, and even shots of the shadows of the beast. The shadow, especially, really did look like a bug if you didn't have a scale from which to judge it. If there was a foot or hand or human shadow to lend some scale, the monstrous size of this bug was obvious.

We were finally moving down the road with Jam (single shot .17 HMR, suppressed) and Aisley (Browning 7mm-08 Remington) in the front, outside arms resting on the door, and their rifles resting in the crook of their elbows. Mandy and I were behind Aisley, and Bear had his .300 WinMag on his arm out the window behind Jam. Martin was six feet off the ground stepping down the paved road at a steady twenty miles an hour. Of course, that was a guess because the speedometer did not work. Only the legs on the sides were working the trek, while the two on the front were just held up off the road, folded back like a truck mustache. There was some road noise, if you call the rhythmic hydraulic sounds coming from the box behind us, but the motor was barely above idle.

"It sure doesn't seem to be working very hard," I said.

The kids were hypnotized by the beast's video display in the dash. Both were intent on watching it designate it's next step on the satellite view of the road, as it's avatar swam in the monitor space. Aisley was touching various icons on the menu at the bottom of the screen, displaying different parameters for the system for oil pressure, ground speed, and including live motion joint articulation graphics.

Jam turned around completely to check us out. He hadn't had his hands or feet near any operator's controls since he'd said, "Go Home."

"Basically, it's just moving the legs back to front," Jam said, "with a little extension from the rear-most leg to assist shifting the body forward. That's why it is so steady. The internal gyroscope and accelerometers keep the cabin completely level, unless I get in the way for some reason with a crazy command."

"I can't believe how smooth it is," I said.

"There are some things I know about it, and it listens to me like I'm it's momma, but Martin is a creation of one of the teams," Jam said, smiling at Aisley as she looked up from the dash video.

"Teams?" Aisley said.

"I know they're going to be as excited at meeting you, as you will be to meet them," Jam said.

As we reached the green belt running into the mesas on the left, Martin veered left and just stepped over the fence. As each leg came up to the fence, it kicked out parallel to the ground like a dancer, and swung over the fence. They planted softly on the other side. If I'd had my eyes closed, I wouldn't have know we'd done anything different from floating above a paved road. The slight increase in the motor's rpm wouldn't have been noted by anybody but an old gear head. The main difference on this side of the fence was that the ground was alive with rabbits, jack and cottontail, fleeing our approach.

There were so many rabbits. The little cottontails exploded out of tufts of grass, invisible until the instant their white tail showed itself. They zipped a few dozen yards before tucking their tail, zig zaggin into another tuft or bush, and melting into the landscape again. Their terminal zigging was something that could confuse dogs chasing them. Some would fly by them on an assault, and maybe even loose their place in the chase, if the rabbit was really hidden. Unless Martin's big claws happened to be passing overhead again, they'd stay put in their new hide.

The jackrabbits were just the opposite, both in size and action. The jacks were easily five pounds or more in this bunch, well fed as they were on this salad. They started out their runs with the zig zag which turned straighter as they got up to speed. They wouldn't hang around but would run out from Martin's approach fifty to a hundred yards then stop, standing straight up. They preferred to keep a watch over the situation.

Looking into the long distance, sparse with creosote and mountain juniper, surprisingly few mesquite, and straggly desert black walnut, I knew I'd be seeing coyotes milling around at three hundred yards. I expected they'd be monitoring our track and waiting for a rabbit to make a mistake. If not now, soon. There is no way fox and coyote could stay away from this buffet, even in broad daylight, I was sure.

"Ok, here's the scoop about this," Jam said. "If we see Javelina, I'm going to shoot them. I don't want you guys wasting any meat with those cannons. If we see feral hogs, just tell me and we'll stop. If any survive, and you have ammo left after the encounter, you got to get out and walk."

We all laughed at that one. Feral hogs have been overrunning the state for decades now, and there wasn't any management scheme that worked as good as high speed lead.

"I aim to do my share," said Bear patting his .300. "If I can see 'em, I'll reach out and tap 'em hard".

"Oh yeah, I'm all in," said Aisley, turning to scan her side of the truck.

"If we see a deer, I'll let you know if you can shoot it," Jam said as he turned back around to watch our progress down the strip. The green was only about forty yards wide, but was brilliant against the winter brown desert.

"What is going on here with this?" Bear said, waving his hand around at all the green.

"You should see it in the Spring, the flowers are amazing," Jam said. "This is a winter mix that we sort of plant and maintain as we go."

"Plant and maintain?" I said, trying to figure what that could possibly mean.

"Martin, time delay 300 milliseconds; display foot prints over the last week, color the waterings blue, please. Pause."

As soon as he'd finished speaking Martin placed all its legs on the ground and stopped. The engine idled down. Almost as fast, the dash video display showed the satellite image of our position, even the truck and it's legs, on the screen. Quickly, in apparently 300 millisecond spacing, the image was populated with chicken footprints. The toenails were often blue, the placement of the prints tracing the travel of the truck over this path the last week. There were significantly different blue spots on the path up ahead on the map. None of the blue areas overlapped in the least but the chicken prints did. It looked like the travel was dispersed across the area as much as possible.

"That's about weird," said Aisley, pointing at one of the large blue circles ahead of us on the display.

"Yeah," said Jam nodding his head, "as you can see Martin tries to make sure not to step on any place any more than another. If possible. We're trying not to make paths through the wilderness. That's why each foot is so wide. Any single foot has as much weight bearing surface as all the tires put together. Theoretically, I'm told, even on two legs it has half as much pressure on the soil than the truck on it's tires. Very light footprint."

He owned us all as he continued his description.

"As we travel, the toenails are positioned to deliver water to the surface which is roughed up by the knobs underneath. If needed. We try to apply the equivalent of an inch of rain to a living plant every week. That's what the tank on back is for. Every pass, either direction, we give stuff a drink."

"But what are those big dots about?" said Aisley.

"This is another thing you're going to enjoy," said Jam. He turned to the screen and touched the nearest blue. "Martin, can you take us over to this, please?"

"Affirmative Jeremy, your wish is my command," Martin said in the sexiest voice I've heard this side of sleep.

"Dude, Martin's got a hormonal imbalance I think," laughed Bear.

Aisley was mumbling something to herself, about questions she'd asked trying to decide why she never heard Martin's voice.

"Yeah, I know," said Jam, "I named her Martin after Dr. King because this was looking like a dream to me. I have a dream, right? As far as answering, she only talks to a few of us. She's a baby, and they want to control who teaches her. The crew made her up, thinking that I said Mar Ten." Jam turned to look at me. "Maybe an ebonics issue? Anyway, the lady lead on that team thought that wasn't good enough for something this beautiful so they loaded her as Martine. I refused to change. I picked the name before they picked the voice."

Jam turned to Bear, and said, "She is easy on the ears though, isn't she?"

Bear smiled and started glassing the countryside. In any direction, there were twenty rabbits looking at us within slingshot range.

As Martin ambled over to the place for the blue dot on the screen, the grade of the land started sloping off to the left at about twenty degrees, but there was no change in the cab's orientation. As we came nearer, we could see a spindley, but vigorous, tree sticking out of a short tower of rocks. More rocks formed two low walls tracking up the hill from the main tower.

"Rest Martin," said Jam, and she did, lowering the truck to the ground and idling down. She still kept the cab level as one side of the trucks tires touched the ground.

"Come look at this, y'all," he said.

We piled out of the truck and walked over to the tree. There was a thin tree exploding willowy branches from a circle of rocks four feet high. It looked like a dry stack done by the same people that did the Machu Pichu[1] construction: very tight, the fit like puzzle pieces. The two low lines of rocks extended up hill like a "V" from its base. Each of these legs was ten feet long.

"Oh wow," I said. I could tell from looking around that I was speaking for everyone.

"Yeah, pretty amazing. This is an Arbequina olive that they decided we should be growing. The wall of stones around it keeps the deer from raking it to death with their antlers. The rock lines are supposed to direct any fortunate rain draining down the hill onto it's roots."

"But why is it such a large blue spot on the display?" said Aisley with some impatience.

"This is rough country, dry country. These olives are noted for having shallow roots, spread wide to get as much of rare rain as possible. So we installed special watering for an experiment. It seems to be working," Jam said as he turned to the truck.

"Martin, water this tree, please," he said in a muffled tone.

Even though the truck was twenty feet away, it still heard him. It immediately rose and started moving towards us. All but Jam started backing off as it towered over us. As it neared, it started taking small stutter steps, inching its way up to Jam while beeping. It was almost a tweet.

"She has Asimov's three rules of robotics installed and is very careful. Strict observance of the rules leads her to believe that scaring us is bad, too. There is another rule of robotics that we're requiring ,too, from what we've learned here."

"I'd like to be part of that discussion," said Aisley.

"And you will," he said. He joined us at the side of the tree, then said, "Martin, water the tree, please continue." Martin moved with more alacrity once Jam had removed himself from the scene.

On reaching the tree, Martin reached over with one of the front legs and gently pushed aside the branches of the tree, the other arm reached into the rock encirclement and came out with a 4" PVC cap. It pulled back just enough for another pipe embedded in the front claw armature to extend, then it slowly positioned inside the ring. In seconds the splashing sound of running water could be heard. Jam motioned us over beside the tree where both front legs of Martin were inside the ring, one holding back the branches and the other running water into a pipe almost flush with the ground.

"We drilled a ten foot deep hole next to each tree. We inserted PVC septic drainfield pipe, which we wrapped in landscape cloth to keep the dirt from falling in, and we fill that every week or so. Capping it keeps evaporation from the deep soil to a minimum. Any self-respecting plant is going to follow moisture down into the earth. We're hoping that training the tree to dive deep gives them a better drought tolerance once they're established." Martin replaced the PVC cap and it's front legs retracted to the ready again.

I glanced down the way and saw randomly placed tree rings, every hundred feet or so, marking a path on the green around the mesas.

"It looks like it's working really good," Mandy said.

"It is amazing the creativity of these kids. I guess they're kids to us, eh Jack?" Jam said. "When all we really have to do is enable them and they start spouting stuff that is so off the wall. Sometimes we try it, sometimes we don't. This is working better than expected. We haven't really planted an orchard but we have 200 trees scattered around this trail over the next mile, which is about two commercial acres of olive orchard. Enough to play with anyway. We should be harvesting some of the first crop in two years."

Aisley had always been our gardener, too, and her eyes were really bright. "Are they all olives?"

"Pretty much. We're trying some other plants. But, when they asked me, I just blurted out that they were making me think this was like a new Eden. Then somebody mentioned Biblical plants. They just ran with it from there," Jam said shaking his head with a smile. "Now, they're looking for landscaping ideas from the Bible. It's hard to believe this stuff is growing out here in the desert isn't it?"

Bear turned back from looking over the wide draw and said, "But what about all the ground cover? There's a ton of forage here. I don't think I've ever seen so many rabbits."

"Rabbits, deer, javalina. Then predators of course. And snakes, but they're so full of rabbit they can hardly move," Jam looked at us and raised his eyebrows. "Keep an eye out though. Martin, demonstrate watering a ground planting."

At this command, Martin reached over with it's front right foot, made a fist with one finger extended, then pressed that claw on the ground near a tuft of grass for a few seconds then pulled it's leg back. Where the claw had been there was now a neat little pattern. The tetrahedral spikes had lightly imprinted the ground and each one had it's own pool of water which was quickly disappearing into the desert soil.

"And that's how we do it today."

"Did Martin do that rock work, too?" asked Bear. "That is really something special."

"Let's say relatives. But none of this will have the impact of what I'm about to show you. Let's mount up. Martin, rest," Jam said, then he stepped over to the lowering truck and opened the driver's door. We all followed, returning to our seats.

In seconds Martin was striding us down the wide green path into the mesas, the bow of the truck pushing a wave of rabbits. The quickly passing scenery and engine revs proving our host was as eager to get us to wherever we were going as we were to get there.

5.

"Martin, go to the overlook," Jam said, and the creature of iron, electrons, and chrome started veering slowly off the green path.

We were making good time. We were quiet, like we'd all been covered up by what we were experiencing. Jam was the only one that seemed to be scanning for game like a real hunter. Aisley and I were hypnotized by the motion of Martin's legs again. Mandy was watching the new footprints getting plotted on the display, as was Bear, and they were intermittently scanning the brush. The low moan of the diesel facilitated the trance state. Most impressive was how quiet the hydraulics were. The extended space between the cab and the bed was totally boxed in, and while you got a sense of the valves switching the flow around, it was not so loud as to be foreground noise. It just blended in with the diesel to give a sense that this was a machine. A well executed machine, purring.

At each step, Martin would lift a chicken foot, starting from the heel, rolling onto it's steel toes, before finally lifting and placing the tire tread encased heel on the ground to start again. In passing, we could see where some toe prints left the little lakes on the ground, while other times it did not. Checking the monitor and the surrounding area visually, proved that Martin kept perfect track on which areas hadn't had a drink in a while. Watching only the motion of her legs, without being informed of the rules, it would be impossible for the untrained observer to note that each foot placement wasn't quite what was expected, if you had been steady walking in a direction picked by a crow. Each step either slightly longer, wider, or up next to the body. Martin was selecting, stepping, and gardening at each step.

"I can't believe how quiet she is," I finally blurted out.

"She's all super tech," said Jam. "They put in some active sound suppression in the hydraulics area in back. Whatever that is. The engine compartment is going to get some soon, too, but we're re-prioritizing almost every day, if not every hour. The slope and scale of what they're doing is ... ," Jam said, his voice trailing off.

Jam must have noticed us in the rear view mirror. "If you're actually hunters, you know games going to be a little farther from the truck, right?" he said as he turned in his seat, catching us all focused on Martin's feet at our sides.

"Who are *they*?" Bear inquired, scanning the brush. Besides Jam, he was the only one of us that was tending towards actual hunting. The rest of us had pretty much focused on Martin so that only game on the left side of the truck was in any danger.

"You'll get to meet our crew when we get to where we're heading but I don't want to spoil any surprises," said Jam, as he checked his rear view mirror to catch our expressions.

"Surprises? I'm already fixing to pass out, I'm so overwhelmed!" said Mandy. "I've heard Jam stories for many years, but this is something else."

Jam looked in the rearview at Mandy sitting in the middle, "Now listen here, y'all, there's a good chance that most of those stories make him look lots better than he should."

"I always try to lay it out like that," I mumbled, looking out towards the brush.

"We'll just have to go over them one at a time and see how much damage he did to my reputation," Jam said, returning to scanning the brush.

"Reputation … Ha! I'd really like that." I meant all of it, too.

In unison the reply was, "Me, too."

Aisley just had to add, "It will be good to get even a little truth perspective on some of those stories." She punctuated it with a sheepish grin to me.

The uniformly positive shouts of agreement echoed around the cab.

We covered the next mile or so in silence except when one of us pointed out an animal that wasn't a rabbit. It was unbelievable the number of rabbits that kept jumping up. Sometimes, it seemed that every footprint had spontaneously generated a rabbit explosion as they burst out of their hiding places. Other animals were there, too: porcupines, skunks, rock and ground squirrels, and sometimes we saw snakes in the open. But, the rabbits made the desert appear to squirm in waves due to their huge numbers.

The actual game we were looking for, deer and hogs, were another thing. We saw some whitetail doe, but no mulies. No hogs or javelina. Jam didn't want us shooting any that we saw, because he had that big muley tied up on the other side of the hill for one of us. Being that it was the middle of the day now, and Martin wasn't exactly deer-stalking quiet, this wasn't surprising.

The carpet of green that marked our path

went around an outcropping of a mesa on our right, and disappeared from view. As we neared the outcropping Martin started veering right to the mesa itself. Approaching the base, it became apparent how steep it really was, the slope approaching 45 degrees. As we took the first couple steps up the hill, Martin again kept the cab level, but the front legs extended, positioning in front of us like anchors into the hill. I had the sensation that the mesa was getting pulled down in front of us by the front legs. They were continually reaching up above us, moving the mesa down past the front grill. It was disorienting. The relativity of it was unnerving, because of the steadiness of the cab. One minute your eyes would confirm that you were moving up the hill, then blink, and they'd convince you that the hill was sliding down in front of you.

"Ok y'all, put your seat belts on," Jam said, as he started belting up. We obeyed quickly. The dash display of the footprints showed that this wasn't a common route.

Jam looked around to be sure we were all buckled in, then he said, "Martin, crawl." Immediately, the truck lowered down, the body coming parallel to the ground, wheels close to touching, the stance widened as it moved. "It's much better to have the tires closer to the ground, with six hydraulic anchors in case we hit a soft spot." The diesel and hydraulics assumed a more aggressive note.

With the truck body now lowered, we could see the summit coming up through the windshield, and it wasn't a calming thing. It looked to be a nearly vertical climb to the top of the mesa for the last twenty feet. Aisley saw it coming first.

"I ... uh ... not sure I want to be inside on this part. I got kids!" she said, her voice drifting up a scale. "I think I'd rather watch if you can let me out," she said as she spun towards Jam with a seriously questioning look, then over at Bear for support.

"Don't worry, we're pulling over to the left on a little overlook pad," Jam said pointing to our destination. Up and ahead to the left, was a level piece of ground, obviously cut into the mesa by a dozer judging from the spoil pushed off down the hill.

As Martin started to turn off to the pad, she began tipping off to the left and Jam hit the auto door lock.

"Sorry about that. I've been meaning to fix that. It used to auto lock when we started moving. I'm not sure what we did to her," Jam said. She was tilted enough to the left side so that we were leaning hard into the seat belts. It was reassuring to have the locks, too.

Unlike when we had been traveling on the relatively flat desert floor, the toenails of each foot were now grasping at the hill. Martin was walking more on her toes now than her heels. While some rocks covered by a foot might shift and pop, the overall footing was secure and seemed firmly anchored to the side of the mesa.

When we were within ten yards of the lookout pad, Jam said, "Close your eyes, please, and don't open them till I say, ok?" He turned to validate his command and we followed orders.

With my eyes closed, I could feel the body of the truck leveling up again and the motor calming.

"Martin, rest," Jam whispered. The sensation of being lowered then the motor idling.

"Ok, open 'em!" Jam shouted.

I'm not exactly sure what the sound was that came out of my mouth, but the others were able to actually form words expressing excitement and awe.

Bear and Aisley were out first, slinging their rifles over their shoulders as they piled out laughing. I looked at Mandy. Mandy stared back. There are times, when the goosebumps are so thick on your body, that your brain is overcome with emotion. Words just can't come. I knew it was like that for her, too, no need to ask.

"Oh.my.God," I was finally able to get out as I joined the others at the edge of the pad. Jam was still in the truck smiling at us, starting to rack his rifle in the overhead.

There on the desert floor, looking like some alien colony in the distance, were four unexpected buildings imagining a partial hexagon, partnered with one metal barn positioned at the open end. The barn, the simplest to get your mind around, was huge. It had overhead doors and regular entry doors on every visible side. The ones on the long side, away from the other structures, was covered by a large portico. The south side of the structure, facing the partial hexagon structures, was almost completely covered by large windows. Even at this range, probably a mile, the barn looked like it might cover a large part of a football field. In the center of all the other structures was a thin tower as tall as the tallest building. It was open on the sides facing the hexagonal sections.

The four parts of the hexagonal sections varied from two to four stories high. Each of the levels was connected, from one to the other, by a wide bridge. From where we were standing, the metal barn resembled a giant brick about to be dropped into a giant cup.

The ground around the buildings had the torn up look of a job site, but whatever equipment had been used was missing. One thing for sure, there had been large wheeled vehicles. I guess wheeled.

Jam came walking up with with a barely understated strut and said, "I guess the surprise worked?"

"Holy cow!" I said.

"Jam, you've set a high bar for surprises on this trip," said Mandy.

Bear and Aisley turned to him and murmured agreement.

"That barn was what we started with. It was living quarters but now its mainly labs and cafeteria. The other parts are the main structure that sort of got me going here. That's the panopticon."[1]

Mandy was doing it cuter, but I was looking at him with a dumb look I'm sure. Bear and Aisley had their phones out immediately, asking Siri about a panopticon.

Aisley held her phone out to us first, as it started reciting, " ... was a type of institutional prison, configured so that a single watchman in the center tower could theoretically see all the prisoners. It was proposed in the late 1700's by the social reformer Jeremy Bentham.[2] The name is derived from Panoptes, the giant with a hundred eyes in Greek mythology ... "

Jam waved her off and she muted it.

"I immediately liked the name of the guy," Jam said smiling at us. We were all facing him now.

"I'll tell ya how this part got started. Rememberin' it now like it just happened. I was having a few beers with a doctor from Austin, that was out for a week of hunting, but he was traveling by himself. He'd recently lost his wife, so I just naturally started hanging around with him to give him some company. We got to drinking one evening and he was going on about his utopian ideas, which him being from Austin, I just shined that leftist crap on. Once I got lubed up I started talking, too. Before long, we had started getting more synchronized. I started on the 'if I was King', and we ended up running over many of those things that you and I had covered."

"I haven't thought of that in a good long while," I said under my breath.

"I bet you real money that when we start talking about it, the years will clear away like a gulley washer cleaning the draws," he said.

The words were barely out of his mouth, before images of us as cowboys sitting around fires, testing ideas, began drenching me in memories. The cold beer and clear nights, lit by stars and mesquite coals, had inspired visions that hadn't yet been colored by experienced reality. Even though I was sure there were plans that didn't live through those nights, weighed down by cases of beer, and there were more than a few of those, there was always a generous core that made a skeleton for the next debate. If either one of us had been made king, we'd already laid out programs that youthful enthusiasm was convinced would solve the world's problems.

"Anyway," Jam continued, now starting to wave his arms around, "One of the things he talked about, was how I had the absolute laboratory here. If we can do it here, in this West Texas desert, it would be something that could work anywhere, maybe even on Mars. He talked about Walden Pond by Thoreau and Walden Two by B.F. Skinner and he seemed to really love them. I had only the dimmest memory from high school."

We all looked around at each other.

"Yep, you know we did, Bud," I said shaking my head. "I know why it was dim, too, but I didn't care for Skinner either. We had to read Walden, too ... as in also. Sat on me the same."

"We had to read Walden Two in high school," said Bear.

Mandy followed up, "Maybe ... me too."

"Yep. That was the end of it really. Forgotten. The stress of keeping up with the scheduling for the Trading Post, keeping the ranch going, everything. It had gotten hollow. I'd taken to drinking, and chasing country girls that were throwing themselves at the rancher. I guess the only thing I can say, is that it wasn't filling up a hole I had in my heart. One more quart, one more booty call. Never filled it."

He looked around at us, we looked at each other. Could have heard a pin drop even in the desert breeze.

"So one night I was drinking by myself, again, and I love that Knob Hill Single Barrel Reserve ... smooth as polished glass," Jam said as he paused to check for recognition.
"Agreed. Usually fills the drink 'em dead flask," I said, and again, we all smiled.

"So, when you get a tall glass of ice flavored up with the first pour, and then you cover it over with the second, then ... well, sometimes it can lead you to ... forget? Maybe do a little sleep walking. This particular night, I completely forgot and ended up waking up to the sight of porcelain. Some how, some way, *somebody* had wedged me between the toilet and the wall at the same time knocking the toilet off it's seal and jamming it against the vanity. So there I am, stuck, with the toilet holding me in position." At that he raised his eyebrows and smiled, then flung his arms, left behind his back, the other like he was trying to put his right elbow in his ear.

"It was a fearful awakening. It was during one of our off weeks, and I was the only one out here. I was totally stuck. My arms were wedged against the wall and toilet at my sides, my head was back in the corner under the toilet tank. It throbbed like the bourbon and gravity and toilet had conspired to massage it to mush. Only my legs could move freely and there was nobody for miles to call, even if I could reach my phone! Which I couldn't."

He looked down at his feet and started laughing.

"I tried to wiggle around to wake up my phone, hoping it would answer me, but, nope. *Hey Siri, Hey Siri, SIRI!'*. When I needed that stupid phone, it wouldn't wake up. I was squirming around like a worm on a hot rock."

"Oh man," said Bear, "I resembled that back in a previous lifetime. They say."

Aisley slapped his shoulder.

We all laughed with some nervous embarrassment. I've never been trapped by a toilet. That I remember.

"I was stuck up in there on my left side, laying on top of my left arm. It was, by then, senseless and totally useless. The wall was to my back and the toilet was to my front. My right arm was pressed into place over my face and held in place by the toilet tank. My right hand was actually free behind my neck. Because I was stuck in there rotated a little onto my belly, my legs, while free, were almost useless. The angle I was trapped in there meant I couldn't apply any real pressure against the wall to my back and even when I did the toilet was jammed up hard against the vanity. Because of the angle, I could only move my right leg forwards towards the vanity and then I could only just touch it. I kicked the stuffing out of the baseboard as much as I could in sock feet hoping to drive myself back an inch to free my right arm."

He looked around at all of us, then said, "Stuck like a rat in a trap of my own drunken design."

"I don't know how long I'd been there when I woke up, but I know I yelled at that phone for at least an hour. Throwing my legs around, trying to pull myself out just a little, so that I could bring my right arm into play. Any little movement to the rear seemed like it might free my right arm so I could push myself out. I was just jammed up tight, pardon the pun. And that's when it got worse."

I don't know about the rest of them, but I could see the reenactment was replaying the real fear he'd felt in that moment. Mandy must have seen it, too, because she walked over and started holding onto his arm. He placed a hand on hers.

"Of course I'd tried ordering God to let me loose, then pleading and begging. But all that time, inside, I was calculating what *I* was going to do. How *I* was going to get myself loose. How *I* was going to conserve my strength for the next attempt, surely successful this time because *I* planned it better."

At this point, Jam took a deep breath, and looked around at all of us.

"That's when I felt the cold chills coming over me. *I* knew it was fear and *I* just needed to keep my wits about me. It wasn't minutes before the nausea caused by that fear started building, and then the uncontrollable fear started, which *I* couldn't resist."

Jam started patting Mandy's hand, smiled and looked up at the sky. Taking another deep breath, he looked back at us. I could see tears welling.

"I was practically face down on the tile

AND projectile vomiting. And I'm not talking about some wimpy watery stuff. I'm talking about the chips and salsa, steak and loaded potato, full good-meal type. The kind of stuff that is easy to clog nostrils and airways. The kind of technicolor yawn that brings back memories of everything you ate in the last 12 hours. By the fourth ejection, I was crying, working to blow it away from my mouth and nose so that I could breathe that stank air. It was pooling up around me, and I could feel it passing down my left side as if I was the puke dam. My prayers were taking on a different tenor. My youthful training brought something to my mind, clear as a bell in that stressed moment, that anchored me at last. I truly and truthfully humbled myself under the mighty hand of God and cast my anxieties on him, (I later searched out to be 1 Peter 5:6). I was mightily troubled at that moment, but a peace came over me. I took it to mean I was going to be with the Lord that very day. And I welcomed it, believe me! But the heaves left and the air seemed to change for the better."

He looked us over and said, "Bro, you should see your faces."

Aisley was the first to speak, "Oh yeah, that's something I was expecting! It better have a happy ending or I'm ruined for the day."

"From there, I sensed ... felt, I can't describe it to you really. A small quiet feeling came over me. Not words. Not a vision. The Lord led me, that's what I am sure about, that I should kick the vanity again. And I did. Strengthened by his presence, I felt my predicament change. The whole side of my body had now been lubricated, and I know my body volume had decreased by gallons, and I was able to move. Then more. Then freed my right hand. In thirty seconds I was out."

"Oh thank God," said Mandy.

"Ok, that's one for the books," I said.

"You know it ain't clean yet," said Jam, "I was sitting there on the bathroom floor, covered in vomit, giving real thanks to the Lord. A sacrifice of thanksgiving, if that means anything to ya, and another scripture popped into my head. Now, you know Jack, I wasn't a Bible reader after we got bigger. Meemaw always made me go to church and sat by me until I could ask to be baptized. It's in me. Spirit's in you, too. And then decades after I'd read the Bible at all, Isaiah 55:8 came into my mind, 'For My thoughts are not your thoughts, Nor are your ways My ways'. The instant this formed in my mind, the concept of God being golden light beaming throughout the universe, super strings of Love, filled me up. Super strings? Where did that come from? Like, what little I now know from the net, the foundation of every particle we know is actually energy. Every single particle of every hair on our head."

"Ok. That's deep," said Bear.

Aisley grabbed his shoulder and looked into his eyes nodding, then they both stared back at Jam.

"So what does that have to do with all of this?" I asked, still stunned by what I'd heard.

"That's exactly how I felt. My life, in the world, didn't change except for the fact that now I knew there was something for me, a path, and it required me to be sober. It wasn't hard for me to leave the booze after that. I became obsessed with studying the Word, but I was also nudged back towards Walden Two, remembered from that old widower. Now it really fired me up."

"In what way?" said Mandy, looking at him, then over to me raising her eyebrows.

"That puke B.F. Skinner wrote a new introduction to his book in 1976, where he said that he thought China was the country that was going in the right direction. China. A communist dictatorship, that had just come out of the Cultural Revolution[3] where millions of citizens had been abused. I knew that the idea

B.F. seemed to enjoy, like most elites, was the regular people getting sent to the fields. That was something that just had to be addressed. But, just like regular, the shiny nature of the idea faded over days, until the work of the Trading Post just papered over it. I had become, however, a regular church attendee."

At this he looked directly at me, wiggled his eyebrows, which led me to say, "I think that's all to the good."

"Any hoo, every once in a while, I'd pick up that B.F. book, and almost every time, it just made me madder. I didn't know what to do about it. It seems like leftists are all about restricting the choices of free people, cultural engineering us. I knew that was just wrong, but lost as to what to do about it."

"Months passed, plenty of time alone out here with the internet. I came across a blog site, Instapundit[4], run by a Tennessee law professor, Glenn Reynolds, which came to be part of my daily, required reading. It wasn't weeks after I started reading that blog, that he introduced me to the panopticon in one of his postings. It just washed over me like a warm bath that it should be tested right here." At that, he pointed down at the community of buildings.

"Wanna check it out?" Jam said, moving back to Martin.

"*Damn straight,*" somebody said. We loaded ourselves into Martin and Bear and Aisley racked their rifles in the overhead.

As soon as we were all belted in, Jam said, "Martin, take us to the panopticon." Martin revved up, and that first step over the edge was a bit challenging. Aisley reached frantically to the hand grab in the front overhead, Mandy grabbed on to me, and Bear grabbed on to the back of Jam's seat.

Heading down the steep hill, it was easy to see Martin's feet hitting the hill on their heels, the claws digging in and spread wide, like a cat stretching its paws. The clawed front arms were swimming in front, selecting anchor points like slalom skiers with their poles. But, this passage was straight as an arrow and steady.

A couple of steps down the hill, and then the questions started. There were cantilevered balconies extending well out of the south side panopticon units. Some were draped with dead and dying plants, while others were enclosed in plastic wrap, giving them the appearance of hexagonal spines protruding from the main building. There were acres of some kind of metal appearing spines sticking out of the ground around the base of the panopticon, like bare corn stalks, and their appearance was odd, in a desert mirage kind of way.

The most engaging feature of the hexagonal sides, was that they had definite clear blue bands that encircled each one. It was so blue and so clear that it was hard to take your eyes off it, but at the same time didn't seem to be a part of the building. It immediately reminded me of the blue of the glaciers in Alaska.

Jam didn't answer any question.

"I told y'all," he'd say, "I don't want to lie to you. When we get down there I'll hook you up with the experts."

We got the message and just rode the rest of the way without questions, however, there was constant pointing bracketed by *"Oh.My.God"*.

6.

When we got down to the valley floor and Martin walked us around towards the north side of the metal barn, it was even more captivating. It was easy to see that the blue bands on the main panopticon building were not part of the structure. The blue light appeared to be floating a few inches off the surface of the building and beaming between panels at each corner. Now we could tell that the ground around the building was covered with metal spikes of varying sizes, from two to four feet, which appeared to have sharply beveled points which flared the sun's reflection at us as we moved around it. Each spike also had a strange rainbow-like halo sphere, barely visible, like a rainbow heat mirage.

While these sights were enough to draw everyone's attention, the thing that really jumped out at me was the missing shadows. It was now past noon on a clear Texas fall day and there was barely a shadow on the north side of the panopticon. It should have been casting long solid shadows.

"Hey ... Hey there's no shadow!" I shouted.

"That's not technically true. You can see

the shadow from the spikes," answered Jam.

"But, Jack's right, there's no real building shadow, except directly underneath," said Bear.

Where the shadow from the building should have been, there was none. Or at least it was not the crisp darkness you would expect from a building this large. Inside that area, where the shadow should have been, the spikes were casting a shadow, however, not as distinct as those outside that zone. The light inside that should-have-been shadow zone was more diffuse, the shadows fuzzier, and, again, there was a faint hue shift[1]. The same shift seemed to affect the spike points, and their halos.

"I know there's no answer you will give to this one before we get out. Right?" said Mandy to Jam, who shrugged, then she cocked her head at me.

As we turned towards the portico, we were each looking back at the panopticon base, when suddenly, the inside surfaces became visible, and we began seeing scores of people and ... robots? ... moving along the breezeways. The bullet shaped devices moving amongst the people immediately made me think of R2D2 in Star Wars, only smaller and flatter. We had just become aware of the inner structure of cells and breezeways, seen the movement of the people, when our view was blocked by the barn.

"Oh yeah, this is your heaven, isn't it, sugar?" said Mandy as she reached up front to shake Aisley's shoulder.

"No doubt," was all Aisley could get out.

"And there's our welcoming committee," said Jam.

Standing against the wall of the building, under the portico, was a small group of young people leaning against the wall. The only common factors were that they all seemed to be wearing cowboy boots and be under thirty. The women were particularly striking if they were wearing tight Wranglers, but the skirts and boots had a special appeal, too. The few men were pretty typical in boots, jeans, some with western cut shirts, others not. They all stayed against the wall as Martin pulled in.

"Martin, rest," Jam ordered.

As soon as we'd settled to the ground, the group moved up and started opening the doors to help us out. There was the door opener, then the greeters, who each had two bottles of water.

The greeting was a variation of, "It's so good to see you. Jeremy told us you were coming and we're really excited to get to share with you. My name is ... " , then they'd hand a bottle of water over. It was passed over with an atmosphere that implied their hand was going to return to them empty. Placing it in your hand, and then grabbing it with both their hands like the greeting from a warm friend, made it feel rude to not take it.

Then, Keila, as she'd noted, immediately opened her bottle, while staring deeply into my eyes, took a drink, then said, "Welcome". It has been more than a long time since such a beautiful dark-eyed woman looked at me like that.

Who hasn't been lured into a yawn by another's yawn? The same thing happened with the welcome drink. I looked around our group and we were all in various stages of imbibing the offering when I finished mine and said, "Thank You."

Keila took my elbow and started walking me to the door on my right side, with Lindsay walking on my left.

"Jeremy said you were all interested in what we're doing here, and we're very excited to show you," Keila said.

I was still a little flustered from the water ceremony, but I looked back, and each of us was being escorted in by a pair of beautiful young people. Even Jam. They'd given him water but they were escorting him quietly, without the elbow support, and following a half step behind. He definitely had a more confident walk than I did. After a couple of steps he leaned over and whispered something to the young man walking on his left and then the older lady on his right, patted her on the shoulder, and then they were both off on some mission inside.

Lindsay stepped forward and opened one of the double doors for us, while one of Mandy's escorts opened the other. Stepping through the doorway of the metal barn was like walking into a 17th century castle. On every wall and most of the ceiling were intricately carved and painted French boiserie panels, a term I'd mastered at Versailles on our tour of France. A portion of the ceiling was covered with the most intricate coffered ceilings that I'd ever seen. Believe me when I say that I'd seen some, because we'd spent an entire year traveling Europe when it looked like it might become unwelcoming to American tourists.

Every panel, starting from the entry door, was more and more intricate in both it's carving and it's painting. All of them were painted. The floor was also tremendous, but who could look down right now.

Bear was already at the wall, looking at it closely, then thumping it. He said, "Foam?" as he looked to Jam.

Jam motioned to the last few sections of the

ceiling that weren't completed, "Closed cell foam, right," he said. The foam had been laid on very thick and where it wasn't shaped it protruded inches into the space.

"How do you get it like this?" asked Aisley, now thumping some panels, too.

At this, Jam pointed at Keila and a young man, and immediately the rest left after a wink or a wave. As they started walking off, Mandy got up from the floor where she had been feeling it's texture, too. The floor didn't follow the design of the wall panels at all. Starting from the door it resembled the typical stained and scored concrete floor but evolved down the hall into an intricate Roman mosaic floor.

"Hey y'all, my name is Randy," said the young man. "This is all an example of how we've been training our mobile CNC platforms."

Mandy looked at me, and I said, "Computer numerical control ... machine tool robots." She nodded and looked back to Randy. He smiled at her like you might smile at your mother.

"If you'll notice, from the door to the end of the hall, each successive panel gets more and more intricate in both it's design and it's paint scheme. That one right there, by the door, with just a few typical trim pieces, is still intricate, compared to most finish carpenters work. It was the first and it took three hours to carve and another three to paint."

Before he had finished talking we were all at the panel, caressing and thumping it.

"Then the process team met, we suggested improvements, gave it another design, and that's this one," he said doing a Vanna White impression to the next panel. "Even though much more intricate with it's carved leaves and animals, this one only took two hours but the paint still took a little over three." It was a white panel like the other one, but the raised portions were now painted in gold and silver. It was striking.

"How did you zero it?" asked Aisley.

"Excellent question," said Randy, and you could tell from his expression that he respected it. Bear looked over at me and nodded with pride. Randy went over and knelt down beside the two panels and pointed to a nail head that was flush with the face of the panel.

"We affix these nails to the studs, and, if you get down here, you can see that it has a little crosshair on it. Each of the machines has a little microscope camera[2] that matches up the crosshairs, and, voila, they're zeroed and know exactly where they are in 3D space. To five thousandths of an inch."

Randy stepped away and Aisley and Bear

bent down to check it out.

"We normally paint over it as the last step, but Jeremy said for us to prepare little presentations for you guys so I scratched this one off," Randy said. "There were cascading issues with setting this; should it be at max, or wall plane, foam depth, et cetera. We had to re-foam this first part twice before we got it right. The production systems are rock solid now."

"Any more questions about the panels?" Jam inserted.

"What do you mean production systems?" I said.

"Each system we ... they ... get going we go out to market with it. There's teams in most large border cities, the master hub is in San Antonio, and they're working with custom builders implementing this in custom homes. We are very picky because these are clearly disruptive technologies. Whereas a good trim carpentry team can do the same work, if you don't get too out there, our bots can complete a 3000 square foot home in a couple of days and that includes the painting. So basically, we're replacing sheetrock, insulation, trim carpentry, and interior paint in one fell swoop."

"Oh man," Bear said. The shock on his face obvious.

We looked around at each other with blank

stares.

"After they sign a non-disclosure agreement, we give them a demo on their site at night after the building is dried in," said Jam, "It specifies that we have exclusive access to the building for two weeks while we work it. No other trade or person can have any access, so that we can keep it quiet. We even put foil over the windows." Jam looked around at each of us in turn. "Locked doors and a 24 hour security presence."

"Once they try us," Jam said, "they want to use us exclusively." Jam was shaking his head negatively. "We can't do that yet. It would let their supply chain know things were happening. We won't even think about working with anyone if our participation is more than eight percent of their total business." At that, he stared hard into me. "We are getting closer to coming out, but we're not there yet."

"How many teams do you have?" asked Aisley.

Randy answered quickly, "Twenty three in San Antonio, which is the original hub, Laredo, Del Rio, El Paso, and starting in New Mexico and Arizona, in the larger cities. All total, closing on a hundred. We can easily add one per week in outlying areas, but only for the largest custom home builders, so the individual impact is reduced. It's still secret squirrel stuff."

Randy looked to Jam, who nodded ok, then he said, "Thanks y'all, see you around."

"How can you add teams that fast?" asked Bear.

"Have you ever read about the PC gray market when they first appeared in the early 1980's?" said Jam. "Once you get the hardware and software mix settled, you can slap stuff together in a hurry. We are limiting ourselves on purpose." He nodded to Keila.

"My name is Keila and I was the lead on the team that was working on the floor," she said.

"Unlike the wall and ceiling guys - ", she started.

"What do you mean team lead here?" asked Mandy, with a smile.

"Oh, we just have small little groups. Less than ten, but usually about five, who look after a problem and try to get it into a beginning specification. We hand that off to the Host for alpha development. By the time it gets to the virtual beta, in the system, we've usually added some other stuff that we thought about. *Lead* is probably not what you're used to in other places. I just try to make sure everybody's thoughts get included, and all ideas are sampled, before we settle on *the* one we want to present. The Host is really the lead and final sifter."

"We'll get more into that tomorrow you guys," said Jam, "let's stick to the small stuff today, ok?" Jam nodded to Keila to continue.

"Small stuff?" said Bear and Mandy as one.

"Anyway," said Keila, "we decided we didn't want to have fixed zero points in the floor that we might have to patch later, so we drifted over to beacons modeled on LORAN[3]. That was a more long range protocol, allowing for some possible outdoor use eventually. After fiddling with frequencies, the Host was able to implement improvements that allowed us to use it within small spaces, and be accurate to within five thousandths of an inch."

"The Host?" I said.

"That's plenty of resolution for a floor, which you ain't gonna see up close, unless something goes terribly wrong!" said Jam, rocking his head, smiling wide, with his eyes closed. "And that's what they call all this!" Waving his hands all around, he said, "The Host."

"Come on, Keila, they're easily distracted so just talk over them," Jam said. At the sound of his voice, it was like she was completely his to control.

"So," Keila said, beginning again, "we've got these little strobing transmitters" and she picked one up in the back left corner, "and we place three in the distant corners of a room. We have the Host demonstrate, with a graphic, what it is going to be like. The next stage is, a bot actually draws the plan in chalk on the floor. Then we get the written approval. Got to have the written approval, because concrete doesn't patch cleanly if the customer changes their mind."

She looked around at us, then continued.

"We started with actual carbide router tools but the dust was crazy even when it was partnered with a vacuum. Now we use a water knife[4]. Matched with a wet-dry vac and we can even work in a house without covering the furniture. The best part is that it's repeatable enough so that, if we want, we can even leave the furniture in the room and just work around it until it has to be moved."

Keila moved over against the wall saying, "And we can get right up against the baseboards which we really couldn't do without it being a hassle for the mechanical router bits." It was hard to keep my eyes on her speech as the distracting brilliance of the work under her feet was impossible to ignore. It was real art.

Continuing, she said, "The nastiest part is putting the acid stain on which will smell up the joint something horrible. That is the real limiting factor of how fast we can proceed on this portion. We can do it with the vacuum sucking up the fumes, but we still have to limit the amount of coverage to protect from fumes. We're still working that. "

She walked to the back of the room, finally pointing down at the intricate mosaic design of Michelangelo's "Creation of Adam" in the floor. Cut into the concrete slab and colored, without a close inspection, you couldn't tell it wasn't mosaic tile. There wasn't a single tile-sized piece that was a square inch and damn few touching that were exactly the same color but it was perfect.

"This one took 48 hours. What do ya think?" she said.

At that, all we could do was murmur our approval. What does someone say to the Sistine Chapel? No words work.

"Thanks, Keila," said Jam, "I think we'd better get a bite to eat before it gets too much later."

"Thank you, Jeremy," she said and turned and walked through the back doors. When she went through it seemed that she was making some effort to keep us from seeing through to the next room.

Jam herded us together on top of the David in the floor, then put his hands on Mandy and my shoulders. "Ok, y'all, I want you to hold hands and close your eyes. This is a pretty good one, too," he said smiling.

One after another, we looked at each other. I know I couldn't, and I don't believe the others could imagine more coming at us to match what we'd already been shown. But, Jam sure seemed confident.

We held hands, in a chain, and he walked us through the same swinging doors. As we heard them closing behind us, the smell of bar-b-que overwhelmed us. He herded us gently by our shoulders into the position he wanted us, and said, "OK."

At first my eyes were blinded by all the light coming through the wall of windows on the south side of the building. As my iris adjusted, the panopticon was the first thing that came into focus beyond the windows, then the large room, then more of the intricately fashioned wall panels and coffered ceilings. Giant intricate chandeliers of unique design hung around the room, some sporting flickering faux candles while others were bright indirect light.

The room itself was large with seating for

hundreds. There were mostly four toppers around the central area, with many 10 seaters around the walls. At the time, there were dozens of people sitting around in small groups.

In large block letters above the windows directly ahead was *E PLURIBUS UNUM*. It was cut deeply into the foam and painted black. Off to the left was the source of the delicious smoke. There was a huge circular pit, with stacks of mesquite on a ramp leading into the pit. The pit was manned by something totally different. There were two bullet headed robots manning the pit and delivering the meat to plates. Except for the plate shelf, they were enclosed in a metal screen.

Jam led us off to a large table against the windows, nearest the pit.

"I know you are going to want to watch the servers," he said, waving us to follow.

Our escorts reappeared, and Keila asked me if I wanted her to make a plate for me. Mandy and I both said yes. Bear and Aisley walked over to the pit with their guides.

Jam, Mandy, and myself sat down at a long table. It was hard to decide which side of the table to sit on. I could either watch the robots serving the meat, or watch the robots and people moving around on the upper floors of the panopticon.

"Is this whole structure the Host, or only this building?" I asked as I sat so I could see the robot pit masters. Mandy sat across from me, on the side away from the pit. Jam sat at the end facing the panopticon.

"Well, we've had discussions about that. Typically, when we say it, we mean the entire structure, but all the big brains are hosted in this building and the standby site in San Antonio, and separating out "panopticon" is a little too many syllables. Some of us have grown to calling it *the pan* but that seems, if not wrong, not quite right. What do you think?" he said, turning to watch as Bear was coached by his sidekick on how to order.

Without missing a beat, Mandy said, "Hive."

Looking slowly back and forth between us, Jam said, "Yeah, I like it. It seems so obvious, really. I can't believe nobody here thought of it."

Bear and Aisley came and sat on each side of Jam. They had slices of pork roast, a small pile of pulled pork, pickles, jalapenos, beans, white bread and corn bread. Nothing out of the ordinary for this part of Texas, except for the pulled pork.

Aisley cut off her first bite of the roast, and

said, "Oh man, this is really tender. There's something ... is it cayenne?"

"I guess you asked for spicy," said Jam, "but there's three varieties. I guess they didn't tell you."

"No," said Bear, "they told us." He took the first bite of the sandwich as our trays arrived. "Holy Moses. That is some good there."

"I knew you'd like it," said Jam. In short order our plates were delivered and Mandy and I started feasting ourselves.

There were a couple of minutes of silence as we chowed down. Looking around the building, there were more phrases on the walls. Behind the pit was "1 Thessalonians 5:16" imprinted in a heavy serif font. At the other end of the building was "James 4:6", also in a heavy serif font. Both were painted black. Embossed above the doorway through which we'd entered was "Ephesians 6:16" but it was painted red against the beige paint of the wall panels.

"Yup, I do like it," said Jam at last. "I really do."

"What?" said Aisley.

"We were discussing what to call the panopticon, kind of a descriptive nickname, and Amanda suggested ... "

"Mandy!" Amanda said.

"Mandy said," Jam said, and smiled at her, "we should call it the Hive".

"Duh on that one," said Bear, "there's certainly a swarm."

Jam stood up, faced the majority in attendance and said, "Mandy," pointing at her, "just thought we should call the panopticon the *Hive* for shorthand."

Everybody in the place stood up and started applauding. And hooting. Hollering. It was a popular option obviously.

Jam sat back down. "That kind of represents why I called you out here. I'm never wrong," he said to me under his breath.

I could tell from his expression that my expression must have represented puzzled. "When I say something nobody wants to change it up. When I called it the panopticon it stuck, which it technically was founded on, but I know everybody got tired of it."

We all looked at him, then looked amongst ourselves, then silently pondered it over more eats.

Small groups of people were continually coming into the dining area to eat, some just came in to sit and chat over a drink. The amazing thing was that the majority were women with a distinctly Western style. The kind you might find in high end Dallas shops.

I've admired it many times. Tight Wranglers have always been a thing for me, yes.

"What's the scoop with the cages around the servers?" Aisley said, finally breaking the silence.

"Oh, I can't spell it out too tight, but from what I understand, computer programs before AI could be tested against requirements and coding that was fixed. Now, with these learning robots, you can't really test all the options. Because they continually learn, you don't know what they learned or if they learned it right. That's why Martin has a restricted access protocol. These guys," he hooked his thumb back to the pit, "are playing with knives amongst people. We all like it better having them caged up."

"Pretty fancy aren't they?" he said.

I hadn't been watching that close I guess.

"What do you mean? Fancier than a robot?" I asked.

"Oh yeah," said Bear, "they got a little bit of fancy knife work going on like those Japanese steak houses. Flipping and gittin', but no wild large movements. All inside the cage."

Between bites, we all watched the servers performance for a few minutes.

"Why aren't you eating?" I said between mouthfuls to Jam.

"Oh, I like to eat a little later. When ... ," he was interrupted by a young couple walking up to the table. They were wearing matching dusters that were mimicking a digital camo but made with different materials for every slash and dot, like a quilt.

"We'd like to go out tonight on the hunt, if there's room, Jeremy," said the man.

Jam looked around at us but we must have been blank about it because he decided. "I'm going to take Mandy and Jack back to the Post after running the fences. When I get back the five of us can go."

"Aw right!" said the man.

Aisley immediately got up and introduced herself to the woman, Sandy, and Jeff her sidekick, and then starting poring over their outfits. They were traditional cowboy dusters made of heavy canvas but with the camouflage hashes made of different materials. In short order Aisley had learned that they were made in-house.

"I have to go see this," Aisley said. Mandy immediately got up to go, too. Robot clothiers? That train was leaving.

"Ok y'all, be back inside an hour. I want to have time to ride the fences with Jack and Mandy later," said Jam.

"No prob," said Sandy.

141

"Maybe, don't let Aisley steer you off because she's a hard questioner and has a Masters in Constraint Programming," said Jam to their backs.

As they walked off, I could tell they were sharing geek welcomes and comparing fields of study. From what little I could hear both Sandy and Jeff were computer science majors, too. At least Mandy was going to get to check out the clothes. Bear was following along behind and I couldn't really tell his mood. Robots and electron mite things were his forte but shopping wouldn't seem as high on the list.

"Dude, where did all these kids come from?" I said.

Jam got up and walked over to the window and started staring out at the Hive. I joined him. There was motion at every angle.

"I had thought about it a lot. It just came to me that I needed to get people out here that were used to country. They had to, absolutely had to, enjoy hunting, and have some serious smarts. And were Christian, because living out in the sticks is no place to test each other's foundations. I didn't want to deal with it." He looked over at me, then leaned against the glass with his head down.

"My first exploratory trip had me going to the Texas A&M Christian club, which definitely wasn't very large for a school that size. I was feeling around for some engineering or computer *volunteers* in a post graduate program. I had no idea what I was doing. There were two girls, Keila was the computery one, Larisha, who you'll meet tomorrow, was the mechanical engineer. I talked to their parents, and texted them my driver's license. I offered to give them bonus money for volunteering but made sure to tell them it was not a job. More like an internship, but sort of paid."

"That was pretty bold of you," I said.

He turned to me and said, "Yeah, some guy wants to give money to take their daughters out to the desert. Insane, right?"

"Insane in spades," I said.

"Yeah, and that, too," he said smiling, "but I went to their small group study. Later, we got their parents on the phone and we all prayed together and things just crystallized. That first year was all about getting this building done. An insight Keila had, has focused us in everything we do. The single most important decision that has stayed as a critical point in every project. More robots, versus big robots. Ants versus elephants. Many, many hands make very, very light work."

I'm not sure why it didn't register before, probably because there were so many large ones, but the hive was alive with and literally crawling with small droids. Standing at the window, you could barely see the tops of the ones on the upper floors, and they were partly hidden even on the second floor. There was nothing on the ground level, it appearing that the entire structure and it's purpose was all on the upper floors. The various steel spikes were underneath, too, but only covered the area immediately around the hive.

"So how many people are there here?" I wondered aloud.

"Three hundred at any one time," Jam said. "It started to ramp up almost immediately that first summer. Their networks were deep. I paid every volunteer $1,000 a week to start for a three week trial. That's real money for a college student in the summer. Then a three day vacation in San Antonio. I have a wonderful old house in Olmos Park, a really nice 6-7, that I rotate them through as they desire, and send them off with $500 gift cards. We got a motorcoach that rotates a crew through every four days. Fortunately they're all good kids, and it's a big lot with the house far off the road, or the neighbors would be bashing me hard."

"That seems very generous for interns," I said.

"It is. They're worth it. You'll get a kick out

of that three hundred number," Jam said and he gave me a comical look I've seen many, many times. I knew the pause for effect so I was going to wait him out. I was looking at the Hive studiously ignoring him. He did the same. Two minutes of silence maybe.

"Uncle," I said finally.

"Gideon," he said, with twinkling eyes.

I shook my head. I honestly had no idea what he was talking about.

"You know. Gideon? 300? In the Bible?" he tried again.

I shook my head and I was feeling his disappointment this time.

"Ok, you'll figure it out," Jam said. "Judges 6. Let's go watch the serving robots for a while." He rose and led off to the pit.

We watched the serving robots for more than ten minutes. I just could not get enough of them. They'd ask for your order and knew right where that piece of meat was on the whole hog carcass. The pit was a circle twelve feet in diameter and the grill was the same size and rotated around in it.

"How many hogs are on there?" I asked the droid.

"Ten, sir," it answered.

I looked at Jam, "Ten? For real?"

"For 300, eats are real," he said. "The fire

and hogs never quit 24 hours a day and you can always find some ready here."

"But don't y'all get tired of Barbeque all the time?" I said.

"It's another Gideon thing," Jam said and smiled at me.

Any time the robot wasn't working up a person's order, they were slowly rotating the grill. When a customer came up and gave it a valid order, it would quickly rotate up the hog in current process and cut up what was ordered. The metal roof over the pit had two main doors where serving robots did their magic. If they were just rotating the grill, they closed the door which left two inches at the bottom open and the droid could reach in there to rotate it.

It was fun to watch them work. If neither robot was serving, they were rotating the grill. They would hook up to the grill through the opening window, and lean back, reposition, hook up, lean back. They looked like happy rocking droids, the two of them rowing the grill around. Jam told me all their droids used gravity and scavenged energy every chance they got.

When Bear had said they were fancy with their knife work, I now knew what he meant. They could take a slice off the hunk of meat, and flip it out of the pit onto the other knife in it's left hand, then spin that around just for effect like I've seen jugglers do with plates. I never saw it drop a single piece.

The cooking droids[6] could take individual ribs from the backbone with two flashing knives in a split second, and separate a heavy joint as if they had x-ray vision guiding the blade. Their cuts were always sure and quick. After watching that, and remembering the testing issues, I was glad they were behind cages, too.

"So how'd it go, sugar?" I asked Mandy, as the group returned from their visit to the clothing robots.

"They can do everything!" she said.

I knew I didn't want to get in that discussion so I was glad when Aisley, Mandy, and Jam started talking about material purchases and surging stitches and whatever. Bear and I went to get some coffee and just stood around and watched the residents. They were definitely easy to look at.

In a few minutes, Jam headed Mandy and me to the door, and handed Bear and Aisley off to Keila. He'd given her some instructions I'm sure but it was out of my earshot. We mounted up in Martin, limbered up the kids rifles, Mandy in front and me behind Jam.

"Ok y'all, I just thought we could ride some

fences in Martin and talk about old times some. How does that sound?" Jam had his seat turned around so his legs were between us.

"Works for me," I said. Mandy acknowledged it, too.

"Martin, let's ride the west fence starting at the southwest corner," Jam ordered, and Martin shifted directions slightly cutting cross country.

Thirty six sections requires a lot of fence. If it were square it'd be six miles on a side, but we learned this place was four miles wide at the widest, with two really long sides. We were going to be traveling a long side. When we hit the corner, Jam stopped and pulled an ice chest out of the back with a bag full of snacks. The ice chest had two six packs of Texas beers and Dr. Pepper. Everything had been considered. Even a fresh roll of toilet paper.

It was just like riding fences in the old days, minus the horses. Martin would slowly cruise along the fence, ten feet off, and would even ask our opinion of an area that might need a patch if we'd become distracted in our lies. Hogs are tough on field fence and, when there was a hole, we'd get out and patch it together. It was so like old times.

"Why don't you have the robots doing this?" I asked.

"This is not a priority. Tt is kind of tricky

with all this antique wire, and I kind of like getting out to do it," Jam answered, smiling. "Besides, nobody balls up a fence repair like you, and I need some comic relief!"

"Funny!"

The real experience was watching Martin handle the inevitable draws and wash outs that come off the mesas. The flat tops of these hills were often a unique environment all their own. My uncle had always explained that the plants on top got two or three times as much water as the plants down below. Seriously. It was mainly rock on top so what little rain hit it got soaked up by small patches of dirt. The flip side of that is a typical Texas gulley washer couldn't soak in, and would be cascading off the mesa, like Niagara. To say that it might roll a boulder was underestimating it.

There's always places, in this country, where you could be riding the fence and come to a gully that neither horse nor person could cross. It might only be thirty yards across, but a hard, rocky, and steep, twenty yards down. You'd have to ride miles around to start on that side of the fence over there. Martin didn't have that problem. When we came to gullies, Martin's only limitation was vertical drop. If the vertical drop was over twenty five feet, we'd have to go around. Anything else was doable, and she did it. Easily.

Like a squirrel hanging by it's back toes, Martin could lower herself down as surely as she could step over a short fence. You wanted to have seat belts on the first time or two, but once familiar, just a hand on the dash was enough. Nothing scary about it. Another interesting feature, was her ability to back the bed up to the the fence in a gully to make a work platform. The additional help, of being able to stack large boulders, made these washouts goat proof like nothing else I'd ever seen. There was no path needed for Martin. Each and every step was sure.

We'd started out with the rifles ready, but after getting started with the windows down, the stereo up, and more than a few empties on the floor, we eventually just enjoyed the time together. Mandy was forever beating on my old stories, checking the validation. Fortunately, I'm just so well rounded that I sound like a liar, because it's hard to believe anybody could live so many lives. It was a time.

The trip was so full of the past that no questions about the Host or Hive entered the conversation, even sideways. We were living the lives together that we'd missed. When we got back to stepping over the fence towards the Post again, it came to me, amongst other mysteries of the day, what Jam had said about calling me out.

"Earlier you said you called me out for a reason," I said.

"Yes. That is so true," Jam said as he looked over at me smiling. "We can flesh that out on the way back in tomorrow."

We were tired so he left us off at our tipi. He was racking the rifles back in the overhead, when he said, "We'll probably be late tonight because they don't clean hogs as fast as me. I wouldn't wait up. I'll be getting you up early in the morning, about 5:30, because we're going to start really hitting it. You're really fixin' to see something. Help yourself to whatever is in the Post kitchen if you need anything, anything at all."

He waved, Martin powered up, and they were skating back off to the Host.

Tomorrow we're *really* going to be hitting it. That phrase no longer represented boundaries. It could have been the cold descending on the desert that caused the chills but I don't think so.

Mandy and I walked over to the Post and grabbed some beer, made some sandwiches, and gathered up snacks. We tried to watch the sun go down from the porch, but the food, on top of all the excitement, made us drowsy. We decided to lay up in bed and watch the sun fade in the smoke hole window, but we faded out faster than it did. We were completely emotionally drained out but it was all good.

7.

The night passed as fast as a starving man attacking his plate. Dreams piled on each other, filling the space to where there was no more room when Jam honked outside the door. This morning, the glow from the light strings behind the tipi liner were way too bright.

"Oh man," I said to Mandy as she grabbed onto my arm. I pulled her upright.

"That was too short wasn't it?" she mumbled as she straightened her hair with her fingers. I'd always loved that moment in the morning. Her beauty always shined through the mess of any night tosses.

"So I guess we forgot to set an alarm. Hey, Siri, what time is it?" I said.

"It's 5:30 A.M., Good morning Jack," the phone said. At almost the same moment, there was a light knock on the door.

"We got some time", said Jam through the door, "I'll load up some coffee for us. I'd like to get out of here in 15, if we can, but don't hurt yourselves getting ready. Just hop in the truck when you're ready and I'll come on back down."

Mandy and I did the morning routine,

changed some things, but covered it all with the same camos we'd worn the previous day. We were in a place where opportunity could present, so we left the tipi with our rifles. We stepped into Martin, racked the rifles, and Jam headed down from the Post with some travel mugs and a large green thermos.

"Mornin' y'all," he said. "Let's get you charged up. The others had a long night of it so they're sleeping in." He commenced to filling the mugs, which went fast, because we took it black.

"So what are we up to today, Jam?" Mandy said as she tested the coffee. She shook her head and shoulders like it might have bit her back.

"If I told ya, it wouldn't be a surprise no more," he said. He looked back and forth between us like he was really enjoying this. I was, too. Mandy gave me that secret look, barely noticeable but blaring to the educated. That look wives have to let their husbands know we're on the same track. Or not.

"Martin, let's head to the Host," Jam ordered the machine, and the diesel and legs came alive at the same time. We were moving down the road again, without so much as a tremble to disturb the coffee in our mugs. Of course, that's not saying much because it was almost thick as syrup. I'd had this before when we were running buddies.

Over the next minutes we shared stories we hadn't covered yesterday. There were stories of jobs we'd had on various ranches in the hill country, or escapades that could only be explained to those who were close. Times where coffee was shared before dawn, just like this, waiting with saddled horses for there to be enough light to head out for the day. Hauling hay for 25 cents a square bale, cowboying, and herding all have stories. The ones where beer was involved offer differing perspectives. Mandy was enjoying hearing them because many of these were actually new to her.

Tossing a bale of hay to find a rattlesnake baled up in it is something that always gets shared, and she was tired of hearing it. Things like getting jerked off your feet by a confused cow dog had been lost in time. Talk about sharing kisses with a rodeo cowgirl, with her cheek full of dip, is something you would never share with a young wife. One story led to another and another, linked chains of memory. We were half way to the Host when he finally got serious.

"This is the thing, Jack," he finally said, using a voice a quantum of energy below where we'd all been.

"We, the group of us, mainly them, have been implementing something that is amazing and terrifying at the same time. For months I've been led to call you because, you, with your real estate experience and experienced interfacing with attorneys ... but that's only part. At the start, because I know you will have my back again, the issues with attorneys and government and the press are something I think you can help us with. I know you can. I'm expecting a deluge and I've never been one to stand in front of crowds too much."

"If your teams are making the kind of money that you imply they are, it would seem like you could purchase all the professional support you need," I said. I was starting to feel the pressure of some new responsibility gelling up.

"They are. The problem is that there are always professionals that can be found on the net or some brother-in-law referral. That doesn't tell you what kind of working relationship you're going to be able to build. Some will rape you for a dollar, all along the razor's edge of legal. Others will not be what you need, but you won't find that out till maybe it's too late. We don't have time for that. This is a cusp event in history and we ... I ... need somebody that is close and trustworthy."

He reached over and grabbed a hold of my shoulder. "I'm pretty sure this is going to be the wildest ride you ever sat. Bar none."

He turned in his seat to look directly at Mandy, "And that means there's going to be a huge role for you, too. I know you're the brains in the operation," he said as he smirked back to me. "I'm so glad you could come and see it for yourself."

"Thank you so much for having us," she said. I could tell from the firmness of her voice that she totally meant it. I could also tell she had some apprehensions, too.

By now, the panopticon, the Hive, was just barely visible in the near distance in the light of the setting moon. It's outline blocked the stars in the sky. The only lights in the entire complex came from the Host. The thing I noted was that there were panels, skylights, along two broad paths over half the roof, that were glowing. I hadn't noticed them before, but my attention was focused on the fact that the kitchen was open. I was looking forward to see what they did for breakfast.

Pulling up to the Host structure, our escorts from yesterday were already waiting as we exited Martin.

"Morning Keila," I said. She nodded to me as she offered her hand for my exit from

Martin. I was happy to take her hand, and looking down to validate my step from the jacked-up vehicle, I noticed the European fan style cobblestone again, but this time I paid attention. It was fit together like the rocks protecting the olives, and without any visible mortar joints at all.

I couldn't help myself. I poured a half mug of coffee out on the stones and it immediately found it's level in the crack between the stones and disappeared. I looked at Keila and she just nodded with a smile.

"Jeremy is going to give you a short demo, but we'll go get your breakfast ordered so it's ready when you get back," Keila said. She led me off without even checking on Mandy. Looking over my shoulder, I could see the young man escorting her had her complete attention. When she looked down, where I had poured the coffee, then she caught my eye with a quizzical smile.

Crossing through the foyer, I made a point of stepping on God's finger on the floor mosaic. There's no count for oddball.

As we entered the great room there were a few people sitting around enjoying their coffee. Some had a burrito-looking roll on their plates. The cafeteria serving lines were partitioned off with panels that looked like what we used to call spiny swift lizards. As we walked by, the intricacy of each piece of the panel became clear. Each of the scales making up the panel protruded from the plane, ending in a point. At each base was a hollow that went deep into the panel. Until you were close, the penetration into the interior of the panel was hidden by the preceding scale's point hanging over it. Thumbing it affirmed it to be foam again but the sound of the thump was different; the sound suppressed.

They moved us on into the cafeteria line. This service was manned by another android. A cute one.

"How may I be of service?" the robot goddess[4] said.

Keila spoke first, "Breakfast roll with bacon," she looked at me, I shrugged, she continued, "melon, coffee, and a juice." She turned to me again, "The mango is really great." I nodded and shrugged. "Mango, tag Jack, pickup in 20."

"As you command," the Androidess said.

I turned to Mandy and held out my hand to the young man escorting her, "I'm Jack".

"Everybody knows who you are. You're Jeremy's childhood friend. We're all so glad to have you here. He needs to have someone around his ... " he looked uncomfortable for a split second, "age." Another longer second, then, "I'm Jon."

Out of the corner of my eye I could feel Mandy's smile shine towards me.

"That's ok," I reached over and patted him on the side of the shoulder. "The alternative to old is not pleasant." He smiled, glad to be forgiven his faux pas.

"I'll see y'all when you get back," said Keila and she peeled off from our group. I think I detected a little smirk towards Jon as she passed.

Jon turned to Mandy and said, "There are more options but I know Jeremy wants to get you out to the Pan for a morning zero." Mandy caught my eye with another questioning glance. "Did that order sound ok?"

At Mandy's nod, he ushered her over to us, and Jam led us towards the door facing the Hive. As we moved off we could hear Jon instructing the android, "Ok, H5, breakfast wrap bacon, coffee, mango, pickup 20, tag Amanda. H5, breakfast wrap bacon, street corn, coffee, pickup 20, tag Jon."

As we exited the building, the cold of the morning hit us again. I was glad our camos where as heavy as they were. Jam and Jon were both wearing long-sleeved shirts that were very light for the morning, I thought, but they seemed perfectly comfortable. I put it off to the fact that it was so still, the cold hadn't penetrated yet. Even in what little moonlight there was, they had a sheen to them I'd never seen on any material except silk.

There were no lights on at the Hive. The moon sliver provided some light to outline the structure, but the steel spikes again grabbed our attention. They seemed to reflect even more light than was hitting them. They were growing out of the ground around the Hive on all sides, except for a little roadway leading up to the center tower and directly underneath the Hive itself. They were various heights, but none of them were above my waist. It was a steel lawn.

Jon had trotted off and now returned with a 4-seater Gator[1] and the three of us took our places. The path to the center tower was a hundred yards away and I'm old enough to appreciate a ride when I get one. Especially at night.

We barely got started when Jam tapped Jon on the shoulder and he stopped just before we entered the zone of the steel field. Jam got out and leaned over to us saying, "Just a minute, something I have to do."

Jam pointed, and Jon handed him a can of marker paint off the dash board. He walked a dozen yards or so, looked around like he was positioning something, then painted a large "X" on the ground. He trotted back and slid into place.

As we moved off, the lights playing on those steel spears would again generate a dim halo which would immediately disappear at any jiggle of the lights.

"Gosh, those spikey things are really weird," I said, tapping Jam on the shoulder as I leaned forward to be sure he heard me.

"They are. They're actually three generations back from where we are now on diffraction gratings," he said giving me that look again. "Jon, could you ask Larisha to talk about that, please."

At that Jon spoke into his wrist. "Larisha, Jon, add some discussion of diffraction grates, please," and he didn't wait for an answer. As we turned on to the road heading to the central tower, the eyes of dozens of rabbits amongst the spikes were ignited by the headlights as we passed. None of them shied at all, as if they were confident this was their home, too.

We pulled up to the tower with a quick stop, and Jam hopped out holding his palm out to Jon. Jon reached into the glove box and retrieved an air horn can and handed it over.

"Come on," said Jam as he headed to a door in the tower. "I *love* this stuff! Jon ... activate zone 2, level 2 and 3, please." Jon was going to stay in the cart.

The tower was also hexagonal, probably twenty feet across. The lights came up automatically when we entered. There was a small space on the floor, with a safety gate around it, and buttons on the wall that implied an elevator. The space was open, and not much bigger than a person. I couldn't stop myself from leaning in to see that it did extend to the top of the tower but there didn't seem to be any mechanism installed. At the other side was a staircase arching up clockwise from the floor and circling up to the next level. Jam was already out of sight, taking two steps at a time, and Mandy was following. I started to take two steps at a time, but quickly realized you really do need to respect limitations.

When we reached the second level, it was completely open towards the Hive, with four distinct zones. Each slice, from the center, was marked off by international danger orange paint on the floors and ceiling. Each pie slice in the tower was facing it's own particular face of the Hive. The back slice, one third of the whole, where we had entered and were standing, was separated from the others by a heavy black line tattooed repeatedly with "DO NOT CROSS" in fluorescent yellow. The other four sections each had some kind of mechanical robotic mounting mechanism, floor to ceiling, clustered at the center, but one was actually holding something that could not be mistaken: it was a black AR held at present arms, muzzle to the ceiling.

Jam handed me the air horn then stepped across the line without hesitation holding his hand up so we wouldn't follow. He said something, "Jeremy, release" maybe, but it was unclear. He stepped back over the line holding the AR and passed it to me.

"This is a .50 caliber Beowulf[2] AR and it's bad ass," he said smiling. "From here to the panopticon, I mean Hive, it is unstoppable."

"It is a pretty rifle," I said. I passed it to Mandy since I only had one hand free. She held it as we looked at the extra long barrel and suppressor. The maw of that .50 exiting the suppressor was awe inspiring even if you didn't know guns.

"Holy crap, I bet that's for sure. This has got to be death to hogs," said Mandy. She took a step up to the line past Jam and sighted onto the panopticon.

"As you know, by now, the panopticon was designed to be a prison and that's what this one is, too. Mainly. This tower station will eventually be armed with one for each section and every level, and certainly able to control any issue that requires force. Deadly or not. Once the convict gets here, they won't touch the earth again till released. The spikes are the ground protection. No tunnels. No running away, either. Always under the watchful muzzles of a very capable system."

"There's no sights," she said as she lowered the rifle.

"Nope, it's all lasers that are part of the robot mount. The systems check their zero every morning before the day starts so all the prisoners get reminded. It's an intimidation factor to keep them knowing that we really are watching what's happening. Someone is working on an algorithm that zeroes these rifles on floors where they *predict* trouble a little more than the others."

"Predict trouble," I said. I know it had to be a quizzical look.

"We'll get into that later today if you want. I don't like the sounds of it too much either," he said.

He took the rifle from Mandy, and stepped over the line again. He placed the rifle back in it's cradle. The robot grabbed it gently, however, there was no doubt it was a firm mechanical grip.

He stepped back over the line, took the air

horn from me and said, "You might want to hold your ears."

Once we'd covered our ears, he stepped to the open wall and let three long, loud blasts free from the can. I could feel in my sinuses the vibration of it inside the concrete tower .

"That was to let everybody know we're about to let fly," he said. "There were people still sleeping I'm sure. The real general alarm, which you'll probably hear later, makes dust dance." He smiled at that.

"Jeremy, static zero test 2-2, please ... standby." A green laser issued from the device drawing a dot on the ceiling, he looked at us still holding our ears. "Not necessary with this suppressed rifle." When we dropped our hands from our ears, he continued, "Execute."

Instantly, before the last sound of his word cleared, the robot dropped the rifle to horizontal and fired, then quickly returned to present arms. I was certainly conscious of the rifle firing and hitting something in the darkness. I thought I might have seen a spark, but it was all so fast. The laser looked like it might have been on a column of the Hive, but it went out at the shot. Amazingly enough, the thump of the rifle, while definitely throaty, did not cause any ear abuse.

"After that, it knows what it has and can

calculate every shot perfectly," he said smiling.

He stepped back from the line this time. "Jeremy, exercise 2 ... 2 ... standby." He turned to us and mouthed *Wow* then said, "Execute."

The next was truly wow!

The rifle lowered, laser ignited, and painted patterns all over that wing of the hive so fast that the beam-traced patterns stayed in my vision. From one side to the other of it's work space, it moved with lighting speed. Back and forth, zig zagging patterns, groups of circles, wavy lines, one pattern after another, it was as fast as any machine motion I'd seen. And it's repetition in space was so accurate the lines were crisply defined.

When it finally stopped, he said, "Pretty cool?"

"Uhm ... yes," I said. Mandy looked at me and exhaled. I realized I'd been holding my breath, too.

"I saw this on a Picasso site one time," Jam said, "one of my few cool ideas. Jeremy, exercise 2 ... 2, Picasso, please ... standby." He turned offering us an exaggerated wiggle of his eyebrows, then "Execute."

This time the rifle laser painted a Picasso bull[3] in space, over and over at lightening speed, to the point that it looked to be a hologram floating in space. Like a giant outline of a bull cookie cutter, it's depth was from us to the face of the panopticon.

"Holy Shit!" I said as I looked over at Mandy. She was just smiling at the image like a statue.

This exercise lasted 15 seconds. After it was over, Jam just stared at us. We stared back without a word.

"Ready to see if it can really hit something?" he said.

"Yeah!" we said together.

"Ok, let me explain a little about what's going to happen so you get it all. There are going to be three droids that start charging around on those two floors. You'll notice that it's dark now but the lighting systems come on in those areas where there's motion so that any prisoner is illuminated in any area traversed. Makes sneaking around rather obvious. Each droid will have a six inch steel disk, a small human target equivalent, which it'll hold perpendicular to the tower. Once the first shot is fired, one of the remaining robots will toss it's disk in the air. The system will shoot the flying disk then the remaining one."

"Aren't you scared of ricochets?" asked Mandy.

"I wondered who was going to ask that," he said as he patted her shoulder. "Brains of the

168

op."

"Funny," I said.

"Not at all. Every one of these bullets is a frangible, packed with lead dust. It blows to smithereens if it touches anything. Super energy transfer in meat, though. We shoot a heavy load that has about a ton and a half of deliverable energy at this range. Unstoppable."

"OK, I'm ready to see if you're BS," I said. I reached over and thumped him on the back of the head.

"Jeremy, zero, zone 2, standby ... execute," he said, which was followed quickly by action.

The second and third floors had droids zipping and zagging around with the iron plates. Fast. As they moved into new areas, LED can lights covered them and stayed on. It was almost too fast to take in. In the first second a shot clanged a plate on the third floor. A droid on the second floor tossed it's plate, which didn't travel two feet before it was sent spinning wildly back against the wall by the strike fired from our level. The third shot came from the level above, hitting the last disk. The flying disk was still spinning and clanging when the third shot found it's mark. The two droids that had held on to their plates froze at the instant of bullet strike. The one that had tossed it's plate retrieved it and stood holding it towards us, too. All the action took perhaps two seconds.

"Holy shit!" I said. "I've never seen anything like that."

"That's scary," said Mandy.

"Yes it is. That's why we're finalizing the fourth rule of robotics. Right now it sort of stands at 'NO robot may take any life without ... ' Which is where we're stuck. How do you control it. Government," his voice started fading, "teams ... whatever." I could tell from his softening tone that they'd tangled with this issue a bit.

"We should be able to respond to violence proportionally," he said, but you could tell he wasn't so sure yet. The thought of robots with triggers is very uncomfortable.

"Anyway, y'all ready for a little breakfast?" he said, motioned for us to cover our ears and then he let out three short blasts with the air horn.

Getting back to the Gator, Jon had his phone out with images that were the target disks. We passed those around as we headed back to the Host. While none of the lead smudges was exactly in the center of the target plates, none of them missed it by half a bullet diameter either.

8.

"Hang on!" said Jon as we skidded sideways up to the back windows of the Host. We ended up close enough that the pebbles launched against the windows made them sing. The percussions made the few people sitting inside look up from their plates.

"Gosh, Jon, you didn't even-" Jam started to say.

"Dude, they need to be awake for what's coming," said Jon smiling wide and helping Mandy out of the back. Mandy gave him such a look.

"It will be a day of clarity for sure," Jon said. Then he looked over to Jam, "Should I go get the rest of the crew?"

"Don't think so," said Jam, "we didn't get in till dark thirty. Let's let 'em sleep a few."

"Ok, I'm going to refill Martin for the trip back," said Jon. With that, the Gator disappeared in the dust.

When we entered the building, the warmth was welcome. The few dozen people sitting around the great room looked up and smiled at us. Keila was delivering two trays. It was surprising that the smell of barbeque and smoke, while present, wasn't completely dominating the room, even though the pit was a large presence.

"Come sit over here you guys," Keila said. "I love watching the sun come up on it." She put our trays down so we were looking out the windows at the Hive. It was starting to get more distinct as the sunrise drove the black out of the sky.

Mandy and I took our jackets off and placed them over our chairs. Jam grabbed an extra coffee off my tray and stood looking at the Hive.

"Hey, Jam, what is that you're wearing?" I said blowing the hot off the coffee.

"It's a special fiber they worked up here," Jam said. "A Kevlar fancy weave." He stepped over next to me. "It's almost like a fur coat. It's warm when it's cold, and cool when it's hot. Light as a T shirt."

Touching his shirt, it was easy to see that the weave was something done with a different slant. It had a shimmer to it. Up close it had a structure of a very irregular knit.

"What-" I barely got out of my mouth.

"I won't tell you more than that. It's part of your trek today," Jam said. He smiled, then turned back to watch the Hive again. I sat down next to Mandy and we started to work on the meal. There was nothing extraordinary about the food other than it was hot and filling. It hit the spot. The coffee was definitely more manageable than Jam's syrup at the Post.

We ate in silence as the sun started painting the sky with red, then orange. Every moment of the growing dawn led to changing impressions of the lawn of spikes and the walls of the Hive. Barely discernible at first, but increasing in intensity as the sun rose, were the blue bands encircling the building. The odd panels at the sides were reflecting light down upon what would have been morning shadows. The field of spikes were all supporting helmets of rainbow, more distinct as dust blew across the site, then instantly less as the dust passed. When the dust was thickest, the helmets over the individual spikes looked like the top half of a regular dodecahedron, each face differentiated by a faint rainbow span of color. It wasn't like watching sunsets where each minute was a noticeable change in texture or color. This field changed each particular moment, and the effect was mesmerizing.

We were finishing our meal, and Jam was leaning against the glass windows on one shoulder looking out at the Hive. He was sipping his coffee when a giant of a woman quietly walked up beside us. When she caught our eyes, she winked, and motioned for us to be quiet. She started stalking up behind Jam on his blind side. Her hair was braided in tight corn rows curving up the sides of her head. They all met along the crown of her head where they became a top knot of a French braid. The braid then wove down the back of her head, becoming shiny black locs as it fell off her shoulders. The Wranglers she was wearing were tight but not sprayed on. Her top was the brightest one in the building, bright yellow with African-inspired geometric patterns circling her body at bust height. It gave the impression of being inspired by a dashiki, fairly open and loose.

Just like a hunter, she stepped when Jam blew on his coffee or took a sip. When he was still, she froze. We continued to eat as we watched the stalk. I made a point of nicking my plate a little harder with my silverware as cover for her. Mandy and I smiled at each other.

As the young woman cleared our table so we could see her boots, it was certain her style was African. Her knee high boots had uppers totally covered with a diamond on diamond design in black and white. The rare red line parting the diamonds was a strong contrast. The stitching of the pattern was dense. It had the silky shine I'd seen in Jam's shirt. Her heel was the typical riding heel of the real cowboy. The vamp and toe would look normal in any Western store.

Over the course of three minutes, she'd gotten within five feet of Jam. Suddenly, he turned calmly taking another sip.

"Come on, Larisha," he said grinning. "I saw your reflection ten minutes ago, when you entered the building looking like a giant canary in blackface."

Larisha stepped up, smiling, and gave him a healthy love pat on the shoulder.

"Pretty good stalk though," Jam said, turning to us. "Of course, y'all's cover was ridiculous. Jack ain't never let his silverware bounce off his plate that much when there's still food to load in his pie hole."

They stepped over to us, and Jam said, "Jack, this is Larisha, one of the founders."

Larisha took my hand in both of hers as I stood, "Oh, Jack, I could hardly sleep last night knowing you were gonna be here." She immediately turned to Mandy, "And you, too, Mandy." She let go of me with one hand and had us both in her hands smiling, as she looked back and forth between us.

"Did you eat?" Jam said.

"Sometimes Jeremy has to remind us to

eat," Larisha said nodding, "but not today. I've been up for hours." She was so beautiful, her dark skin set off by the yellow of her top, and her form so fit. I was conscious of how hard it was to keep from staring. Every time she caught my eyes she was smiling wider with perfect teeth and twinkling black eyes. Even standing, I was over-matched. With her heels she was a solid two inches taller than me and stood totally erect. We might be the same height, but I got her by at least sixty pounds.

"Let's have a seat and you can start prepping them," said Jam.

"Gotta get my coffee mug," said Larisha. She practically skipped to the other side of the cafeteria.

"She is so beautiful," said Mandy. She looked first at Jam, then bounced it off me.

"And smart ... Oh my God is she smart," said Jam. "She was in an engineering masters program at Aggieland, headed to a PhD. in aeronautical engineering."

"Oh?" I said. What can you say about that much beauty and brains in one tight jeans package, too?

Larisha came back with her mug. It was to her scale. It was a 32 ounce metal mug and, of course, it had 'TAMU Farmer' etched into it in the mandatory maroon.

"Have a seat, lady," said Jam. "I was just telling them about your degree plan at A&M."

"You're a treat. How'd you decide on that?" said Mandy.

"I was one of those that was told I could be whatever I wanted when I was young," said Larisha. "I fell in love with space through Star Wars and Star Trek, but Firefly was a series that fit my Texan sensibilities more. They really fired my imagination. I focused on school and grades to get to the space program. But, in high school I started a growth spurt that didn't stop until six feet plus. They do *not* take astronauts that big! I decided I'd design their rides."

"Yep, she's special all right," said Jam, "tell them what you told me the first time we met."

"Oh, well, he came out to Aggieland looking for some suckers to get involved in his *project.*" Larisha waved her hands pointing around the room. "Of course, he couldn't really tell us what it was."

"I can barely understand it now!" I said. Jam and I exchanged smiles.

"Tell them what you said first," said Jam.

"Well, my parents are both doctors, one white, one black. We lived in Houston. A black face was supposed to be a Democrat vote. I know people that ensure you know they're yellow dog Democrats before you get too friendly. I just wanted to share my tilt, too. No sense wasting time in a relationship if one party can't bend a little, and believe me, if you've ever known a Yellow Dog-"

"Tell them what you said!" said Jam. "Please!"

Larisha looked at him and smiled, then turned back to us. "He finished his no info, no nothing speech, and looked at me expecting some kind of question I think. I just said 'I'm an MLK Republican'. You should have seen his face."

"An MLK Republican!" said Jam laughing. "Ain't never heard nothing like that. And her face? Like a rock."

We all laughed at that. I have to admit it took a certain anxiety out of my calculations.

"I've had to be hard at times," said Larisha.

"Get them warmed up on what you're doing with them this morning," said Jam rising from his seat. "I'm going to get another caffeine charge. Anybody else?" He gathered up our cups as we nodded assent.

"Was MLK really a Republican?" asked Mandy.

"Both sides claim him and he never really said. He never said he wasn't either. The fact is, I want to be associated with the party of Lincoln. The party that stood against the Klan, and the party that wasn't part of Jim Crow. They both suck now. Freedom is what I want. I believe in individual freedom and personal responsibility. You tell me where that fits best?" spoke the hard Larisha, and then the smile returned.

Jam walked off carrying three cups, shaking his head with a smile. He obviously knew what was coming next because after a few more steps he stopped and turned towards us.

"It is an announcement that you can't tell me what to support. My God, my family, my country. And ... ", she stood up and put her arm out, reaching above her head. Her open hand was certainly seven feet high. "I'm six foot one, 180, and I *can* ... " A flashing inside out roundhouse kick, as quick as I'd ever seen, came to rest against her open hand, then she finished the warning, "kick your butt!" Her booted foot at the end of a straight leg then came down impossibly slow.

Mandy and I both, simultaneously, said, "OK then." The people around the room hooted, hollered, and applauded. There were lots of Aggie whoops. Jam caught my eye, smiled, and continued towards the coffee.

"That's on the far side of impressive," I

said.

"When I was in high school, people tried to herd me. Once I got confident and some training, not so much," said Larisha. She walked around the table and sat next to me.

Mandy and I were fixated on her.

"We're supposed to skim you over what it's like here at the Host," Larisha said looking between us. "The first thing I want to do is take you to a planning meeting that I'm facilitating this morning. A few weeks ago someone came up with the idea of having full grown trees designed, built, and installed. We saved it for y'all."

"What?" said Mandy. I looked across them both with my best ignorant face.

"This morning we're advancing that tree idea," said Larisha. "Our planning groups are kept to five or six people, if you can get that many interested in a project. We'll flesh it out, bounce it off the Host, and when we're ready, call for the community to vote on resources. You'll see."

Jam came back with the coffees and said, "What time are you going to start?"

"The team has been waiting for the word since you zeroed," said Larisha.

"We don't have a fixed schedule out here for very much," Jam started explaining, "because we're all free people with our own biological schedules and desires. However, if you want to get a team working with you for profit or playing for fun, you'll always have to compromise some. Generally speaking, the planning teams like to start early so they can spend the day screwing off or working around the ranch. Getting some manual labor, any sweat, limbers up the mind some."

"Them kids *want* to do manual labor?" I said. I must have looked crazier than I sounded. I wasn't sure what they were doing out here but ranching is full of hard. I knew Jam had plenty of it on a spread this size. On the other hand, between you, me, and the fence post, none of the hands I'd shook so far were hard enough to hint at ever having been ranch hands.

"Sure," said Larisha, "we're proud of the physical bodies that we have and we are replacing labor so-"

"That's enough," said Jam immediately and authoritatively.

"They're going to see it right away," said Larisha defensively.

"Of course," Jam said, then turning to us, "just accept and enjoy the things you see today and we'll cover the theology of it all tonight."

I know I was caught aback by *theology of it,* and glancing at Mandy saw she was, too.

Whatever it was going to mean, Larisha was living proof that they were for sure proud of the physical body.

"Ok, cowboy up. We're fixin' to cover some ground now," said Jam, and he led us over to the right side of the building.

9.

Jam opened the doors for us and led us into a large open area appointed like a shopping mall in some respects. There were trees of various sizes in large planters encircled by integrated benches, coffee tables, chairs and sofas. The floor was made up of the fan cobblestones again. The main focus of the space seemed to be living spaces or offices. Along the sides of the building were two stories of rooms, and the middle section reached up to the peak with three levels. The three story wall touching the peak in front of us had a water feature, the kind where sheets of water come racing down the face. Honestly though, it barely registered. The first thing to grab my attention was that associated with each door, on every floor, was a cantilever walk protruding into the space between the bank of rooms. The railings on their sides were covered with large leaves showing absolutely no overlap. Reaching over the railings were LED lights on arched hangers aimed into the greenery. At the railings were dozens of people leaning over and watching us quietly.

Once again, the impression was of a

shopping mall with lots of hanging displays, and green-covered mezzanines lighted for Christmas. But in this case, all white light. Very white light.

Jam nodded up at the groups, and then started waving them away, "Don't y'all have anything better to do than gawk at us?" he shouted, wearing a smile.

This did not have the effect I was expecting at all. Most of them started softly clapping in unison as they started moving off. Some were quietly singing "Halleluja" until the doors closed behind them. The only sound left was the water feature in front of us.

Jam stepped over to the water feature then turned around to face us. "They're all yours now Larisha."

"Isn't it beautiful?" shouted Mandy. "They made me swear not to say anything after we got the shopping tour yesterday." She started drumming on my back like a rider spurring on their horse. "I was going crazy!" She was practically hopping.

Larisha walked over to the right hallway, but stopped as I stepped over by Jam to look up at the water feature. It was smooth, sheets of water running down a surface that was broken only by edges, fractions of an inch high, that outlined a Christian cross. The water feature itself was twenty feet high and maybe ten feet wide and the cross was positioned inside that space, allowing a border of a foot. As the sheets of water passed over the arms of the cross and it's little ridges, it gave the stream it's first distinct disturbance, defining the arms. The outline of the vertical member made a raceway for the water to stream to the bottom uninterrupted.

"Oh My God," I said.

Mandy and I shot a glance at each other, and then she said, "Oh Yes, dear." I could feel the hair on the back of my neck rising as a wave of goosebumps washed over me. They washed across my body like the water streaming down the water feature itself.

"Awright now," said Jam. He touched us on the shoulders and guided us after Larisha. As we turned the corner, the appearance of the wall forced me to reach out and tap it. This wall was solid concrete but with the detailed appearance of any normal Texas Hill Country masonry wall. Each stone, it's face apparently uniquely cracked from the quarry. But in this case, the entire wall was concrete and not limestone. The texture and appearance was German stone masonry in the smallest detail but the color was green concrete throughout.

"Tilt wall," was all Jam said. He motioned

me around the corner. On this side, the concrete was the same construction but this time there was color. The stain or color of the concrete was very close to a standard brown and gold nicotine-mix limestone, slightly odd in that the colors seemed to run together.

"You know you wanna scratch it," Jam said. He took out his knife, opened it, and handed it to me butt first.

"Yeah, damn straight," I said. A tentative scratch showed the color was imbedded in the mix. I looked towards Jam on that discovery.

"Go ahead, that's not my favorite knife by any means," he said.

This time, I gouged it hard at several places. I dug at the face, sides, and down between in the faux mortar. If there was color, it was always deep into it. The tilt wall give away was that the color of the stone stopped an eighth of an inch before the plane of what would be the mortar line. It was nearly a perfect recreation. In turning around to hand Jam the knife, the other walls showed they'd obviously learned plenty. The other walls had become indistinguishable from a standard mason-built limestone wall. The interesting thing was that each panel exactly joined the others, barely visible, like an interleaved masonry wall, without the vertical expansion joint typical of tiltwall. Looking down the hallway past Larisha there were more intricate brick and exotic designs. The color choices had obviously been highly experimental, too.

"All tilt wall?" I questioned.

"ALL tilt wall, and better every day," Larisha said. She held the door open to the second room, and waved us through.

Mandy went right in, but Jam touched my shoulder to stop me, and whispered in my ear, "When I grab my ear, walk over to let me whisper to you. No matter what."

We both looked at each other, smiled, and immediately agreed on the old signal for the handoff. Back in the day, we'd used it to signal the other that we needed some support of one kind or another. It was not a specific signal, something that demanded a certain action. It could mean something as simple as 'I'm tired of this conversation, please take over so we can leave' up to and including, 'the shits about to happen, get ready for heavy rolls'. Whatever it had been, we'd intuitively known our roles. As soon as he saw that I recognized it, he continued into the room heading for a seat in the back corner.

When I'd come through the threshold, I was confronted with a small conference room. Very large monitors covered the top of every wall.

On the back wall was another embossed scripture, Psalms 111:2[1]. In front of every chair was a yellow sticky note pad with a pen. Also, sitting with them, was something that appeared to be a necklace with some small digital camera attached. Everybody else at the table already had a Bluetooth headset on and the necklace. Mandy and I headed to the two empty chairs. Mandy was already getting re-introduced to Keila, Jon, and Sandy from last night, and the two new faces, Adric and Kez.

"Jack," I said to the massive young man who stood to shake my hand. He was the only one so far that made me think he might have done some manual labor, judging from the width of his shoulders. His black beard was densely packed, but closely trimmed. His head was completely shaved.

"Adric," he said. He shook my hand with a grip that generated a wince. Shaking that hard hand confirmed he'd been a working man fairly recently.

The other new face introduced herself as Kez. "Which is short for Keziah."

"That's pretty," said Mandy. "Where'd that come from?"

"It's Biblical. The middle one of the daughters born to Job after all the troubles covered him up," she said smiling, "and their father gave them an inheritance among their brothers."

"And," said Jam nodding rapidly, "in all the land there were no women so beautiful as Job's daughters."

"Your parents nailed that," I said. I just blurted it out. Mandy gave me one of those looks, which I could feel without looking. As all husbands know, speaking truth at the wrong time is just wrong. Sometimes very wrong and long lasting. This was probably right on the border. This young woman was truly stunning. Guessing, I'd place her as the youngest in the room.

A petite little thing, Kez was in the set of beauties that included Zoe Kravitz. I'd always admired everything about that particular lady. Kez's hair was bigger, and curlier. I have no idea if Zoe had ice blue eyes like Kez, but these could definitely hold your attention. It was easy to imagine them being visible out of a fog. Her bangs on the right were meticulously braided strands that hung down to her shoulders. It made me wonder if Larisha and Kez did each other's hair.

Like all the residents we'd seen so far, she had the Wranglers. These were pressed and starched, and the crease of them was impossible to ignore. She wore her jeans over her teal-colored boots which had heavy scuffs along the sides where the stirrup wears. Her blouse top was a plaid mixture of blues that enhanced the effect of those eyes. Unlike a typical western cut shirt, her's was set off with frilly lace lines running along the front and back implying the Western-style yoke.

Her smile was so welcoming that words will never do it justice.

"My Mom chose it because it was the first example of female equality," said Kez, "but I've got darn tired of spelling K-E-Z-I-A-H."

"She's also got a PhD in Computer Science," said Jam, "Which means she's built through and through."

"Amen," Adric and I intoned at the same time. We caught each others eye, and turning back, I noted Kez busting out a blush. It's been a good long while since I've seen anybody blush, but this one was especially surprising because of her skin tone. It was when she turned her head to the side to shake off the blush that I noticed the little Star of David[2] tattoo below her right ear.

"Stop it y'all!" said Mandy.

"Yeah Sir, Jeremy, this herd," said Larisha, "gonna be tough to circle up." She looked at me with a slightly lighter stare than the one Mandy had used to fix me.

"Anyway," said Larisha, "the purpose of this meeting is to gather up ideas about our new project. The subject: Artificially generated tree. We aren't making decisions here, we're just trying to see what we can catch up in our trap. Everybody, ready? Hey, Jack, thirty minute alarm, hon."

"Uh ... what?" I said.

"Alarm set for thirty minutes," the computer answered.

"I guess we need to get a nickname for you," said Larisha, "How about Little Jack?" At that, there were some giggles.

Everybody rose from the table, grabbed their pen and sticky pad, and started walking clockwise around the table. They'd stop, scribble something on the note, and stick it to the wall. They would continue around reading the notes others had affixed below the monitors until they stopped to post another.

"Larisha introduced this idea of free thinking batches," said Jam. He motioned for us to stand.

"Not my idea," Larisha said. "Saw a marketing guy do it once. The idea is you go around the room, reading everybody else's postings and posting your own on the wall ... *any* idea, as many and as fast as possible. Whatever pops into your head, until we're out of time. You have to participate, too. Only Jeremy sits them out." Larisha gave him a hard look but he smiled back. I got the impression this was a pretty regular scuffling.

"Ok. I can do that," I said. I joined the snake circling the table. The first note I passed said 'concrete bark', which I said out loud laughing.

"You can't talk about anything yet and no suggestive sounds," said Larisha between postings. She looked over at both Mandy and I, then went back to scribbling a note.

On the first pass by Jam, he pulled on his ear. I went to him, bent down to hear him say in a whisper, "Just nod and smile at me, then go right over and put an idea up."

I nodded and smiled, and went over to the wall and wrote 'big' on the tag and walked on, not at all sure what it was about. Big idea from stupid hint? Big stupid?

In short order, there were scores of tags all over the room at shoulder height. Most of them were one or two word suggestions. Initially ideas went up quickly. By the end of the period, we were wandering around rereading tags, and rarely pasting any new ones. When the alarm announced itself, Larisha said, "Hey Jack -"

"Huh?" said I.

" ... set an alarm for fifteen minutes.

Change directions. Hey, mister man, you didn't hear me say Little, did ya?"

"Alarm set for fifteen minutes," the computer answered.

"Oh-Kaaaay now", said Mandy, "I'm a little reluctant to be gettin' in on this, but that there's funny!"

"We are going to have a come-to-Jesus on this I can see," I said laughing. I did not laugh alone.

Everybody started walking counter clockwise around the table. It was crazy, but it actually felt like it changed the way the session was working. Walking around seeing the tags in a different order, did stir some thoughts. Everybody did seem to be posting quicker for a few minutes. It stirred up more crazy, I guess, because Jam pulled on his ear again.

"Same thing blah blah ... blah blah ... and a little more to make it seem real ... blah blah blah," he whispered.

I took a step back and looked at his laughing face. It was certainly a little strange. I nodded, and walked around the room a little trying to think of what to put on this great hint. Then, out of desperation, I wrote 'not scrub', and stuck it to the wall. 'What Is That?' I said to myself. That one was completely out there past the fence. 'Dunno,' self answered.

Everybody that walked by that tag bent to get a good look (I guess they couldn't believe their eyes either) but didn't say or do anything. It didn't gen much in the way of new tags either. No fodder there.

When Jack the computer noted the end of the period, everybody just went back to their seats. Larisha started walking around, pulling down the tags. There had to be a hundred, probably more. She placed the stack at the head of the table in front of her chair.

"Normally, this is a one step process," Larisha said, looking directly at Mandy and I. "I read them in and the team votes good or bad as soon as they hit the main monitor. In this case, we'll do a two step because we all want to ensure your vote counts here."

"Ok," I said. I was unsure of what was really going to happen, but I do like my votes to count.

"Hey Jack, record list. Display one," Larisha said. She started reading the tags off. As each sticky was read, it popped up on the biggest display over the door behind her. She read them into the system as quick as she could pull the notes apart.

There was an odd thing when she got to the two I'd put up for Jam. She said, "Big, status mark" and "no scrub, status mark". Nobody stirred. I turned to look at Jam, he just smiled and wiggled his eyebrows at me.

If it took three minutes to read all the tags I'd be surprised.

"Properties, please Jack," Larisha ordered. She smiled in my direction and nodded.

"There are 127 items," noted Jack the computer.

"Process for voting Jack, on my mark," said Larisha.

"The computer is going to read them off and pause fifteen seconds between items. After it is read, you are supposed to vote 'good' or 'bad'," she said. She tapped her headset and pointed, Mandy and I donned ours. "Now, we usually get a little exuberant here. Even loud. The label turns red when you have five seconds left to count your vote."

"Hey Jack, test vote ... ok, Little Jack," she intoned staring directly at me, "say 'good'." Then she smiled.

I just looked at her tipping her head from shoulder to shoulder. Tic Toc.

"Please?"

"Good," I said.

"Thank you," she said. "Hey, Jack, test vote Mandy."

She nodded her head towards Mandy. Mandy turned to me, and answered 'good', but she made it two syllables.

Larisha turned her chair to look at the main monitor and loosed the vote. "Hey Jack, process item vote."

The read off started immediately. Larisha was right about exuberance on the others. On this pass there was laughter and mocking and shouting for every item. Ridicule was a definite requirement for many items, but not Jam's which were posted through me.

At each vote, the item was removed from the main monitor and the majority 'good' were placed over on the monitor on the right, the 'bad' placed over on the left side. It was fun winnowing the list. There were few that didn't get a defender, with many of the ideas passing through this screening. I was expecting serious mock on the entries I'd done for Jam, but they would have been unanimously approved if I'd voted. I held back to hear what the group would say, but they all just approved them without comment.

At the last item, Larisha reorganized things again, saying "Hey Jack, archive the 'bad' items under subject conference room 'new tree'". At this the left monitor blinked to black, and the right monitor rolled all it's items over onto the main screen again.

The items that had survived the voting pass

redisplayed on the center monitor over Larisha's head. They were reordered. I wouldn't have felt more out of place if I'd been a turtle on a post. The two items I'd posted for Jam were at the very top of the list. If now was the time that we were going to discuss our posts, I had no idea where that was going to lead. I knew I wasn't going to have any comments on those two.

I turned to Jam and he wiggled his eyebrows at me again. When I turned to Mandy, she shrugged with a smile.

"Alright, y'all, I'm about ready for a rest stop," said Larisha. The group dropped their headsets and evaporated from the room. I couldn't have been more relieved. As we exited the room, there was a table that had been put outside the door with taco fixings. There were several large thermoses of coffee and hot water for tea, as well as some juices. Of course, the taco fixings were predominately pork in various incarnations. Topping it off there were eggs and sausage, grilled vegetables, and seared serrano chilis.

As we encircled the snack table, Jam pointed, "The little boy's room is down that way, I have to go talk to someone for a minute outside. I'll be right back." I could tell he was avoiding me from the twinkle in his eyes.

"That's fun," Mandy said as she fixed her tea.

She offered her cup to me, an inside joke. I've never liked tea in the morning. The Navy broke my caffeine sensor so I can drink pots of coffee all day, and have a half dozen serranos at any meal with no problem. On the other hand, a sip of strong tea in the morning will have me yawning into the toilet in no time. Finishing up the taco creations, I stood back and looked around. There were other groups throughout the structure on the different levels standing around their own snack tables.

"Yes. And weird, too, I think," I said.

"What's weird?" said Jon walking up to us with his tacos.

"Oh, I don't know, the things Jam had me put up -" I almost got out.

"That 'big' tag spurred up a thought," said Jon. "I've been working in the oil patch. I've always wanted to do some titanium art welding and that's why I put up that one." He was smiling, biting his lip, and nodding his head slowly.

"Which one?" said Mandy as she turned to us.

"Titanium skeleton," Jon said. "I'm thinking the corrosion resistance and strength ... just wow! Big!"

Kez came up with a bound up taco, too, and jumped right in with, "We need to address how to handle the shielding gas in close quarters."

At that, Mandy and I just nodded at them and wandered to the center of the hall. The chatter between them did not decrease because we walked away. It was obvious they were way into it.

We were slowly strolling to the far end of the hall, no directed purpose to our steps. As we walked, the floor continually surprised me with it's smoothness. Even though the cobblestone fan design was obviously natural stone, the interface between each stone, just like the portico, was minute. I literally could not force a credit card between them.

A trace of our path would have shown me bouncing off the walls. Each wall panel along the walk was different in some way. The tilt wall had been perfected in color and texture to various masonry styles from every period. One of my favorite was the beam and stone that early Hill Country Texans used. The supporting cedar posts were implemented in intricate detail. The concrete had been waxed, or sealed, so the faux wood concrete had that sheen of well worn cedar. The colors were very accurate and their placement in the tilt wall had become precise. And then, proceeding on down the hall, the designers had gone wild on modernistic and arty things.

"I just love these outcroppings," said Mandy. She was staring up at the lighted gardens above us, and sharing smiles and waves with the residents. "It's like I imagine real hanging gardens."

"That's a good description," I said. I left my wall thumping and scrapping, and put my arm on her shoulder. "The way they are staggered so that light can reach each one from the skylights, and the LEDs. I keep thinking Christmas in a mall."

"That works for me, too," she said. "How do you suppose they get all the leaves lined up like that? It's crazy. It looks like a wall of leaves. Almost like wallpaper, and no overlap. Do you recognize the plant?"

"Nope," I said, "We're going to have to ask them when we get back in there." By now we'd reached the end of the hall, and were held back by a plastic *Do Not Cross* tape. At each end, there was a waist high column supporting the tape. It looked suspiciously like a one armed robot on wheels. If I were to guess, and I am, I'd say the decorative ring around their bases, regularly imbedded with dark glass beads, were their multiple eyes.

Beyond the tape, there was an area of the

floor that was incomplete. It extended the final twenty feet to the wall and spanned the entire thirty foot width of the hallway. Along the floor were several different robots, all frozen in place. Each of them was bug-like in that they all had six legs. The diversity of their shapes hinted at wildly differing functionality. There were two distinct queues of the bugs. The delivery line was loaded with floor pavers apparently. The other line was heading back out the door empty.

The largest worker bot, and most numerous, was a carrier made up of a large ball which rotated around an axle. The ball was two feet in diameter. At the end of each axle were three legs. Supported by braces from the axle, over the main body, was a flat panel. These ball bots, in the delivery queue, had large rocks secured to the top panel by small arms from the panel itself. The largest rocks were two feet in their largest dimension, but that was where the similarity ended. Each stone was shaped at one end to fit into the squares of the paving design. The rest of it seemed to be it's natural form, minimally shaped with slots, and maybe tenons, carved into the rock.

"Oh, you're going to love this stuff aren't you?" said Mandy.

This time, I gave her the look, which she

reflected right back to me. *Not* winning.

"You better not get caught up in the computer stuff and leave me all alone," she said. When she said this, I turned toward her and put my arm around her. I gave her a kiss on the cheek, but she pretty quickly withdrew.

"It is a bunch, isn't it?" I said. We put our heads together and giggled. The distinctive sound of boots had me turn to see Larisha and Kez heading our way. The two of them, both so young and beautiful, were quite the sight. It would easily take two Kez to make one Larisha. Behind them, I noticed the other people starting back into the conference room.

"We left this especially for you, Jack," said Kez.

"What?"

"Jeremy told us that you had great interest in geek stuff so we knew you'd like this, too," she said. "It kind of sets the tone for where we're heading - "

Larisha shoved her a little.

"Heh ... Ok," Kez said, "Whatever. Start it up."

"Hey Jack, enable this labor zone, please," said Larisha. She didn't have anything that I took to be a communicator. This place must be completely wired. Or something.

Kez stepped up next to us and started

pointing out the action. The big ball robots rolled up to the edge of the pavement and the platform rolled over disgorging the stones to wiry armed handlers. The handlers worked in conjunction with a fat beetle-shaped bot that squirted some type of sealer, through several nozzles, along a couple of edges. The wirey ones slipped the stone into it's final resting place. From the time the stone was tipping off the platform, grabbed and sealant applied, then slid into it's final resting place, was a single fluid motion. It was practically poured into place, it's fit exact and sure.

"I have to admit," said Kez, "we don't really know how its working now. It's outgrown us to a great extent. I was the lead to getting these little suckers going, Larisha specified the construction ideals defining their parameters, but they've learned so much more."

We all looked around at each other on that statement. I let out an audible breath. We all shook our heads and then turned back to it.

"Yepper," said Larisha. "Look at the way the stones are fitting together now. I specified that we'd try to do a thick layer of natural stones just because I've always been fascinated by how long Roman roads lasted, but check out how they slot together. All over." It was obvious that she was as impressed by it as we were.

She was so right. Pointing around the madness of the construction site with all the little bots doing their synchronized dance, Kez clued us to their various roles. The roles they'd initially thought they assigned them anyway. The floor surface was smooth and perfectly flush, but underneath was a spaghetti bowl of stone working together by an apparently unknown algorithm. Every thirty seconds or less, another stone was moved inside and positioned to fit exactly into the puzzle. The only regular part was the square head of the stone that fit into the fan pattern of the floor. They were making a two foot thick floor of natural stone knitted together.

In the few minutes we'd watched, the floor had grown noticeably. It was like watching a stream of harvester ants work on a tree. But, in this case, they were building instead of stripping. Single file, going in each direction, no wasted movement, this was another hypnotizing show.

"Wouldn't it be faster to use flying drones?" I asked after a few minutes.

"Sure, it is," said Kez. "The problem is the noise. You can't hear yourself think with drones the size it takes to move some of these stones. Most of them are about twenty pounds. We started with flying drones, but this way they can work all night. Listen."

Standing completely still, there was no noise. The sound of the big balls crunching some gravel as they moved across the open ground, and the slight chink of the stones fitting together, was all there was. A dog scratching at a door was louder.

"We should get back," said Larisha, "I don't like to let them loose for too long." She smiled so sincerely.

"Ok, I know Jeremy misses your supervision," said Kez. We were still hypnotized when Kez tapped our shoulders.

"They'll probably be completely done by the next time you see this," she said.

I looked over my shoulder as we walked back to the conference room. I wanted to make a mental note of exactly where things stood, so I'd be able to tell what kind of progress they'd made. I'd turned just in time to see the 'Do Not Cross' robot tape-oids reposition a couple feet towards the far wall.

10.

Larisha held the door for us as we returned to the conference room. It was now a hub of activity. The only person not participating was Jam, who was occupying the corner, and looked to be napping. However, he raised his head as we entered. All the others were talking quietly into the microphone of their headset. From their actions, it looked like each had a designated monitor around the room, or some screen real estate shared on one. They were driving the system with their voice and their hand motions. Like multiuser gamers, they were crosstalking and laughing as they went. Each of them had a necklace with a camera bob on it, and when I entered Kez put her's on and gave one to Mandy and I.

"Have the camera pointing out," said Kez, "and it will assume your finger is the pointer. If you position your hands like they're on a keyboard, it will image a keyboard on the tabletop for you to use. We're all linked together, but we typically drift into groups of expertise or interest. But, in reality, you can just talk to it. The Host is smart!"

Pointing around the room at each person in turn, "Jon is the welder metal worker, Sandy botanist, Larisha mechanical engineer, Adric civil engineering. You might want to just sit next to someone until you get the hang of it."

"What do you think?" I said to Mandy.

"Well, I've always liked plants," Mandy replied. At this, Jam got up and pushed a chair over next to Sandy, who waved her over with a smile.

"I think Jon and welding are more in my line. The engineers have always scared me," I said moving over to Jon. Again, Jam moved an empty chair over.

"Ok, dude," said Jon, "this is the thing ... we're just snooping around the net as fast as we can. We find a page that appeals to us, we just say 'mark'. If there's a picture or a piece of text, you can just circle on the desktop and the gestural[1] computer figures out what's going on."

"Let's get you logged in first. Just say 'Jack at," he pointed to a monitor across from us, "number 3."

"Is this a joke?" answered the computer.

"We're stopping this now. Jacky at monitor 3, please," I said. Everybody at the table looked around at me with a smile.

"I like that," said Jam.

"Me too," said Mandy.

"So now, unless you preface the statement with 'Team', you're just talking to the computer," Jon said, "Team, We got Jacky on-board now."

There were a flood of acknowledgments over my earpiece. "Yeah", "oooh" (made into three syllables), and "Jacky" said with a lustiness that was clearly Mandy playing. When I caught her eye, she winked.

Jon was covering his mouthpiece with his palm "What I'm going to do is walk you through the way I work it, which isn't standard because there isn't one, but I have my approach. Ok ... ready?" I nodded assent, "Hey Jack, tie in Jacky to this convo."

"Jacky and Jon mirrored," said the computer through my earpiece.

"Search, titanium stock," Jon spoke quietly into his mouthpiece but it was crystalline in my ear. Pages of titanium vendors and different size stocks came up. Jon moved his finger around on the desktop a little, and the cursor positioned on an American vendor. He clicked it by tapping the desk, in an outsized gesture, with two fingers. He scrolled through the site pausing on small round stock, .25 inch, which came in very short lengths. "I think we have shipping container loads of little pieces like

208

this. Surplus end pieces we buy for cheap stock," he said.

Jon covered his mouthpiece, "When I'm thinking about materials, I think in little parts. I don't worry about labor cost around here. I figure we can build anything we want with little pieces. In this case, the advantage is that we don't have to worry about the weld shielding so much. Easier to manage a quick short weld."

"Ok," I said into the mouthpiece and it came into my ear sounding like I knew what he was talking about. I looked around and nobody was paying attention to me at all. Mandy was getting a very animated talk from Sandy and judging from their monitor, they were going the other way. Big! Unlike my team, which had me as the slug, Mandy was already waving her hands around and chattering up a storm. I didn't even want to get in the middle of that conversation that had already launched.

"Argon shielding for titanium welds." Jon said. Again our monitor filled with all kinds of welding supplies, small plastic shielding pieces, and tanks of gas, once again focusing on the small. He scrolled through them, making notes, tagging, and then it was off to other areas.

"Team, Adric and Larisha, I'm sort of leaning to using small round titanium stock we have already. Could you, please, see what we'd need to consider for strength at whatever size Sandy has us going. We may want some serious beams."

"Sure," said Adric, "I was just going that way, too. Sandy?"

"Mandy and I think we should beat the Texas record. We're leaning towards bur oak. The largest in Texas is 81 feet, so of course, this one should be 101," the earpiece announced with Sandy's voice. When she said that the heads at the table snapped towards her.

"Why bur oak?" said Larisha.

"Huge acorns", said Mandy, "and I love to make decorations with 'em." An image of a single acorn practially filling a palm flashed up on the monitor.

"And deer love 'em, too," I said. "They don't bounce twice on the ground before they're eaten."

"Disease resistant, long lived maybe 400 years, great food for wildlife, with those giant acorns, and pretty," Sandy said, as a picture of a majestic bur oak painted their monitor.

"Not to mention the fact that they only really grow around deep, rich, wet soils. It would be another miracle proof to get it growing out here," added Sandy. She looked around at all of the team, but ended smiling at me.

The group looked at the picture for barely a beat, then they started going around again with each hitting their areas of interest, new images flashing across all the screens non-stop, and giggles. It was fun, and the conversation was lively. Some of the monitors were making scrolling lists of things, too. I didn't care to find out if they were driven by humans, or not.

The group churned out connections. As items on the approved list were touched, they changed colors. It seemed that the more attention an item got, the warmer the color. Once again, the items I'd entered for Jam were literally glowing at the top.

"Adric, could you help me look over 'not scrub', please," Larisha said.

Whoever got an invite invariably said, "Just fixin' to look at that, thanks." Adric did too.

I was embarrassed by how much actual information they were able to pull up on 'scrub'. Brushes, cleaners, leaning towards brush in the landscape. Desert plants. The amount of things they found was amazing as they hammered on something that was not even a whim, less than a whim. A place filler from the vacuum of my mind.

"Team, hey, I just wanted to say about that-" I barely got out, before Jam thumped me on the back of my head. It was then I noticed that he'd pulled his chair up behind me. It was the first time I noticed he was wearing a headset, too.

"Free-form, nothing you have to worry about," he said. That look in his eyes assured me that was actually totally true and I should just leave it alone. "No worry." He smiled and scooted his chair back.

As the time passed, the frantic energy of the group started dissipating. Some put down their head sets and took off their gesture interpreters. Others went to get coffee. On returning, they just sat watching. The room was getting quieter and quieter. The monitor across from Sandy was starting to focus on one particular tree she had displayed. The engineers were working with her to spec dimensions. Outlines of the crown, then the roots, various dimensions of a grown tree, were being collected and stored in the Host system.

Finally, there was a shift as Sandy and Larisha started making suggestions to Kez about diameters of wall thicknesses, root holes, watering requirements, even humidity. As Kez started working her magic, she was entering commands via pseudo-code sounding words. I'd had some computer science in school, and it sounded vaguely familiar, but obviously a skill set not used for decades is pretty empty. Now, everybody but Kez and Larisha had quit participating and we all drifted out to the refreshments table again.

"Oh man, that was great inspiration with that 'Big' tag." said Sandy. She poured herself a water with lime.

Jam slapped me on the back, "Just amazing how he fits right in, ain't it?" They all agreed, including Mandy, even though they didn't know about the vapor of the ideas. I'm pretty sure she could read some surprise in my face, and I, in turn, could see that reflected back at me.

"We're running a little late," said Jam. "I got some things we need to talk about, and I want the whole group here. I'm going to trot back to get Aisley and Bear so why don't you keep them busy for a while. I bet Jacky ... is that with a 'y' or an 'ie'?" He squirreled up his face.

"Hmmm, I guess just a Y," I said shaking my head. I made a mental note to myself that I should, for sure, recollect this day if this nickname stuck. After all, a nickname given so a computer wouldn't be confused is pretty special. And stupid. 'Oh, your name was already taken ... by a computer!'

"So," Jam suggested, "I bet Jacky will

really like your corn field, Sandy. And Mandy-".

"I'm going back to the clothes shop," said Mandy, not even waiting for an answer. She didn't wait for an escort either.

"Okay then. Later y'all," said Jam, and he was off, too. Everybody else just nodded at us as Sandy took my elbow and started leading me around to the other hallway.

"It is so exciting to have you here with us," she said. "We're going to do some really special things now that you're here."

I guess I must have been slow-walking due to that comment, because she started being more forceful in dragging me by the arm. The idea that I was anything to this amazing little community was plumb crazy.

As we turned the corner, I had to stop and look at the water feature with it's cross again. She quit tugging on me when I did. I hadn't noticed before, but the splatters of the falling water that escaped the pool were just disappearing. They were disappearing into the paving stones and leaving no puddles. Damp stones, but no puddles. Does everything take care of itself here?

Sandy started me off again, walking down the hall under the multiple mezzanines. They were brightly lit and leaf-tiled, just like the other side. The tilt wall panels making up the walls on this side were much more finished. It was hard to tell they were modeled concrete. The colors were very natural and accurate. I had to tap a few on the way down the hall, again, to confirm they were tiltwall. They'd implemented American, Flemish, and other brick styles that I know have names. Stone and brick, mixed colors, and mixed sizes, were all represented. I was dumbstruck. Again. They'd been trying everything and succeeding.

The last few compartments on the right were successful attempts at various half timber constructions[6]. The very first one was of finished timbers where the intervening space was filled with a plaster appearance. Of course concrete did this one just fine. The second one was another attempt at the Hill Country cedar and limestone building technique. This time, the appearance was of rough hewn timbers. These fake logs even had faux branch bases, individual unique cracks, tool marks, and even checks in the "wood". The places where the branches had been cut off actually showed the grain. It was very realistic, impossible to discern, even up close.

The last panel was really special to me. It brought back memories of having seen it in Europe, once again in the German end of culture. It had exotic patterns of colored bricks. I had to walk up and marvel at this one. It was hard to convince myself that it really was a tilt wall concrete panel. Of course it was, but the micro detail of each individual part was an amazing copy of reality. The finished timbers had detailed cracks and tool checks in the "wood". The brick colors finished up very close to the mortar level, and there was no color bleed. It was accurate in every detail, even if you looked very close. Amazing barely described it.

On reaching the end of the hall, Sandy turned to me and stopped before we approached the last compartment. Unlike any of the others, these wall panels were glass on both sides of the hall. They were two stories high on the left and three stories high on the right. Inside it was brilliantly lit and that light spilled into the hall. Made of smaller glass panes fit together like a stained glass window, they were exuberant displays of workmanship. They exhibited arches, interweaving the design with plants, leaves, waterfalls, and flowers. Like all the other rooms, they were a standard width that looked to approach fifteen feet. A noticeable difference, however, was these rooms were without floors to the upper stories and freespan. From what I could see at my current position, they were filled with panels covered with leaves from floor to the high ceilings. The space between each panel was barely eighteen inches.

"This has been my focus for close to a year now," said Sandy. "I want you to move up on it slow to get the full effect. One step at a time." She pointed down at my feet. I took a step.

"What do you see here?" she said.

"Tall ass panels covered with vines and lighted like the halls," I said.

"Yep, doubled up rabbit fence, for strength, to the ceiling."

She nodded and pointed at my feet. Another step. Sandy gave me that questioning look again.

"Same, but more of y'alls little robot bugs," I said. I was smiling because you just couldn't help it. More of the six legged droids were moving along the panels like spiders on a web. Their bodies weren't much bigger than my fist but their long legs made them look like daddy long-legs. Because I couldn't see down the lanes yet, the ones on the end seemed to be moving along their own lanes until they went where I couldn't see. They would pause over a leaf, for only seconds, then move to the next. When they were over the leaf, their little body moved concentric circles over it, then it would lift an edge by the stem before moving on.

"I had them wait until you got up here to start a leaf audit," said Sandy. "We strive to keep the systems at optimal performance. Every leaf is laser etched[2] with it's date of maturity. They remove them as they age out."

I cocked my head and raised on eyebrow at that one.

She said, "Stay."

I've heard that one before and understood. She turned and propped open the door to the compartment, walked in, and pulled a leaf off the panel. Turning back to me, she grabbed a small magnifying glass from the table by the door. She handed me the leaf and glass.

"Look near the stem underneath," she said.

I started scanning the leaf, it immediately looked familiar but I still couldn't place the species. Turning it over and glassing, I saw a very light but distinct scar between two veins near the stem. Applying the magnifying glass, it was obviously a small QR code. It was barely surface deep.

"Oh nice. Never seen that before," I said.

"It's done by laser and basically just burns the cell surfaces. Very shallow. Notice how there's already a replacement coming on," Sandy said doing a game show hostess point. From the location where she'd pulled the leaf, there was another leaf already in position but ten percent as large.

"What kind of plant is this?" Looking at the leaf up close kept ringing bells, but nothing was on the tongue.

"It's a hyacinth bean^3 vine," she said. "It's one of the fastest growing plants around and, as it turned out, right in the middle of the bell curve representing phloem constituents." She was staring up at the panels.

"Uh ... huh," I said.

"Sorry. It's products of photosynthesis, that are distributed back through the plant, are very similar to many agriculturally significant plants. Therefore, we thought we could use it as a graft host."

"One step," she said, and pointed down again. She took the magnifying glass back from me.

"More little droids. There's some pots in the middle of the rack."

"In order to keep xylem water transport to the plant simple and strong, each row has it's own host plant so water doesn't have to be lifted. It also means the phloem products are distributed to our grafts laterally."

At this she stepped right up to me, looked me in the eyes, and said, "Shut your eyes, please, and don't open until I say." She grabbed my elbow again as soon as my eyes closed, moved me a few feet, and turned me toward the compartment.

"Ok," Sandy said. The excitement in her voice was obvious. I might even be tempted to say bubbling.

"Oh My God," was all I could say. I could now see the back side of the panels where side-by-side, in rows extending to the high ceiling, were ears of corn. The effect was of a wall of ears of corn three stories high. They'd obviously been started at different times because there were zones distinguished by their size. Larger ones had silks already. Still more mature zones had the dead silks flagging their successful pollination.

"Oh My God," I said again.

"You already said that." Sandy was hopping in place now.

"It is ... It is ... I can feel it coming," she said before she let out the loudest Aggie Whoop I think I've ever heard (sober).

"Are we doing it or what?" she said as she grabbed my hand, and almost skipping, dragged me into the compartment. The warmth of the room, and the smell of green corn plants, hit me like a wall. On the table to the right of the door was a collection of oddly-shaped safety glasses. They almost resembled diving masks. She grabbed two pairs, put one on, then turned to place one on my face. They extended down all around my head to the level of the bottom of my nose. Along the sides, the temple pieces, there was a thickness, and panels, suggesting replaceable modules.

"You don't actually have to keep these on in here during the day, but we flood this compartment with CO_2 at extremely high concentrations at night. During the day, for four hours in the morning, it is the closest it gets to ambient air. After that the ramp up starts at noon till 1900, at which point it's toxic to humans. You will feel more comfortable here with additional oxygen though." Then she tapped the modules on the side of her face, then mine. A very low hiss was discernible. "It's best to get in the habit."

Bending over to inspect one of the corn ears showed it growing out of a thimble-sized cup, and it in turn, was connected to the wire which made up the welded wire fencing. Each of these ear sockets had two inches on each side for the ear to grow. Every one had the stalk of the host vine fused through its base. Mature ears were growing side by side.

"Oh My God," I said. I guess practice makes perfect?

"Oh yeah. That's what I'm talking about!",

she said, doing the game hostess point again. "This room has 30,000 ears of corn growing at any one time." She turned, fixing me with her gaze. "That's equivalent to one acre."

"One acre ... in a room,"[4] Sandy said with emphasis.

"What does that come out to?"

"The first time I finally got cloning the lateral meristem right so I could hand it off-"

"Whatever that means," I said, trying to stay focused.

"When I finally got it so the droids could clone the ears, and they were able to plant all the racks, and they mostly lived after dozens of failures. It was a struggle. Anyway, one acre averages about 170 bushels of shelled corn in the field. We do better because we control pollination, have 20 hours of light, optimize temperature, control individual leaf health, and the droids hate bugs bad!" She was dancing to music I didn't hear yet. She went over to several holsters by the door where she grabbed up a laser pointer. She started illuminating a couple of adjacent leaves on the rack near me.

In the time it took me to recognize that she was painting two specific leaves, every daddy long-legs droid on that rack, six of them, came hustling down to that area. In this close proximity, it was easy to see that they really were using the fencing like the web of a garden spider. They had tiny tweezer claws at the end of the front two arms that were softly clacking like a nervous sow's teeth.

"And that is?" I said.

"That is how much they hate bugs. There's a flying drone that paints any bugs with the laser and they are supposed to come pick them off. They never miss either. Even tiny hopping bugs." She was smiling as she teased the drones with the laser, just like a cat. When she stopped, the droids started departing from the hot zone. She grabbed a leg of the closest one and it froze. "Exercise the left tongs, please." The tweezer claw cycled then she let go and it scurried back up towards the top of the rack.

"See ... they swarm and if they can't find anything they go right back to work. Each has her horizontal row to baby."

"That is pretty amazing. Really amazing."

"They're so thorough now, that we don't even let the flier in but every couple of days. These guys clean the leaves and search for bugs and monitor each part of the process."

"How many bushels?", I said.

"In a 20 day cycle, which we're also reducing with extended lighting, we got almost 190 bushels."

"*Oh My God* ... shelled?"

"Shelled."

"That's about ... probably ... " I stuttered while trying to do the math in my head. (190 bushels x 50 something pounds per bushel?)

"*TEN* thousand *SIX* hundred *FORTY* pounds ... in three weeks," she said, exhaling a sigh of success.

We both snapped a look at each other. "*Oh My God!*" we said in unison.

"What do you do with all that corn?" I practically shouted.

"We eat as much as we can in as many different ways as we can, but really, you've tasted the majority of it already," she said giving me a mischievous grin.

"What?"

"Tons per week we pour on the ground around the ranch feeding those feral hogs," she said, laughing. "I guess you didn't notice how white that fat was on that BBQ."

"Bear sure knows after seeing it up close last night," she added softly. "He's a heck of a shot, too."

"He is, we haven't been hunting all that much together." I was now wishing I'd taken him more so we'd have more stories to share. It was starting to sound like they had made some good ones last night.

"Oh yeah. Beginners luck I guess," she

said, nodding. "Jon shoots a .300 mag, too, and he shared some bullets with Bear. They got him on target with them quick. Then we went out and Bear did something the first hunt that Jon has been trying to do for a year,"

"New bullets?" I mumbled. I'd hand loaded, chronographed, and sighted those Hornady 168 grain A-Max bullets for Bear. Depending on the shooter, of course, you could regularly cover three shots with a dime at 100 with his rifle.

"Jon's been shooting 180 grain Remington Copper solids. He's looking to get a couple of head shots with one bullet. He's gotten two with one bullet several times, but not both head shots."

"So what did Bear do?" I asked. I was trying to focus so as to not look too surprised.

"We set him in a blind, low over the corn, and we hadn't driven off two minutes when we heard him shoot. Him being a newbie and all, we turned around to check on him in case he had an accidental discharge. He'd laid out three. Head shot all."

"Oh My God!"

"Uhm ... yes ... He is. Mine, too," she smiled. "I think Jon was bummed that he told him what he'd been looking to do, because who even thinks to take that shot?"

"So now he's got a steeper one to beat," I clapped and smiled at her. "That's the father of my grandkids!" At this, several people on the balconies started clapping, too.

I looked around and we all clapped. I waved and smiled, as they started wandering away. Out of the corner of my eye I caught Sandy waving them off.

"So did you get anything?" I inquired gently.

"Does a bear go in the woods?" she smiled. "We have to shoot at least 10 every night to keep this group in meat. Jon got five, Bear and I both got four. About average night I'd say."

"That's a lot of shooting."

"Not on a ranch this big. We corn ten areas miles apart every day which means most places aren't even hunted for almost a week. Place is ate up with well-fed hogs."

"You sound like a pretty serious hunter. What's your gun?" I said, tapping her shoulder like a buddy.

"I shoot a 6.5 Creedmore; about like your .260, only better," Sandy said, smiling that smile gun nuts smile. "I'd shoot it more but we all have to take our turn at killing for the crew. Jeremy absolutely insists, especially for his stew." She grabbed my elbow again and directed me towards a door adjoining the corn nursery.

"I spent my youth slopping hogs and I've got memories. Plenty of 'em. No problem for me to go out every night for a hog hunt if I could. There's always room for extras on the rabbit hunt though."

"What do you mean?"

"You know it. We can bag a 100 rabbits driving a mile down any ranch road, and if we wanted, 200 driving back the same way. A quick hunt, super easy to dress, but ... 150 a trip?" Sandy turned to me and scrunched up her face, "All those little bunny feet." She shook her head and cringed.

"Anyhoo ... I want to show you my lab," she said. She opened a door into a completely dark room.

At the door's threshold, I almost made out a rustling sound. The lights came up when my foot passed into the room. On the left side of the room were microscopes, vent hoods, packages of new plastic petri dishes, and the typical vials of unknown to me things. On the right side of the room was another cabinet, half the size of the vent hood, but loaded with scores of the thimbles that had formed the base for the ears of corn. Several droids, positioned outside the box, four of their arms passing through holes in the side, working smoothly on the inside. On the far end of the box were petri dishes, with something that the droids were taking minute specimens from, placing them in the tiny thimbles, and completing the operation by topping off the thimble with some type of gelatin.

Two arms rotating and selecting from the petri dish, two arms selecting, filling, and stacking the thimbles at a pace that could never be maintained by any human I'd ever seen. I've seen fast factory workers where muscle memory allows them to do things at speeds no ordinary person could do. But these droids were processing something at rates it was obvious no person could hope to approach. Every few seconds, a new loaded thimble went in the rack. Sandy went and leaned on the table overlooking the production hood and stood there watching the operation. I joined her.

We just watched together. Silently, the only sound in the room was the slight rustling of the droids doing their work. Every movement was quick and exact to the thousandths of an inch[4a]. I presume. There was no clatter.

After a moment, I said, "So what's happening here?"

Sandy looked over at me and I could see tears welling up in her eyes.

"These petri dishes are seeded with

thousands of cells that are a monoclonal cell culture that will generate the ear. I spent years at school researching the two clones of the lateral meristem." Sandy turned to me again, and I'm sure stupid was written all over my face. The tears were really welling up now.

"Is something wrong?" I barely got out.

"Thousands of hours spent under hoods like that one to generate a process that I could hand off to Kez," she said. Then she wobbled and the tears came in earnest. She crumbled to the ground as I tried to steady her.

"Okay Okay, you're okay." It was all I could say to a woman I'd barely known two hours. What could I do? She hadn't looked sad, but the tears were real, and she was starting to sob. Sandy was on her knees on the floor with her hands on her thighs slowly rocking back and forth. Intermittent sobs racked her. I was frantic. What is safe to touch in a lab?

"Can I get you some Kleenex?" I blurted out finally.

Without looking up or stopping her rocking she said, "Cabinet on the right, bottom shelf."

I was quickly back with the tissues and she looked up at me with a tear streaked face and the biggest smile.

"Uhm…are you ok?" I said.

"I'm so fine, so good. I … " she barely got

out before she went back to rocking again with her head down. The sobs were gone, and I think, maybe, I could detect ... giggles?

"Should I go get someone?" I said as I stood up. I'm past the age where I know what to do when a young woman has an emotional thing.

"No, NO, I'm really just great," she said as she let out a huge sigh. "Thank you Jesus!" With that, she was up on her feet wiping the tears away. She grabbed me and hugged me, then pushed away from me and gave another huge sigh.

"Wow!" she said.

"uh ... wow?" I echoed, much quieter. "Do you want to talk about it?" In my heart, I knew I should want to talk about it. I really did want to know how you go from sobs to giggles so fast. On the other hand, tomorrow maybe. Next week better.

"Sure. I had a Jesus moment. I haven't told anybody since grade school about having to slop the hogs. I lived on a poor, poor farm with my family when we were young. Five of us. No indoor plumbing. Daddy had to drive to the neighbors to pick up 250 gallons of water any time the cistern ran dry so we'd have any at all. Couldn't afford to dig a well. We grew what we ate or what we hunted up. That's why I'm a great shot." She jacked her eyebrows up and did a slow nod.

"We kept a wooden barrel outside the kitchen door which we'd keep full of corn chops, everything left after we picked the corn, which was run through a hammer mill. We'd mix any kitchen scraps into it and stir that slop, a slop like kids don't know today, with a hoe that had holes in it so we could really turn it over. Every morning before school my job, as the oldest, was to take two 2 gallon buckets of slop to the hogs. Sometimes those pigs would jump into the slop as I poured it, because they wanted it so much, and it would splash back on me. And then, I still had to go to school, because I didn't have but two dresses. I couldn't use them both up in one day. Water was always the issue."

"What? Where are you from?" I said.

"I was raised up near Detroit-"

"Detroit?"

She gave me a side-eyed look. "Detroit ... Texas. Red River County. One of the poorest in the state, if not *the* poorest."

"Oh," I said. I'd never heard of Detroit but I knew the county was northeast of Dallas. "That sounds ... "

"Crazy, I know," she said. "My Dad was an off-the-grid redneck and thought we could just make it alone. No asking for nothing and definitely no handouts. He would have kept the plumbing out of the house if the county hadn't threatened to condemn us."

I was just standing there, listening, and barely understanding. My family came from the rough edge, too. Not this rough though. This was the difference between ranching and farming. God grew grass, we ate the mutton and steak. Her father had to have been one hard man.

I smiled at her, and said, "That's a character builder."

"Oh yeah, heard that more than once. The thing is you go to school smelling like hog slop, you get teased. A lot." She smiled.

"I'm missing something here," I said.

"It's really a long chain that I didn't see till right this very minute," Sandy said. She turned and leaned over the droid hood again. She was looking down towards them, but her eyes were focused on something far off.

"When I went to play with the neighbor kids, on big farms, their hog feeding chore was filling a trailer with corn from a silo and driving it beside the pens auguring shelled corn out into the troughs. I got high on the idea of that golden corn then." She turned and looked directly at me.

"Then 4H corn contests, BS biochemistry with a minor in genetics ... of corn, PhD Genetic Mosaics in Maize ... everything kind of predicated on my idea that no other little girl should have to be called piggy because she had to slop the hogs." She let out another sigh.

"And up until this very minute, I'd thought I'd been driving," she said, looking over her shoulder at me.

These people were getting the full inventory of my stupid looks, so of course, I reiterated it, and said, "Huh?"

Sandy turned and came over to me, took my hands in hers, and looking past my eyes, said:

"For we are God's masterpiece, having been created in Christ Jesus for good works that God prepared beforehand so we may do them."[5]

She cocked her head as she stared at me, smiling, and I could feel the hot waves of goosebumps starting at the base of my back.

"Would you mind if I said a little prayer of thanks?" she said. I nodded and she held my hands and put her head against my chest.

"Dear Papa, thank you for showing me your handiwork in my life. Help us to always know you stand with us, ready to accept us if we but accept you. Thank you for bringing Jacky safely to us, and return him and his family to their homes safely if they choose not to stay. Bless this congregation. In Christ's name, Amen"

Sandy stepped back from me, shook both my hands twice, smiling, then let go and said, "You know, we should probably be getting back."

We walked back to the conference room in silence. I didn't pay any attention to the people in the balconies above us or those that passed other than I nodded "Howdy" to them. I had waves of goosebumps crawling over me. I was feeling the welling behind my eyes that experiencing huge emotion can have on an old man. Old-ish, really.

11.

Sandy was a couple of steps ahead when we got back to the conference room. I could hear the group talking over each other as she turned the corner crossing the threshold. In the two steps it took me to catch up to her, the room had gone quiet.

"Pause," I think it was Larisha who said it.

"Are you ok, sugar?" said Jam. Larisha stood up after putting down a laser pointer on the table and came and put a hand on Sandy's shoulder.

"Sure," said Sandy looking around the room. "Jeremy, I just had a God wink and Jacky was right there with me." At that, she turned around to smile at me as did all the other eyes. Bear and Aisley were part of the group now, obviously intrigued by the tech of the gang, but swallowing laughter. The set of eyes I was looking for weren't there, really.

Sitting in the corner was the face of my beautiful wife, or most of it anyway, peaking out from underneath a hot pink camouflage shrug in the style of a ghillie suit. It was full of pink, red, black, and gray strands making up the body of the shrug, with some hanging over her eyes. It covered most of her torso, was hooded, and long sleeved. As soon as she caught my eye, she was up out of her seat, wiping back the pink ghillied hoodie. The shrug had pockets at the end of the sleeves, large enough for gloved hands, which she shook off to put her hands against my face.

"What is that?" I said, fondling some strands of the ghillie suit.

"Baby?" said Mandy in loving concern.

"It's fine. Sandy had a thought that brought her to tears and it worked on me some, too," I said. When I said that, all the other members of the group looked to Jam and they all shared a smile. I would say a knowing smile, but whatever it was, what I'd experienced wasn't quite clear to me.

"It's kind of like when you hear a really beautiful piece of music that touches, you ain't it?" said Jam. "A piece so beautiful your soul feels it deep down, in a place you don't go to much."

"Yeah ... I guess," was all I could say. The welling-up was not as under control as Mandy led me to my chair. Jam seemed to be addressing the emotional switch itself directly and I could feel it.

At that, a quiet chorus of "Amens" rolled

around the room, and I watched the wave. Mandy pushed me down into my seat because I'd froze.

Larisha sat down, grabbed up her laser pointer, and said, "We were just fixing to get started reviewing the presentation so far. You haven't missed anything, so I'm going to start it." When she said that I, was under my own emotional control again, but looking back to what I'd been feeling. Looking over it close.

"Hey Jack, rewind, please," she said. The large monitor over the door went black and started again. The monitor was covered by the image of the state record bur oak. The observer's point of view started rotating around it slowly.

The animations alone I would have bet would take weeks in a normal world, but they were as seamless as everything else we'd seen while we'd been here. The viewer's perspective flew around the bur oak and then around the bare earth at it's base. Ditches, three of them, started sinking into the ground. Each ditch started radiating from a central location that was being punched straight down into the earth.

"What's happening here," said Bear.

"The presentation is all about making this titanium tree," said Larisha. "That's our project right now." She traced the ditches coming from the center hole with her pointer as she spoke.

I looked over to Bear and he cocked his head at me and quietly mouthed, "Titanium tree?" Aisley did not even look over. She had been captured already.

"Those are lateral roots," said Sandy, "that we're going to make sure extend past what a tree of this size would have. Then they're going to angle down to the depth of the tap root. We're hoping to make a little more surface water collection area, because if it does rain out here, we want to soak it up."

Sandy reached out her hand and Larisha put the laser in it. She pointed to the sides of the screen hitting some icons and the scene changed into a surface and subsurface cross sectional view. The lateral root ditches, after traversing some distance, were sloping steeply down into the earth.

"This is the biggest change in the structure. I personally think is going to be really great," said Sandy, as she traced the line of the sloping tunnel. "Larisha wanted some deep support because it's going to be so high. Because of desert, I wanted a deeper tap root. We're doing it all."

Sandy looked around the room, waiting for comments.

"How much room do you think you're

going to need to get to welding down there, Jon?" said Adric.

Jon shrugged his shoulders, then said, "There're some new, more compact drones being shaped right now for spot welding and some for shielding gas, and I'm betting ... ," he held his hands up making a circle 16 inches in diameter, "this'll do it."

At that Jon, Adric, and Larisha all looked over to Kez.

"Hey Jack, make the ditch diameters 18 inches, please," said Kez. "Hey, Jack, demonstrate the welding droids at the farthest point from tap root center."

Immediately the scene zoomed into one of the projected lateral root ends. Two droids appeared in the hole, and started spot welding individual short pieces of titanium rod together.

"Hey, Jack stop motion please," said Larisha.

The scene stopped.

"Jack, Step," said Larisha.

She stepped it through the scene. A welding droid delivered a rod with it's ends already shaped to fit exactly flush in the proper place, just like the stones in the floor earlier. The welder placed it's electrodes over the ends to be welded. The drone supplying shielding gas placing it's paws around the weld site, injecting with shielding gas, then "flash". Tic toc, on to the next, again and again.

"Instead of just showing them created, the rate of growth of ditches and structure ... is it ... to scale?" said Aisley.

"That's a good question," said Larisha turning in her chair to face Aisley. "What we generally do is let the system work with a budget of droid time. Some call it DTs. We assign a number of DTs and let the Host show us how it thinks it would go. This particular one has a 4 DT per linear foot budget. It's kind of amorphous: droids per linear foot, droids per area, droids per volume. However we decide to scale the resources for a project."

"Can you see that?" said Aisley.

"Sure thing," answered Larisha, speaking over her shoulder, "Hey Jack, display droid resources."

At this command, the scene was overflowing with legged dots representing all the drones working the site. There were hundreds. It became impossible to pay attention to the tree because of the swarm of drones scurrying across the site.

"One thing we've learned, if we micromanage the actual production it adds a layer of confusion. Or maybe I should say it confuses us. At this stage, generally, we just watch the project grow to see if we understood each other. After a while, then we add the droids to see if they're working efficiently in the virtual presentation. Then, we go for a test ride. What do you think? Too busy?"

"Too, too busy," said Aisley.

"Amen," washed around the table again.

Larisha took over the session again, removed the display of the drones, and over the next hour we watched as the team refined and polished the titanium tree. We stepped through the presentation and model repeatedly. Each person had their area that they questioned or offered improvements. Bear and Aisley had become integrated into the group as easily as if they'd been calved into it.

Weird ideas, again, were welcomed as easily as breathing. At one point, Bear made a suggestion about the lateral roots, offering that they be barbed to add a structural strength enhancement. I'm sure it was because of his love for archery hunting somehow. Even though they all laughed, it was implemented immediately after Sandy confirmed it wouldn't affect the placement of tissue grafts.

When the root structure, lateral and tap, were finalized, the size of the project was immense. As we were watching the work on the trunk of the tree, I could finally feel the scale. The trunk of the tree at ground level was 90 inches in diameter.

"Holy Moses, how big is that thing supposed to be?" asked Bear.

"We're shooting for the record, this is Texas after all, and we specified 101 feet," said Sandy.

"I'm pretty sure things are working," said Sandy, "but I want to stop at this level before we go any higher. I'm not sure if we have to exactly copy the xylem, the woody part, that delivers the water to the top."

"I thought you said ... " I started to say, hooking my thumb back in the general direction of the corn field room.

"That was one of the hardest things we've done botanically so far," said Sandy, "because each kernel of corn is individually fertilized. Apples, pears, zucchini, other handy things are so much easier. Clone gametocytes, trick them to thinking they're fertilized, then grow out pericarp making the drupe pear, cherry, or whatever."

"This ... " Sandy traced the outline of the tree stump and roots with the laser "this is truly BIG. I just want to get the root structure in and developing before we get too carried away."

"What are you talking about?" asked Bear. He hooked his thumb in the same direction as I had. You could tell he was on to something and was going to chase it down, even if it wasn't his area.

"They have a corn field. In a room!" I said.

"What?" Bear and Aisley said. They glanced at each other as if they'd heard me say the moon was cheese. Looking around the room to seek support for their disbelief, was stomped on because of all the nodding.

Mandy grabbed the shoulders of her camo shrug to shake it at them and said, "You've both seen the dress shop. Duh."

"Ok y'all, we're gettin' into the bushes here," said Larisha. "We need to get back on the trail."

As the team started working again, Sandy was leaning into Jam and whispering something that made both of them do exaggerated, unselfconscious nods. They were wearing relaxed smiles, and whenever I looked their way, they were looking back. That feeling you get like someone is watching you? This was much bigger and enveloping.

The team wanted to see the final height and build, so Jack displayed the titanium tree completely. It was a hollow titanium rod reaching into the sky. The crown of branches reached out almost as wide as it was tall.

"Oh, look at that wasted center," said Jon,

"I think we need some tree house in there."

"I'm all over that, too," said Adric. The smiles traded on this exchange energized a rapid-fire burst of ideas. Tree houses are popular for little and big. In no time there were balconies above some of the limbs. Hobbit doors in heaven.

"We just need to make some drone space to carry us up to the different levels. This is getting a little ... ," Larisha had started to say. Her statement was distracted by her laser-pointing the empty central column and stretching it large enough for a wide person to fit inside.

"There ain't nothing about this that says we can't be carried from space to space riding a ladder-climbing droid," finished Kez. "I love it."

"Oh.Yeah," "That's it," "Got it," "You go girl" and other affirmations filled the room.

I looked over at Mandy and she was smiling so brightly. The infectious joy of the group was covering everyone. The beauty of that smile on my wife was making me emotional again.

She noticed me looking at her, smiled, and reached over and patted my cheek.

In the space of minutes the tree was redesigned so that the center had a square titanium shaft with sides made up of ladder rungs.

Tree houses had always been one of my favorite *forts* when I was young, and this was a magnificent plan. And in that warm memory, once again, I was drawn to stare at Mandy. The life we'd lived started like the acorn, with nothing, and then kids, and houses, and eventually undreamed of success. There were times she trusted me to mortgage everything. And here we were in the middle of something that was huge, that was giant. I was overcome with the feeling that we'd been walking this direction our entire lives.

Mandy caught me staring at her again, patted my cheek again, and pushed my face towards the monitor. As soon as she let go, I turned back to her, and gave her my best loving smile. I think. She smiled back with that big eyed, "what?" face. This time she pulled the hood of her ghillie over her head and went back to watching the show. She gave me a side glance, then pulled strands of the ghillie down over her face, smiled even wider, and turned back to the monitor. How lucky can a man be?

"I think we can reduce material on the outer shell some," Adric said, "since it's eventually going to be oak, right Sandy?" His eyes never left the monitor's redraws.

Adric went to working on his monitor, and said, "Hey Jack, reduce exterior shell material and use it ... ". He pointed with his hand pointer to an image of a longitudinally sliced long bone of a bird displayed on his monitor, "in the fashion of the ... " he paused looking around the room for a second, absently tracing the interior spaces of the displayed bone with the cursor.

"Adric, would you like it to be pneumatized with trusses and struts?" said Jack the computer.

"Uh ... sure ... let's see a sample, please." Adric let the system have it's head.

In moments, the tree had become a central square pipe, surrounded by webbing defining the outer surface of the tree. The spaces between the outer shell and the inner square column were now filled with a geometric webbing freeing up heavy titanium structure from the previous design.

"Where's all this coming from?" asked Sandy. She smiled around at everyone in the room, settling on me.

"Jack, compare this tree with the model, side by side, please," said Kez. On that order, the monitor instantly displayed a giant bur oak in full leaf on the left, with it's larger mirror image in titanium, sans leaves and bark, on the right.

You'd have thought the room itself was moaning with pleasure. It was astounding to see the actual parent model for the tree and it's new titanium child displayed side by side. The monitor point of view was circling them both to display every angle, and except for the Hobbit balconies and height, they were twins.

"Do you really think this will grow out here?" asked Mandy, cocking her head towards Sandy.

"Well, it's darn hot in the summer," Sandy said, "and this is a bottom land tree. I think if we water it, since the roots will be pre-formed, why not? Hey Jack, display the water tubes in blue, please.

"When I was looking into this irrigation part, I learned that the giant redwoods use something like 200 gallons of water a day. These blue tubes are actually PVC septic lines paralleling every foot of root installation. I figure we can deliver 50 gallons a day to each section without too much trouble.

"The reason I don't think we should go any higher than the first 10 feet on the trunk is that we need to make sure we have a grip on the cell culture, transfer and graft integration. After we're sprouting on the trunk we'll build up."

Sandy looked around smiling, then said,

"Hey Jack, display the graft processes, with daily estimates of time required in the bottom right. This will pretend we've already solved those problems."

This time the display showed the entire titanium tree, it's surface filling with rings of solid color, whose appearance aged, into something looking like young tree bark. As one layer filled out, the next section above was started and the one below started sprouting into a shag carpet of new leaves.

"It's getting faster as it goes because it thinks it's getting smarter about it," said Kez absentmindedly. "This unsupervised AI is-"

"I love this stuff," Jam burst in. The room moaned approval again.

By the time the entire tree had been covered with a lush green shaggy carpet of leaves, the counter in the bottom of the monitor displayed "74".

"That can't be right, can it Larisha?" Jam queried the boss pointing at the number.

"Jeremy, you know as well as I do that Jack is ... " Larisha seemed at a loss also, "unexpectedly ... prescient?"

"There ain't no way!" said Bear.

"I'd say farfetched myself," Aisley said. She was slowly shaking her head from side to side.

"Jack, how much is the tree required to grow, per hour, to meet your projection for completion?" said Larisha.

"0.719175454-" the computer started answering.

"To 3 decimals, please," instructed Larisha.

"0.719 inches per hour," Jack the computer noted dryly.

"Jack, does that include root structure?" requested Larisha.

"That does not include root structure," droned the computer.

"What is the DT density as reconfigured?"

"The current project resource bill of materials calls for 1861 workers and 48 Mdrones."

Larisha turned to the group and said, "Who thinks it will be able to grow up in 74 days?"

Looking around the room, the default answer was a definite shrug.

Adric was the first to speak, saying, "I don't think it's close to possible, but if I've learned anything here, it's that the impossible may be likely. A hundred foot tall structure, built from scratch from small pieces in 74 days? Sure!"

"Amen," said Jam. At that, the room joined in. The locals in the group were clearly onboard, or at least had some faith in the prediction. My group was just as clearly leaning skeptical, but respecting the reality that we were breathing in here.

"Once the main structure is covered by grafts," said Sandy, "if this is right, the tree should start recognizing the limbs designated as mature limbs and it will start dropping the suckers. I'm thinking it might look pretty much like a real tree within three years. Crazy."

At that, Sandy leaned over and shoved Jam, "Jeremy wants to say something."

"Ok," said Jam, pointing to Bear and Aisley. "I sorta introduced some of this to Jack and Mandy this morning, but I need to bring you guys up to snuff."

He slowly rose out of his chair and said, "I hope y'all don't mind if I pace while I talk. I'm fixin to talk a little about what drives some of this, from the periphery anyway."

Jam looked around the room, and said, "Y'all have heard this scads of times. Won't hurt my feelings if you leave."

Everyone but those in my party rose, smiled at us, some gave me the thumbs up, but in a bare minute they were all gone and the door was closed.

"I'm guessing," I said, "that when you said scads of times, you really meant to say boo-jillion. They cleared out like scalded geese."

"Not sure if that's a real number, but it sounds close, and the answer is yes," said Jam.

"So ... earlier at the overlook, I told y'all about B.F. Skinner's "Walden 2" and how it put a burr under my saddle. Then the intro to panopticon. Basically, what we're doing here, is saying that we aren't interested in ordering free people's lives. But convicted prisoners in the panopticon, they get it full bore. Good and hard. When we plan something, everybody out here tries to find a way to counter Walden or Walden 2. For example, the dress shop."

Jam walked over and flipped some of the strands of Mandy's ghillie suit.

"All the communists, and B.F. is no different, always plan to have standards. They plan standard food, standard work day, and standard suit of clothes for the people. Larisha was the first one to pick that out as a task, because she's got a lovely style. She's always been so outside the normal size of most manufacturers that she always had to sew her own. Her and Kez fixed up the dress shop so we can let our creativity go wild with whatever we want. We're FREE to create. The droids give us real power, in depth, to do it."

"Yeah, they do," I said, and we were all nodding.

"So after a bite for lunch, we're going to

tour the pan ... I mean, Hive. As we walk around, if you see anything you don't understand, ask someone how that relates to Walden. Most everything over there does in some way, unlike this tree, which is more a test of the system. This was a spark of an idea laid out to show *you* how free to new ideas we can be."

"So everything is related to pushing back on Walden or Walden Two?" said Aisley.

"I wouldn't go that far. I will say that Thoreau was some lying shit that only city people could believe. I know for a fact that Jack ... eee ... and I know that sitting under a bush, or plank, in the rain waiting to get back to work is no joyful thing. And the stupid is obvious and deep all around if you've ever spent any real time in work gloves. Heck, one time he claims to have shoveled out a cellar[1] of over 8 yards, through tree roots, too! Then he wrote 'It was but two hours work'."

Jam shuddered, and said, "You can only try to pass so many of those by me before I'm going to look at that horse's teeth."

I knew immediately what he was saying. I could clearly picture 10 yards of sand, loose and dry, being dumped on my front yard. If anybody was capable of moving it at that speed I've yet to meet them. A quick figuring at 5 shovels per cubic foot, being extremely generous so the math would be easy, that metrosexual would have to be shoveling about 10 shovels per minute, not counting roots. Also, not counting having to toss out of a grave-sized hole. Big Bull indeed.

"Oh man. That's lapping over my boots," I said, knowing my group had history, in our own lives, proving Thoreau a crank. Every one of us in this room started out country.

"One thing that has been kind of bothering me," I said.

"Yes, sir," said Jam.

"Why do they always call you Jeremy," I said in a mocking tone, "and why do they always clap when you walk up. I woulda thought they'd be used to you by now!"

"They always tell me they love Jeremy," he shrugged, "and I quit trying to get them to change on that one. And the clapping ... they're not clapping for me."

"Who then?" I said.

"You, cowboy."

12.

The five of us walked to the cafeteria together without a word. Passing through the fountain area with it's trees and seating area, there were people sitting around deep into their tablets. Others were working in small groups around a single tablet. Now, when they looked up at us with a welcoming smile, I assumed it to be directed to me. I just nodded not knowing where I fit into this situation. It was passing odd. Far past.

"I want to see the corn field," said Bear from over on Jam's flank. "Oh yeah," Aisley added.

Jam called a young lady from one of the groups over, and told Bear and Aisley that we'd meet them in the cafeteria.

"I'm going to check this out, too," Mandy said, and she turned off to join them.

"Hey Jam," I leaned close and whispered in his ear, "I'm pretty confused. What have you told them-"

"All I've told them is that you have a skill set we absolutely need to move forward to the next step. We've been seeing it building for several months, and we're all gaining more confidence at every success. On the other hand, we know the powers that be will work in earnest to stop us when we make ourselves known. You ... I won't say you alone, but I know you can help us over this step and I'd like that. If you so choose." He put his arm around me and patted me on the back. "Really. No pressure."

As he finished, I was aware that every set of eyes at this end of the building was on me. It's been a bunch of years since I had any stage fright at a business presentation, but here I was feeling a cold sweat. I was getting focused attention, and my role was still completely unknown to me. It certainly wasn't fear, but it felt like it might be a close neighbor to it. More like a very questionable house guest.

"Let's go grab a bite to eat and I'll clue you in some," Jam said. He opened the door to the cafeteria.

This time the cafeteria was almost completely full. There was an empty table on the periphery of the room, which seemed obviously set aside for us. Passing through towards the food line, the same looks and smiles followed us at every step.

"It makes you kind of nervous doesn't it?" Jam whispered into my ear. "Like being the turkey invited to Thanksgiving dinner?"

"Ok, that's not really a helpful analogy," I said. "I hope you'll help me understand soon, because I was loving every part of this until just while ago. Now ... should I be looking over my shoulder?"

"Nah, dude, come on," he said. "There is nothing about this that won't be one of the biggest things you've ever done, and twice as fun."

He led me into the line, cutting in front of several people already there, but they just smiled and handed me their tray and silverware. I apologized for it, but every one, to a person, seemed eager to be able to stand aside for me.

The food choices still focused mainly on pork, the big special today being tacos of 'pierna de puerco'. The pit and it's automated carvers were busy, too. Every fruit and vegetable that was displayed, now made me wonder if it was another one of the magical presents derived from the work of Sandy and her cloning crew. One thing was pretty clear, most everything that was available, and there was plenty, were things that had short harvest times. Peppers, tomatoes, green onions, herbs, okra, squash, small fruits, and multiple varieties of each, were in the presentation. Of course, corn tortillas were there.

Jam headed us over to the vacant table against the wall, and I could see that the Hive was alive with motion now. Three large rough terrain construction cranes, large trucks, swarms of small drones, many man-sized ones, and so many white hardhats. The action on the Hive at every level grabbed my attention. When I came back to earth focus, I almost stumbled. I became aware of the piles of dirt, framing ditches, outside the windows. Centered on the area Jam had marked on our trip to the *zero* this morning, were now ditches sinking into the desert floor. It was clear to me that the titanium tree had already started becoming reality.

"Sit over here against the wall with me, please," said Jam.

We unloaded our trays onto the table as Aisley, Bear, Mandy and their guide came into the cafeteria laughing and gesturing.

Bear saw us in the corner and gave us two thumbs up, and said, "Hail yes." It was loud enough to echo through the space.

At that holler, the occupants of the cafeteria let out an Aggie whoop that I haven't heard since the 2013 Cotton Bowl when Oklahoma really caught it. The volume of this endorsement visibly startled Aisley, and led Mandy to replace her ghillie hood, which sparked more laughter into the space.

"Look, Jack…eee," Jam said smiling at me, "I really want to do the dog and pony show today for all of you, and then talk about your roles tonight. Just us back at the Post. It won't be something you have to spend a lot of time thinking about, and ain't going to cost you no money.

"Let me tell you a story. I don't know why this came into my mind. It just percolated in. When I knew you were coming out, and I'd be asking your help, I got a little anxious." He was looking down, slowly shaking his head from side to side, Then he looked up. "So … I was driving down to Sanderson one evening, almost twilight. It was a cool evening, and I had the windows down. That was before I had a jacked up truck, just a regular F-150. So I'm cruising down the road, watching the clouds change colors minute by minute and keeping an eye out for deer. It was a beautiful evening. Sure enough, a half dozen does are walking across the road down the way, right to left. I let off the gas, put my foot over the brake, and coasted towards them honking. The whole time, I'm reminding myself that I'm not about to dodge a deer and head into a rock or telephone pole, but they walk on across so I start speeding up.

"I barely got going again and, *bam,*

something hit me on the side of the head. Hard. Put me right to the edge of consciousness. I skidded to a stop on the side of the road. Feeling my face was wet, I discovered blood all over me. The first thought I had was that someone had thrown a rock at me, but I was miles from anything. Who'd be sitting on this deserted desert road? As I gathered myself up, and my head started to clear, I realized there was a place on the side of my face that ached, but the blood, it didn't seem to be mine. Getting out of the truck, the door was all mashed in and the mirror gone. Laying in the road behind me, was a dead muley doe with her neck broke."

"Holy crap!" I said. I hardly emphasized it enough.

"That's right. Stupid animal from the left had tried to make it across in front of me and hit me on the door, bashing me in the head. Try buttin' heads with a 50 mph deer and see if that don't make some stars."

"Good thing it wasn't a buck!" I said. "But, heck, you got a pretty bony head as I remember."

"That's been said more than once," Jam said. He turned to his food and started filling his smile.

"So what's the point of that story?" I asked.

"I'm not exactly sure. We have some

beautiful stuff happening out here. I know you agree. But it might be perilous, like them crossing deer. Me getting you involved, at a part I know is going to raise some hackles all around, but maybe we won't even see the real danger coming at us. Pretty sure about that. I can see some fear, then even more relief ... that's where we're all going to live for a little while I think. When I tell you what I want you to do, you'll laugh it's so easy. I think we'll be scared, then intrigued. Here's hoping," Jam said. He raised his glass and we clinked.

Jam started working his plate and I joined him. Between mouthfuls I was totally distracted by what he'd said, and watching the happenings outside gave me the excuse, I guess, to ignore the others. The little drones working like swarms of fire ants marching to and fro along the paths to their task, the larger ones normally associated with someone in a white hat. The cranes were lifting panels and stuff around, fast, very fast. I've always loved watching cranes work.

"Holy Moses!" said Bear, walking up on us. "Every minute there's something stirring around here."

"Hey, Dad, you should have seen the dress shop, too," said Aisley.

"Yeah, it would have been the first time

you didn't threaten to cancel my credit card," Mandy interjected through her pink ghillie. She tossed her hood back and arranged her plate on the table.

"Is that ditch out there the tree we were working on this morning?" asked Aisley, to no one in particular. She was focused on getting her food down to the table, too.

"Ok y'all," Jam said with some seriousness, "I want you to cover everything you're interested in today as fast as possible. I guess you've noticed that the heavy equipment is back. I had everything cleared out for your arrival so you could see the main focus of what we're working towards, without being distracted."

Jam took a bite of taco, and that led the rest of us to grab a bite of something, too.

"What you're going to see now," said Jam, "is the symphony of all the parts working together. The thing that is going to impress you, if it hasn't already, is that productivity is geometrically related to droid density when they're in close proximity. As they work, they optimize continually."

He took another couple of bites and we did, too.

He was conducting us! When that thought crossed my mind, it was quickly followed by another. *We are the disruption!* This one had an effect such that I actually quit chewing for a moment. I have no idea where that came from. *The* disruption.

"One thing you can really help us with is the Walden angle," Jam said. Those words came through a mouthful of taco.

We all looked around at each other as we stuffed tacos, too. I didn't get a glimmer of recognition from anyone.

"I loaded both on my phone earlier," said Aisley.

"Good. Maybe you can find the place in Walden 2 where B.F. talks about the duck pond when he first walks his crew around," said Jam.

At that, he started eating with some real focus. Us, too. Aisley was looking at her phone, tapping the screen, and whispering to it intermittently. She still managed getting fed.

"Okay, I think I found it," Aisley said. Talking through taco herself, and showing a little *see food*. "Here goes, 'The pond is our own work, ... It covers some swamp land and stores a bit of water against a dry spell. As you see, we have a few ducks—more for the children than anything else, though we get an occasional dinner from them.'" [1]

"Yep, that's it alright," said Jam shaking his head. "Ain't nobody living around any animals that don't understand that's some Harvard elite, slick as goose, shit. If you have animals for the kids, like a yard lamb, they give them names and you aren't never eating even one. If you actually got enough production that a few won't be missed, you got so much crap on the ground, you are stepping light around that pond, and you aren't likely to swim in it." He looked around at us all smiling.

"And that's what I want to make sure you learn today," Jam said. "We're not talking pie in the sky here, trying to make believers of some city boys and girls with piles of sweet smellin' crap. We're talking fat cattle, and I want to make sure you leave here able to present that to whoever asks, because I think they just might."

This time, everyone was leaning in, and the faces around the table showed eagerness.

"So ... I'll have everybody come round by groups, and y'all can do with whoever you want. And, whatever you do, don't be shy about moving over to whatever interests you. You can change minute to minute because we want your interests to be your guide. We live that way. We're free children of the universe."

More eagerness in our faces, accompanied by nodding this time.

Then Bear, leaning over to Aisley, said "I

think we're the children here, eh?" Mandy swatted him on the shoulder.

"Ok," said Jam standing.

"We're about ready y'all. When I point your team out, stand up, and we'll let the lead give an intro." The moment he started speaking the crowd went completely silent. Everyone started shuffling over towards us, smiling, and organizing themselves. They were arranging themselves into little clusters, apparently by a gathering of similar hats.

"Oh, I'm sorry, Larisha," Jam said, "you got that list for me?"

Larisha raised her hand then bent back to her phone, Jam's phone dinged and he opened it. He leaned over to us and said, "Really, ya'll are the only ones that know less than me."

"Ok, first group is Agriculture," he said and looked up from his phone.

Sandy stood up on this one and another half dozen. They all smiled, so sure and confident, it was hard not to want to go to their group right off. Most of the people in her group had cowboy hats in earth tones. Sandy gave a short speech that covered existing production that was feeding the Host, corn field in a room, projects that were in the works like the titanium tree, and other outlandishly, apparently possible things, done with CRISPR[2] gene editing.

I raised my hand. Bear and Aisley whispered in a huddle deciding if they were going to start choosing, or wait to hear the list.

"Ok then, Jack-eee's on one. Then," Jam said checking his phone again, "construction tech." He pointed out Adric.

Adric stood and a dozen stood with him. He introduced CNC techniques with concrete, automated heavy equipment, and I didn't hear the rest. I was thinking about the cranes running free. Without people driving?

I raised my hand again and the entire group giggled.

"Listen, cowboy, you can only ride one horse at a time," Jam said. He took his hat off to give me a swat.

We went on through Deep Knowledge (Aisley), Distributed Processing (Bear), Environment Sciences, Marketing (Mandy), Robots and Exoskeletons(Aisley and Bear, again. Duh!), and Panopticon Philosophy. After Aisley picked, Jam leaned over and asked her to look up "working hours" in Walden Two.

I raised my hand, to more laughs, on each of the choices. Every presentation was full of detail. I mostly understood. They sounded challenging, and so very inviting. After the first three, Jam would just blurt out a day of the week. "Distributed Processing"/hand up/giggles/"Jack-eeee on Friday".

Finally done, he totally ignored my choices, and assigned me Panopticon Philosophy. "It's the one you need to understand more than the others. It's actually the main part of what you need to understand."

"Ok. If you say so," I submitted.

The entire group applauded, and it made me blush, because I could feel every single eye. Then they started filtering out.

Jam turned to Aisley again, "Did you find that passage?"

"I think so," said Aisley. "Is it the one where they work 4 hours a day?[3]"

Jam raised his hands, and shouted, "Hold up, y'all, just one thing. Raise your hands if you only work four hours on any given day."

Only hysterical laughter met that announcement. Jam waved them off, and they all left except the leaders of the groups we'd selected. They came up to sit at our table.

"Now y'all, it may be hard to sort it out when you're covered up with everything that you're going to see today," Jam said, looking at each of my group in turn, "but this is a capitalistic endeavor where we do lots of sharing. That boy B.F. said, I think it's right above that four hour work day thing, that profit was always bad[4]. Profit is why we work, how we keep score, but we do some serious sharing with community. We hope. We're planning to. We have very few requirements for labor, we don't need no Ivy League B.F cultural engineering for the free man, so don't even go down that path. If you get distracted ask for an interpretation from your guide."

He looked around at us first, making sure we were nodding, then shrugged at the others.

Jam stood, arms wide, then waved us off like he was shooing chickens, "Ok, y'all, lets hit it."

13.

I was standing at the edge of the little ramp leading into the car, when the crane put the hook block directly over it without an instant of correction. The droid hanging on the hook block connected the car to the block, and in so doing exposed the "100T" lettering on it. When our little group stepped aboard it was not going to tax this heavy lift tool.

Above us, much closer now, but still without understanding, were the blue bands going around the buildings of the Hive. They were obviously related to some kind of panel on the building face, but the panels weren't generating it. It was just a clear, pure glacier blue, hovering over the panels in horizontal stripes across the hive. Each band ended at a mirror on the building corner.

Kez entered the car first stepping to the back, then Larisha. Sandy stepped into the car holding my elbow, then Jam followed and slid the gate closed. In the center of the car was a pole that had wrist straps on it like subway cars. There was room for another six people without crowding.

"I'd grab a strap," said Jam, as he did just that.

I reached for the strap, and as my hand slid into it, I noticed that Kez and Larisha were facing each other with their fingertips touching their ears.

"What's going on there?" I said. They bent their knees a little as they turned towards me. Again with the smiles.

"You ready?" said Jam.

"I'm-" I barely managed to get out of my mouth.

"Hey, Jack, four - ", said Jam. As the number of the floor left his mouth, it was obvious we were inside a different kind of vehicle. It was like a car fixing to drop off the summit on a really big roller coaster, but this time in reverse. It seemed there was a slight pause as we left the ground, but we leapt to the fourth floor as fast as any vertical trip down I've ever taken. I'm not absolutely sure I ever fell out of a tree any faster. The acceleration pushed me hard to the floor, and I would have crumbled if not for the wrist strap. I was barely able to recognize how the shadow of our car momentarily dimmed the blue bands circling the building.

" ... please," finished Jam. He turned, looked over me like he was expecting to see stains on my jeans, then smiled. I wobbled a little as I regained my footing.

"Good job. You'll fit in fine," he said.

"Maybe," said Larisha laughing. She dropped her hands from her head, as did Kez, who reached up and slapped her on the shoulder.

"At least we know his heart's still in pretty good shape," said Sandy, smiling widely.

The car was grabbed by two arms protruding from under the floor at level four, pulled up flush, and Jam slid the gate open. Those first few steps onto the landing were still wobbly. Sandy and Kez walked over and sat on a bench against the wall, one of many spaced regularly along the deck between doors.

Once we'd cleared the car, and Jeremy closed the gates again, the car fell out of sight as quickly as it had delivered us.

"Sheeeeeuut!" I said. "That was a serious ride."

"You want us to set it to your speed?" Larisha said with a smile. "We didn't know how you'd take it, but we wanted you to see our capabilities. All the major construction machinery has already been converted to pilotless Mdrones." She walked over to look off the edge.

Joining her at the railing, we looked over at

our ride now sitting on the ground. The hook block had already been disconnected, and the crane was positioned over a panel laying on the ground.

"What is it doing?" I queried. In actuality, I was stalling for some time at the handrail because my knees were still a little rubbery from the trip up. "Better yet, what is that blue light band?"

"Well, in general," said Larisha, "I can tell you pretty much how that blue band came about. Sandy was the one that brought the idea to the table. She noted that large buildings shade productive ground. Somebody joked about moving the photons around to the other side." She paused to let that sink in. "Then the host came up with the idea of using diffraction grids to redirect photons hitting the sides to reflectors at the corners." She pointed at parabolic mirrors at each corner. "So here we be, moving photons around to the far side, to defeat the shadows."

"Amazing, huh?" said Larisha. "A whim made real."

"We've tested it pretty close already, and most of the wavelengths needed for plant growth get moved over completely," Sandy said from the bench. "That's why there's no distinct shadow on the other side, even on the brightest day."

"But what about the blue?" I said.

Jam walked over to me shaking his head, "There's some things we don't know about what happens here, and this is one. The Host tells us that it's like the blue ice on glaciers, something about absorption of wavelengths, but diffraction grids don't absorb. It's the high energy wavelengths acting crazy, and we don't know why."

I looked around at everyone and they all just shrugged in turn. Kez shook her head, and then her whole body as for emphasis, "We've looked. Some. Not a lot. We got bigger fish."

I looked around at the group and they all just smiled back. Again.

Larisha took over the moment of silence saying, "So ... You noticed the spikes, too. Their pointed tips are gridded, too, which makes that color changing mirage around them."

From this high angle, the mirages on the spikes were wavering about equidistant between each other. It's substantive presence varied as dust swirled into them and, at those times, the colors of the rainbow were almost visible, before evaporating.

"The colors show better from ground level," said Larisha. "The density of interference layers is greater."

I looked at her. What can you say? She just stared back with a half smile as if she was waiting for questions.

"You've probably noticed," Larisha said, "that we use tiltwall quite a bit in constructing the panop ... Hive ... and the efficiency ... one of the things on any site is scheduling crane time. With these automated systems we can work 24/7 with no break." She turned around and leaned against the railing facing me and the others.

"Where was all this stuff yesterday?" I blurted out, and turned towards Jam.

Kez and Sandy were smiling and whispering to each other on the bench, and just glanced over at me, then went back to their conversation. They were sitting next to the first cubicle that was closed by a door, and between us were several awaiting door installation. I was getting accustomed to pretty women staring at me.

I surveyed the immediate area opposite of where we landed. This section of the fourth floor was not complete yet. Extending off to the left, it was a completely open deck. There were slots a foot wide running to the back edge and parallel to the existing wall. The slots looked to be where the dividing walls of the cubicles would go. There were another six slots on the floor to complete the level. At least two dozen compartments were already completed on this floor. All but the last few had doors.

The area beyond Kez and Sandy, off to the right, appeared as a fun house mirror. It was a repeating view of the same benches and the doors extending into the distance. The wide doors were spaced every five feet. Each had a panel at the bottom, as big as a five gallon bucket, flush with the floor, and latched with four clasps. A waist-high slot that could only be opened from the outside judging from the latch. There was a hole in the panel where a doorknob should have lived. A brass quick-attach plumbing fitting protruded from the top right of each door near the hinge. Between each door were the metal benches mounted to the wall.

"We just wanted for you to get the whole effect," Jam said, "without all the construction equipment being a distraction. We park it on the other side of the hill, in a small box canyon, when it's not working. Which is practically never. You'll really see us working now."

He'd barely finished talking, when a half dozen small droids scurried over. LEDs on their back started blinking yellow. I hadn't noticed them as they were sitting quietly, lined up along the edge of the balcony, when we landed. Attached to their backs were several spikes like you might find in a railway yard which gave them the appearance of flat turtles. In a nimble maneuver, as quick as the lift I'd just experienced, they divided up and marked out a blinking path from the handrail to the nearest slot in the floor decking across from where Larisha and I were standing.

Larisha started moving over to the benches. Jam waved me over to where he was leaning against the corner of the closest wall. In the ten steps it took us to clear the space, the droids started blinking red. We were joined by two large flying drones, man-sized and flashing red, positioning themselves above the smaller droids. They started repeating, "Danger, leave the designated area" as they hovered, passing slowly back and forth overhead.

The boom of the crane moved over to where we'd just arrived and a large tiltwall panel appeared, no slower than we'd popped up. It was hoisted over to the slot in the floor without any hesitation whatsoever. As the panel started lowering into the slot, each flying drone picked an end and steadied the panel with a metal paw.

I stepped over to the side so I could get a better view, and Jam grabbed my shoulder, stopping me from turning the corner.

The droids on the floor swarmed the base of the panel and started inserting their pins into the base as pinned tenons. I hadn't seen it earlier, but there were two mechanical arms resting on the building's roof that now steadied the panel at the top. The droids at the base inserted their pins into the panel, attaching it to the floor. As soon as they'd finished inserting the pins, which happened faster than I can explain it, they were back into their formation at the gate, blinking yellow once more. The two flying drones were hovering a short distance off the balcony and were no longer flashing.

Out of the corner of my eye as I watched the small droids return to their danger area zone, a larger droid on wheels rolled around, avoiding me smoothly, and moved directly to the pinned locations on the panel. Waist high and cylindrical, an argon tank with appendages, this machine had arms with fingers like hand fans that screened it's actions, cupping the pin site like a smoker cupping a match. Once covered, a hiss of gas, then the white light that leaked past the screens casting huge shadows against the wall, and the crackle of a welder. It obviously had no trouble sparking an arc because it moved from location to location as if it was merely pausing to inspect the work.

As soon as the welder cleared the first weld,

I looked over at Jam and the group, and pointed out there, mouthing "Can I?"

"Sure," said Jam, "just don't move too fast and they'll watch out for you." When he said that, all the others nodded in smiling agreement.

As soon as I stepped around the corner, one of the flying drones moved to hover over my head while blinking yellow. The prop wash was strong but it was pretty quiet, quieter than any drone I'd ever seen on YouTube. I squinted up at it for a second to see if it was going to talk to me but it was mute.

Walking over to the first weld site (the weld droid was already on to the seventh), I bent down and got a look at an absolutely perfect weld, shiny in an unfamiliar way.

"What is this?" I hollered out, as I turned my head back towards Jam. The drone was doing a station keeping hover the same distance above my head even though I was now on my knees.

From around the corner, Larisha answered, "Titanium".

"Of course," I mumbled to myself. As I started to stand, all the drones started blinking red again, and I went back to where Jam was posted.

Jam and I were standing at the corner as a

floor span was hoisted over the edge, hanging horizontally from the hook, and headed to it's home at the top of the panel. Stepping to the side to watch it get attached to the structure, I looked back to see the others chatting completely unconcerned with the activity. Different droids worked the roof installation, but it was basically a mirror image of the floor attachments. They swarmed off the roof to do their assignments, in this case hanging down like bats.

"Man. This is just crazy," I said, turning back towards the group, "but it's obvious that it's all in a day for y'all."

"Not really," said Kez, "I would just say the shock factor no longer lives there for us. This is the future and it just IS." Kez stood up and motioned me to follow her to the railing. I walked the dozen yards to meet her. As I arrived, she pointed to the place where the titanium tree was supposed to go, and was.

"You surely didn't see it when they dropped you off, but the Host made superior changes to our design while we were eating. It's digging the hole for the root structure and welding up the titanium structure as it goes down. The colored stuff on the top of the tap root is cedar veneer. It's manufacturing and wrapping the titanium structure with it in order to give an organic base to apply the cell culture grafts. And that," she turned towards Sandy, and raised her voice a notch, "it's decided that instead of growing sheets of cells in petri dishes it's growing them all in solution and *placing* them, individually, to create a sheet to be applied to the structure." Sandy smiled and nodded at us in the negative.

"Close," said Sandy, "It looks like we'll be growing cells in solution, filtering them out onto little fish scale-shaped rice paper filters, and applying *those* seeded scales individually to the xylem shell. Everything is subject to improvement."[1]

"What?" I said. It wasn't disbelief[2], exactly, but it would have been if this were any other time. It was simply a short verbal blurt of surprise.

"Sandy ordered a couple of dozen bur oak by next day air this morning as soon as we'd decided, and we're already behind," Kez said as she shrugged.

"It's crazy isn't it?" she said almost to herself. "We barely made a decision and it started cutting titanium bar, asked us to throw it some cedar posts, and they're off to the races."

I looked down on the activity below us. The ground was alive with drones of several different sizes driving the titanium tree into the earth. There were scores of small drones crawling in and out of the ditches for the tree's roots. Others climbed in and out of the trunk and it's tap root. Larger, cylindrical devices with hoses extending into the trenches, positioned regularly along the root ditches. The cylinders looked to be modified wet-dry vacs. The ditches were just getting started, and the small mounds of dirt, in geometric patterned mounds next to the vacs, seemed to match the progress based on the volume of dirt. The intermittent whining symphony seemed to confirm my suspicions of their vacuum purpose.

The thing that came to mind was the reconstruction of the fire ant mounds immediately after a rain. Each ant unit working diligently to recover the home from the flood, each moving her little spec of earth to the top and dumping it to make the symmetrical mound at the surface. In this case, the little mounds were everywhere along the length of the tree's construction, geometrically regular in their size, and related to the ... vacbots?

I turned to Jam and said, "What are those? Wet-dry vacs?"

"Exactly," said Jam, "They're modified a little. Come on, we'll check that out later. This is what I've been bustin' to show you since you pulled in." Walking off past the ladies on the bench he put his hand into the access port on the door and pulled the door open slowly. It was obviously heavy.

Immediately above the door was etched "451".

14.

Jam opening the cell door exposed a sink, mirror, and toilet all attached to the inner side. That would have drawn my attention, if the inner walls hadn't been the brightest pink I know I've ever seen. I have heard, neither acknowledging nor denying the experience, that the drunk tank in Williamson county was painted exactly the same.

The ladies all went through the door before me and found space on a single bed along the right wall. Judging from the chains supporting it from its side, it could fold up against the wall. Larisha had just cleared the door when she wrapped up the resident of 451 in a serious bear hug. Jam was shaking his head, smiling, and pointedly looking at the ceiling as he walked past them to the corner.

Focusing beyond the wrestlers, the rest of the cell came into focus. There was an opening in the middle of the far wall the size of a door. It was covered with heavy opaque plastic, and duct taped over the opening. It was rattling slightly in the West Texas breeze. Jam was now sitting in a metal folding chair in the back left corner. Next to him was an upholstered secretary chair, with arm rests. The left wall was poorly decorated with ripped out pages from different books, randomly taped on it's pinkness. The other two ladies were whispering and giggling to each other again.

"Hey, lady, let him get a breath!" said Kez laughing.

Larisha pulled away long enough that I could see the man enjoying the attention.

"Hi, I'm Mark," he said, raising his eyebrows, "I'm pretty sure I'll be with you in a few."

At that, Larisha put another bear hug and kiss on him that was fully returned.

"PDP PDP PDP PDP," sang Sandy in a cute little girl voice. "This was a *scheduled* meeting y'all."

"PDP?" I questioned looking over to Jam.

"Public Display of Petting," he said, "and it looks like they're doing it right. Y'all need me to spray you down with a hose?"

At that, they released. Larisha looked over her shoulder at Jam with a stoney look, glanced over me, then blew a kiss to Mark before joining the other ladies sitting on the bed.

"I've been so waiting for you to make it up here," said Mark. "Every minute, I've been wondering how to lay out the plan. I'm glad

I'm quarantined up here or I would surely have interfered with Jeremy's schedule."

Mark nodded over at Jam, then waved his hands towards the left wall decorated with the pages. They were from a couple of books, judging from the various sizes, and cut or ripped out, taped to the wall in an organized pattern. The fact that there was tape still stuck to the walls in other places, some with corners of paper still attached, gave the impression that they'd been moved around. At the moment I turned towards him, I noticed what I first took to be a skeleton hanging on the wall, dressed in international orange. I jerked around in astonishment. Every joint was represented by a wafer the size of a quarter and it was complete down to the wrists. The "bones" of the installation looked to have been made out of thick straws, the kind they use in the bubble tea shops.

"Oh Lord!" I said. "You have to tell me what that is or I just can't go on!"

"That's a panopticon exoskeleton," said Kez. "I've set up a demo for you after Mark gets done with his part." She was wiggling her eyebrows at me.

"I've been reorganizing my presentation almost hourly," said Mark, "because I didn't know what would grab you. Jeremy just told me to go with it." He was finally able to slow the rush of words.

Excluding Jam and I, he was clearly the oldest in the group. He had to be ten years older than Larisha. The barely detectable wobble to his stance when she released him explained the cane leaning against the wall by the sink. I could understand the swoon, too. He was the same height as Larisha, a blocky build seen in special forces types, with a tight haircut to match. The left side of his lower body was detectably slack in a way that suggested childhood illness or major trauma.

"Start wherever you want," I said, "as soon as your blood slows a little. I don't want you to stroke out."

At that, Mark blushed in a way you don't see in a man in his early thirties.

"Holy cow, look at that!" said Sandy. "Maybe I should take some lessons so that I can do that to Jeff."

Larisha leaned around Kez and said to Sandy, "Lessons aren't free, sugar."

At that Sandy elbowed Kez, and Kez passed it to Larisha as they all laughed.

"Ok, OK, we have a lot to cover here," said Jam. At that he kicked the office chair over to me. I looked to Jam, laid my palm out towards the plastic covered door, and mouthed,

"What?" and he answered by pointing for me to sit my ass in the chair.

As I was getting settled in the chair, I scooted up against the decorated pink wall so I could keep an eye on the exoskeleton. Mark had seated himself on the lid of the toilet. On the wall at eye level, was a white board close against the wall, in the space between him and the exoskeleton.

"Ok, then," said Mark, "I thought what I'd do is walk you through a day from beginning to end that we have designed right now."

"Uh ... whatever," I said.

"There are lots of things we address specifically. based on opposition to two specific books, namely "Walden" by Henry David Thoreau and "Walden Two" by B.F. Skinner," he waved his hand towards the wall of book parts, "so if you wonder why we do something, just ask."

"Why those specific books?" I said, scooting back a little to look at the pages hanging on the wall. I might have recognized Thoreau's style on some of the pages, but the closest one, noted as page 117, had a section highlighted that said "my beans, the length of whose rows, added together, was seven miles already." I immediately had that sensation of stepping on the same dog crap pile again. I

286

remembered how I'd hated reading that book for all the things in it that didn't describe any reality I knew. I took it to be a prank on the simpleminded.

"Never mind, I think I remember now myself," I said. "Let's get it. I want to move to exoskeleton." I glanced over the bright orange exoskeleton and scooted away from the wall a little closer to Mark. He leaned towards me resting his elbows on his knees.

"If you've read any of Walden Two, you know it's stuffed like a Christmas turkey full of cultural engineering. He, and his group of ivory tower adherents, are always structuring some kind of design for society that tells free people what to do. On the other hand, we're working on convicted criminals, trying to save the dregs."

"Ok," I said. He was looking at me like he wanted some feed back, but that's all I had.

"Good. The very first thing is that we believe that human beings should be responsible for everything they choose to do. That's really our guiding principle. We also don't think that putting a person in a cage really does anything."

At that, he grabbed his cane, hefted himself up and took a couple of steps towards me and tapped a page on the wall over my head.

"From Walden Two I'm pretty sure, 'Offenders are seldom improved by being sent to prison, and judges therefore tend to reduce or suspend sentences, but crime unpunished, then increases.' "

He stepped back, more carefully than he'd leapt up, and returned to sit. "We are sentencing people to training days. If they successfully complete a day, good. If they don't, it does nothing to shorten their stay. We've devised as many privileges as are possible within the confines of a secure confinement, but the key thing is that the person decides. They decide, they're responsible, and they have to own the consequences."

He seemed to be looking at me for another confirmation so I just nodded and said, "Ok." Again. That didn't demonstrate it, but I have been known in the past as someone with insight.

"The first division of time that I want to talk about is that time from waking to 0800. That is the start of the day, but there's already been serious decisions the trainee has had to address. For one thing, we don't wake them unless they set an alarm and it has to be set manually every single evening. The first system alert, after their alarm, comes at 0800 when there are two zeroing shots from the panopticon tower. That marks that they've already failed to meet their obligations for that day. No credit."

"Wow," I said. I was thinking what it must be like to realize you're late to work by the sound of large caliber bullets slamming steel within earshot. "Only slightly better than a sharp stick in the eye."

The gang giggled.

"But I love this," I said nodding to the group, "All those punks today that can't get themselves motivated to be a real employee, or spouse, it just puts it to 'em. Most of them have been waiting for some angel, more likely crystal-hugging fairy, to come around and bestow adult thinking. Until that happens, they just feel justified in nothingness. Always waiting for the train but they ain't even at the station."

"Amen brother," said Jam.

"Yes. But that is the end of the period," said Mark. "Like I said they will have had to remember to set the alarm and there is a time limit to that. Anytime between 2000 and 2200 they can tell Jack ... Uhm ... what are we calling you?"

"We're calling him Jack-eeeeeeee," said Jam.

Giggles around again. I just mouthed

"Thank you" to the peanut gallery along with a three finger salute.

"Ok then, but there are decisions the CT ... " Mark stopped, noticing the look of confusion on my face.

"Sorry, that's the acronym we use for the convicts. Confined Trainee. There's decisions they make for themselves from the first moment they arrive. The first thing they must understand is that they're required to participate in the training day. No exceptions. They will remember to set the alarm every day, and they have to wake up for it[2]. Breakfast is not served without a typed request, and only until 15 minutes before the 0800 login. They have literally nothing but opportunities to fail at getting to the task at hand.

"Until they have proven they can follow the training schedule for 30 days without incident, they have a dietary choice that is also as monotonous as a factory schedule."

He was looking around the group and I followed his eyes. They, to a person, nodded. A couple shuddered.

"The second decision that sticks for 14 days at a time is the choice of a Thoreau diet or Soylent[1] diet, and no, it's not Soylent Green like the movie."

"I'm a little afraid to even ask what the

Soylent diet is," I murmured. "I'm old enough to remember the movie."

"It's a complete food replacement," said Mark, "and that's my personal recommendation."

"Why?" I said, even though you could tell from his voice that it was an educated assessment.

"I'm quarantining myself just like a CT, living through everything we've chosen for this beta version. There are a few of us in this beta, and that is one decision that is pretty easy to make after you do the Thoreau diet."

"Which is?" I said, cocking my head. There was no way I could guess what he was referencing here. It had been decades since I'd read the Walden book so I casually glanced over my shoulder at the hanging sheets. Hoping a clue would be highlighted, I got distracted by the exo again.

"Hoe cakes!" said Sandy.

"Nope, not what you're thinking," Mark said as he rose again, dabbing at another page with his cane, then reading, "Bread I first made of pure Indian meal and salt, genuine hoe-cakes." It was not highlighted on the page.

"You'll have to make up your own mind, but I can tell you that eating corn-flavored mud pies baked in our pits is barely more appetizing than a real mud pie. However, it does temper hunger pains."

"Well, given that choice-" I started to say as Mark nodded to Larisha and she raised her wrist and whispered into the wrist band. Instantly, the sound of a panel getting dropped just above the sink, then a tray appeared through the slot.

Mark handed the tray over to me. On it was 12 yellowish, coarse-edged little cakes with some fired color and grill marks, each thick as a little finger. In addition, there were three bags with a cream colored solution in them, perhaps a pint each. Each had an attached straw, and the bag had a fitting that was obviously waiting for the straw.

"So what you're looking at there," said Mark, "is the actual choice they are given on arrival. From our experience, people tend to take the cakes the first pass. Try one."

I picked up the first little cake and took a big bite because I am a taster of life. The mouth feel was exactly as described, perhaps a cake made of granite sand with a slight cornmeal flavor, powered over by smoke. It wasn't displeasing but it sure wasn't a ribeye. It was one of those foods that volumizes as you chew. I put the cake down still working to swallow the first bite.

"From our experience, people tend to look at the quantity thinking that gives them snacks throughout the day," said Mark. He reached over and took a cake, a big bite, too, and then a smile.

"Pretty apt description don't you think?" he said smiling. "Cornmeal and salt. If you were starving you'd look forward to it I guess."

"Barely," I said.

"Amen," echoed around from the group.

From the way they all laughed at that I knew I'd missed an inside joke. That feeling of being the guest turkey to a Thanksgiving dinner returned.

"Now, try the Soylent," Mark suggested.

I took one of the drinking bags, inserted the attached straw, and started drawing. It wasn't unpleasant and it was a relief to wash the mud pie down. Nice creamy mouth feel but very little flavor. I imagined it with strawberries.

"I could do that I guess," I said.

"Yes you could," Mark said, "and you would, I'll wager. The thing about the hoe cakes is that they leave you with cravings. They squelch the hunger pains but that's about it. The Soylent seems to meet everything because I don't get any cravings at all. And, I'm the one that has done it exclusively longer than anyone here."

"How long is that?" I said. Who wouldn't want to know how long someone was living on fake food?

"On any single stretch, 45 days," Mark said, lifting his head. I took it as a prideful stance from the set of his mouth.

"Anyway, you can see that's a pretty important decision totally left up to the CT. The very next thing they have to decide is if they're actually going to participate in the training program, because that impacts the feeding schedule."

"What? What does that mean?" I said. I was starting to figure this was going to be a conversation where I primarily offered two words: *OK* or *What?* I was now trying to up my game a little. Very little.

"This presentation comes from another Thoreau ditty," Mark said.

Before he could move, Jam was up and being guided by the pointing cane. I turned in my chair to look.

Jam read, "Simplify, Simplify. Instead of three meals a day, if it be necessary eat but one; instead of a hundred dishes, five; and reduce other things in proportion."

"I guess if you're making the rules, that's making it pretty necessary," I said.

"Oh yeah," said Larisha. "We're making the

rules."

"You can imagine," said Mark, "that if you have all your food in your possession at the start of the day, you might snack it away out of boredom pretty early in the day." He got a wicked little smile on his face, and a cant to his eyebrows.

"Ok," I said. Again!

"So that is a real problem. If you don't participate in the training, you don't pace your food intake, and you have nothing all day. All the meals served at 0800. No books. One hour out at 1800 under close supervision of their individual robot guard and wearing ... the ... exoskeleton," Mark looked towards Kez. "Sorry, I'm not trying to steal your thunder."

"No problem," Kez said. "But Jack-eeeeeee, you and me got a seeee-rious date to handle that stuff later. No questions about Baby right now. Okay?"

"Okay," I said. I'm sure I'd agree to anything she ever said. Her eyes were as blue as her hair was black. Another stunning representation of God's blessings showering down on us. That recognition was one that never would I have attributed to God in the past. Osmosis I guess. Pretty disquieting.

"So, one of the things we do," said Mark, "if you participate, we deliver your meals on a normal human schedule, breakfast, lunch and dinner, which breaks up the day and keeps you from getting ahead of yourself. You'd be surprised how important that routine becomes. Of course, like I said, breakfast always has to be requested by keyboard."

I nodded at him this time instead of opening my empty mouth.

"So at this point, we pretty much got you set up. You've decided what you're eating for the first 14 days at least, you know you're responsible for setting the alarm and getting to training on time, and you know the blast that wakes you if you oversleep."

I nodded again.

"Then there's only one little operant conditioning stick we want to use to flog you even before we start the day. In Skinner's book ... you understand if I call him BF from here on?" Mark said and waited for an answer. The laughs around the cell made me know this was obviously something they enjoyed.

"Sure, why not?" I said.

"So BF is of the opinion that young children should be tested daily with authoritarian cultural engineering rules. In typical leftist fashion, it's all about making rules to be followed. We're going to use his style of operant conditioning to impose strict discriminative stimuli that determine if you're able to get to assigned work on time."

"Jack-eeee has some military experience, so he'll get it," said Jam.

"What were you always told about keeping appointments?" said Mark.

"It was something like, if you're not fifteen minutes early you're already late," I suggested.

"Exactly," said Mark. "The problem many CT's have trying to keep a real job is that they figure being 15 minutes late is not a real problem. Typical human error. Fifteen in the morning, fifteen at break, lunch: pretty soon it's real time noticed by, and resented, by the other employees actually trying to keep the company schedule. We fix that here. Mimicking the real world, we inject time for traffic and weather and other issues by inserting a random timer in front of the 0800 login." Mark smiled big at this. "This one is mine!"

"Every morning the CT's get a 'login now' message that blinks on their screen for 30 seconds. They can not login until they get that message, and there is only one per morning. Ten percent of the CT's get one anywhere out to fifteen minutes before typical login time. IF they miss the login, they miss their login for that day. They lose their chance to get credit for that day. Another wasted, uncounted, day. That means everyone in the panopticon, that is not a zoo animal, is watching their monitors intently, very intently, from 0745-0800 six days a week."

"I'm liking this, too," I said, "I'm liking this a lot."

"It's a recommendation gleaned from the leading behaviorist of the 20th Century, one BF," Mark said accompanied by laughs again. He raised his cane guiding Jam over to a page on the wall.

Jam began reading the highlight from a page above his head, "A group of children arrive home after a long walk tired and hungry. They're expecting supper; they find, instead, that it's time for a lesson in self-control: they must stand for five minutes in front of steaming bowls of soup." Jam turned smiling at the group.

"I'm pretty sure," Jam said looking at me, "that people aren't going to have a problem making convicted criminals be tested for self-control by an automated system suggested by the leading behaviorist of the 20th century. And, he recommended it be used on children."

"Oh yeah," said Larisha, "We're tracing rules!"

"For even when we were with you, this we warned you of, that if there were any, which would not work, that he should not eat."

2 Thessalonians 3:10

15.

Mark pulled the white board in its small, rectangular wire frame, away from the wall. At the bottom of the mount was a device, about the size of two D-cell batteries, with a little periscope leaning in towards the paper. He pulled another piece of the white cardboard from the back of the frame, and placed it on his lap. He pulled the system necklace fob out of his shirt, and began moving his hands over the paper in his lap like a typist, a really fast one.

Watching him sitting on the toilet's lid protruding from the door while keying into the ghost keyboard, was surreal. He was playing it like a concert pianist, rocking his head to some inflections, and nodding the completion of passages.

"Ok," said Mark finally. He looked at me again, and noticed my questioning. "I find having the keyboard displayed distracts me. I just watch what goes up on the screen." At that point, he turned the wire frame towards me, so I could see that the device at the bottom was actually a projector displaying a monitor on the paper.

"One of the things we require is that every

CT must do the first login to the system, and request breakfast, via a keyboard. It's going to be a skill that may not be too necessary in the future. However, it absolutely requires that they prepare for the login, instead of just shouting it across the room if they find themselves late, for whatever reason."

The screen showed, much clearer than I expected, the typical computer login sequence and it's completion. The only noteworthy thing was that it was an empty screen like the early days, displaying "UserID" and "Password", instead of filled to overflowing with images and advertisements. There was a large alphanumeric string in the bottom right corner. The bottom left corner had an open circle the size of a dime.

"So, as we derived from BF," Mark started again, "we're going to be sentencing people to training days, and I'm sure you want to know *exactly* what that means." He grinned over at Jam.

"Ok. Sure," I said, "But I've been kind of curious why you call him BF. I don't want my warped sense of things to color something that has a different meaning for you guys. If you could explain that one, please, before we get started."

Sandy was practically sliding off her seat to

301

answer as she looked around the room at the others who all nodded her onward.

"I've been waiting for you to ask that!" Sandy said. "Butt F'er, probably just about like you thought. Jeremy showed us how he was all into taking apart the family for the commune, how governance was going to be in the hands of the few technocrats, and all those other things the world is finally rejecting."

Then Kez got into it, "Both Thoreau and BF are a team that we try to mock at every opportunity. They treat humans like lab rats, and Jeremy selected us all for not being rats."

"Most of us anyway," injected Mark, which got a laugh.

"All these pages on the wall," said Jam, "are the trophies we've scooped out of their dip tank."

Rotating my chair to look at the wall closer, it was obvious what was going on there now. There were dozens of pages taped to the wall, most of them with some highlighted phrases, and a significant number of them with check marks of one kind or another on them.

"So you're checking them off as you bag 'em," I said looking to Jam.

"Correct. And anybody that finds another one, we add it and give them a shout out at dinner. I like to gather up some flowers for them, if we can, because I think these bozos are the backbone of leftist thought. Anybody that can mock them good deserves recognition."

"Backbone?" I muttered at that. "There's scores of university professors and students studying both those guys. I'm certain you can get a PhD just analyzing a small part of what either one of them wrote. But, then, leftist thought. Universities. I echo."

"Look," Jam said, "Thoreau reminds me of a spoiled kid, the child of a successful businessman. He takes a bus for the first time, then goes down to Haight-Ashbury and preaches like he knows what he learned about humanity coming over on the bus. BF strikes me as a very intelligent person, but incorrectly believes that he, himself, or those in his class, deserve to rule us. Both of them are clearly, totally anti-Jesus in their own words. That's not the last strike against them, it's the first proof."

Jam was rolling now, "There is just too much BS in Thoreau's Walden book for it to be considered real enough for a person, in touch with reality, to respect. Pretty words, plenty crap."

"You'll probably hear the phrase, DAD, around here," said Larisha, "and that is our short for both of them ... Dumb and Dangerous."

"I'm sure that could get a few people shouting at you," I said quietly.

"Maybe," said Mark nodding over to Larisha. "Get the larger one please." Then he continued, "But the pages you see on the wall are our trophies, and you'll know them better as we go along. We've already skinned quite a few."

"I don't want to get into this right now," said Jam and he stomped the floor. "Can we just move on and we'll try to point them out to you when we remember or you ask?"

I nodded eagerly. *Anything* to get to the exo.

Larisha moved across the cell after pulling a piece of poster board from underneath the bed. She walked to the wall near me, reaching up to place it on the wall. There was some kind of sticky to it's back. It had a border of black which supplied contrast to the pink walls.

"This is the monitor for your introduction now," said Mark looking to me. I watched her stick it to the wall over her head. She was positioning it between the door and the hanging exoskeleton. The way it was hanging next to it, I could almost imagine it reaching up to look out that 'window'.

That's not the only thing I could imagine. The distraction of Larisha reaching up to place, level, and correct the new device was magnetic: an instant and irresistible attraction. She wasn't as dark as the border of the paper, but her skin was so clear and even and smooth. The cornrows curving up the side of her head to that cresting crown on top mirrored the graceful curve of her neck onto her shoulders. Her skin was taut and covered her muscles like the tiger's moving in it's stalk.

Once my eyes started moving down from there, they were dropping as if accelerated by gravity to those Wranglers. There was a curve that set an old man's heart to striving in remembrance of times past, feeling each arch in the-

"Pssst," came from behind me, and the plastic covering taped to the opening at the other end of the cell popped in the wind. Had it been doing that the entire time? I broke contact with memories, embarrassed, to see Sandy smiling at me, pushing her open mouth closed with her hand.

"What?" asked Larisha still smoothing the new monitor, then looking over to Mark.

"Oh ... I think Jack-eee was just as attracted as me!" Mark said. At that, Larisha gave the installation a last pat, then turned and gave Mark a slap to the shoulder that was more than playful. She then looked to me, slowly shook a

lone finger, "You could hurt yourself old man."
It's been a while since I felt such heat on my
cheeks.

"Man, she has it." said Sandy.

Larisha sashayed back to the bed, and I was
sorely tempted, but forcefully kept my attention
on Mark.

"Ok! Finally," Mark said. "Someone gets
called 'old man' besides me." Mark was
nodding and smiling around the group. They all
enjoyed that, too. I smiled to be polite.

"So let's start it," said Mark. At this, you
could tell it was about to get serious. A slight
furrow formed above his eyes as if to help
focus his eyes on me. The even green of his
eyes was transfixing. Information was going to
be transferred.

"Hey Jack, posit one, please," he said, and
instantly the newly placed paper monitor
brightened, and wavering words came into
focus as the system corrected for imperfections
in the surface. In seconds, the single phrase on
it was crystal clear.

"To live under the American Constitution is the greatest political
privilege that was ever accorded to the human race. - Calvin Coolidge, at
the Whitehouse December 12, 1924."[1]

"The first hour of instruction every single
day is going to be reading the Constitution. To

quote Coolidge again, and I'm more than happy to, 'The Constitution is the sole source and guaranty of national freedom.' A person that was sentenced to prison in the past rarely cared, was frequently ignorant of this, and was never required to understand the laws and traditions that support our freedoms. Those times are over.

"Any person that is incapable of living amongst free men is going to be required to know what is expected of free men," Mark looked around the cell and collected nods of affirmation. "We demand action, we demand responsibility, and we demand, at the very least, exposure to our laws and rules. Daily."

"This is another DAD thing really," said Jam. "This time it's Henry." He rose to point to a sheet of paper on the lower left corner, reading, "I have lived some thirty years on this planet, and I have yet to hear the first syllable of valuable or even earnest advice from my seniors.[3]"

"And that is total ignorance of history and the ignorance of youth. Squared," said Mark. "And we're going to expose some knowledge from our seniors, and without putting too fine a point on it, our betters."

"That sounds good," I said. "But what about the old horse to water thing?"

"You can bring the horse to water," said Mark, "but you can't make it drink. If it wants to leave the shed, in this case, it most certainly will. Every single time. It's a simple choice really. Time off or time alone. No man chooses to be alone."

"I had a friend - " I started to say.

"Had!" interjected Jam, and everybody in the end of the cell was smiling when I turned. It seemed kind.

"Yeah," I began again, " and He went to prison for failure to drink in moderation, time after time, and he told me that people would decline GED classes and stay in their isolation cells." I thought I was sounding knowledgeable for the first time today. Maybe. In my humble opinion.

"I'm absolutely sure that's true," said Mark. "We did quite a bit of research on-site, and in the literature, about prison training programs. Their failure, in our opinion, always comes down to getting people to believe in their betterment and it's enhancement and benefits in a distant future. That's not what we're talking about here. We're talking about constantly reading about what is required and necessary, and immediate *daily* rewards."

Mark just sat there staring directly at me with an intensity that I hadn't seen in anyone here, to this point. If he was waiting for me to inject something, I was going to stand off on this one just like the horse we'd been discussing. His face was expressionless, his green eyes fairly glittering, then he raised his right hand, extended his index finger into the air marking the point, then dove it onto his thigh.

After some seconds, he said, "We're offering a standard office laborer's day, actually hours shorter, with lots of reading of things they don't have to be interested in, for immediate gains like five hours a day outside the cells, more food variety, and fellowship with other people."

At this, he raised his right hand again, this time with two fingers, waved them past my face and drove them into this thigh again. Marking another point?

"Yeah, but how are you going to make them read it?" I whined. I was sure that the horse analogy was firmer here than most places it's used.

The cell erupted with shouts and claps. Mark's face was taken over with a wide open smile and he clapped, too. Jam was in the corner smiling but shaking his head. Kez and Larisha were giving each other high fives and Sandy was the mirror image of Jam.

"Ok y'all, what the hell is going on here?"

"It's just a little wager we always have for newbies," said Jam. "You're a little better than most, but not like Sandy and I thought."

"What would that be?" I said, reviewing in my mind what in the world would lead to a wager. The turkey self-image returned, with added depth this time.

"Basically," Mark started off, "the review of the panopticon that you've received up to this point is something that every newbie gets. The high tech, the explosive amazing advances, all of it, but this is the stage where we actually approach human cultural engineering. Making people read."

"I got that, I think," I said, and this time I was definitely feeling like the center of attention.

"The thing is, most people are stunned by what they've seen up to this point," Jam said. "They just sit there nodding in agreement to whatever we say. Who can grasp all this, right? It is a little prank on you, a teaser maybe, but we have 5 standard levels at this particular step, which Mark was noting, and we all wager on which one you'll question the premise. I picked the first one, cabron." Jam squinched up his face and shook his head at me.

Looking around the room, Mark held up

three fingers, Sandy and Jam one, Kez and Larisha two and they were waving them like VE day, laughing loudly.

"OK then ... how's that rank?" I said. Wondering. They all dropped their hands but not their smiles as we turned to Jam.

"Upper edge of the curve," he said. "Few people ask it on the first one, most never ask. That look Mark gives could freeze you pretty good, huh, cowboy?"

I turned to Mark, "So you saw me as a cabron first off?"

"Not really. Not having had any interaction with you, I didn't want to give you too much credit. Larisha and Kez stood out, but I'd never even seen you. I figured it would be a safe bet that you were better than most based on Jeremy's stories but ... " then Mark just shrugged with a smile.

"So how do you do it?" I said.

"Nobody is more patient than a computer," Mark explained. "They just read out loud at their own pace, the computer tracks their progress at every word, every pronunciation. Even if they can't read English at all, it will just, word by word, walk them through the documents. But, and this is the part I think you really need to experience to see what I mean, it won't let you pretend ignorance."

"I don't pretend," I said.

"Good one," Mark smiled. "The thing is, the computer tracks your speed. If at any time you don't get a word, it will stop, blow it up on the screen and wait 5 seconds for you to try again, then it will pronounce it and you must repeat it within 10 seconds. Totally boxed in structure. You read, one way or another. You can repeat after the computer or you can actually read, but you're going to be going through our documents."

"What happens if I just refuse to participate?"

"If you refuse to participate," said Jam, "you are acting exactly like any four legged animal. We don't expect wild animals to get out of the zoo if they are good for X number of days. You don't see 400 pound lions on the street, with probation anklets, saying they were good for five years. You actively choose to stay as long as you choose to be a non-participant."

"But when you said it wouldn't let me fake ignorance, which won't be a problem for me, what did you mean?" I said to the assemblage.

"The computer tracks your performance," Kez started explaining, "and it corrects and assists you. If you try to sandbag it, slow walk it, it matches you and stays at the lower level for the rest of the day. If you hit a standard deviation below your normal performance, it stays at that level and you can't raise it back up. At half a standard deviation below, the text is yellow, when you're within 10% of a standard deviation low, the text is red. Imagine being a quick reader and having to repeat one word after the other, *after* the computer says them really slow. Interminable."

"What if I don't want English?" I said, sounding confident that I'd caught them on something.

"Not a choice[2]," said Jam. There was finality in his statement that was unmistakeable.

"And when I don't play?"

"It all just goes black," Mark said raising a clenched fist. "The first time you refuse to repeat after the suggestion, you're done. You've made the choice to stay another day."

"Wow," I said. "I think amen works there."

"Jeremy told me you'd been a Naval officer," Mark said. "Tell me you didn't have to focus on reams of message traffic, most of it meaningless to you, in order to sift out what was critical for your division." Mark reached over and slapped me on the shoulder.

"We're just insisting that people that refuse to play well with others, work to understand, or at least be thoroughly exposed, to what this free society is all about. Period."

"The thing is," Mark said changing his tone, "you should spend some time in here on this lesson so you can really grasp it. What do you say?"

I turned and looked at Jam who said, "It really is a big part of understanding what we're doing here. Everybody else does 3 days to start. I know you'll get the gist of it on the first lesson."

Offering another prediction, Mark said, "Maybe." He closed that off with a smile.

16.

The packet in his hand was immediately familiar, and had me concerned that maybe I hadn't clarified the situation completely.

"Just in case," said Jam, handing me over the MRE toilet paper packet.

We were standing in the open door to the cell, and the attached toilet cum office chair, was right behind me on the door, along with the sink, mirror, and frame for the monitor display.

"Ok. You're starting to make me a little nervous here," I said taking the TP, "I agreed to one hour I thought."

"One lesson is what you agreed to, which is an hour unless you have to ask for a timeout," Jam said pointing to the TP, barely keeping that smile under control. "Your password is *bold17*. When you get started, you'll get a better feel for the system if you start as if you couldn't read, and follow it for a while. After about five minutes, speed up, then play around with the limits. Like Mark said, as you start slowing down from gathered stats, the text will change colors. If you see red, you're fixing to get stuck. If you need to take a break just say 'timeout' and it will stop. 'Go' restarts it. Any breaks do nothing but make the day longer. No penalty."

"That sounds plain enough," I said stepping back from the opening. It just now got through to my conscious that the door was six inches of hybrid concrete, swinging easily.

"We are going to lock you in," said Jam. "If you get dumped, or done, just pound on the toilet seat. That's the only place you might be heard. The walls are solid, but we'll be listening for you." He was really smiling as he slowly pushed the door closed.

Larisha popped her head over his shoulder, and said, "We're betting on you again." Her comment just made it into the space before the door closed. Then, the clunk that signals two large masses mating. The sound of the lock rotating into position was a sure sounding thing, too.

I sat on the seat. With no back rest, this was not going to be the most comfortable session.

The screen was inert. I took a deep breath and let it out slow. They're probably trying to test me with some BF patience thing. Another breath. Glancing around the cell, it was pretty large. Ten by ten maybe. With the bed folded up it was clearly bigger than any prison cell. TV prison cells anyway, which is all I know. Swear. Empty screen. I wonder if this is some stupid snipe hunt where they're just going to see how long I'll sit here before anything happens. Breath. The plastic over the opening was breathing with me slowly, not enough to make it pop. Breath. Come *on*! This is getting pretty ridiculous, if I'd have known they were going to be jerking-

Password:

As soon as I saw it I realized I didn't have any idea about how to do a keyboard. For some reason, I'd thought I was going to be talking to it, even though I'd sat through their directions, which were only now coming into focus. I guess I should have been actually thinking.

Quickly reaching around the back of the monitor, as I'd seen Mark do, I found that piece of poster board and it had a little necklace hanging on a corner, too. Putting the necklace on with the eye out, and placing the board on my lap a keyboard image appeared. My keyboard skills allowed me to get positioned and logged in. First try.

To live under the American Constitution is the greatest political

Oh. It's only going to do ten words at a time I guess. They told me to play dumb, so this is going to be very easy.

To became the only word centered on the screen three inches high. Then, the computer said it with a pleasant female voice. I repeated it nicely, I thought. The whole line came up again, but this time 'To' was dimmed. I started measuring: one Mississippi two Mississippi three Mississippi four mississ -

Then *live* took over the center of the screen. One Mississippi two Mississippi ... oh, this is crazy I can't believe I'm counting seconds.

"Live," she said.

I echoed it back.

"Timeout," I said, and the system froze immediately.

Ok, that works. Sitting there looking at the stupid monitor I realized I was good at playing dumb, but it looked like it was going to be tiring. More so than I thought originally. What in the world did she mean they were betting on me again. If I just read through it and finished fast then I wouldn't have tested the system like they suggested. Was that it? Or failing to finish the lesson from going too slow? I couldn't go any slower. Jam told me to test it. Test the range. I pivoted on my seat to look around the cell and inspect it closer.

Man, there's room enough in here to get a good workout going. I bet you could even play a mini-handball game. I got up and walked to the plastic-covered door. You could see through it barely. Whatever. Would this be part of the bet, too. Are they betting I won't check out the door? Are they betting I will?

My pocket knife cut the plastic covering the opening easily. Pulling it apart so I could see out, the crisp fall air freshened the cell, and I could see the mesas in the distance. I'm facing south. Attached at this opening, there was a balcony of sorts. *Slash it open.* The balcony was something like the ones that had been over the Host halls, four feet wide with railing, but this one was all covered with dead vines and leaves. It extended out ten feet. Putting my knife back in my pocket and pushing through, the expanded metal floor supported me easily. It did flex enough for me to be glad there were handrails. I used them and stepped out.

Walking out to the end of the balcony confirmed that these were the things we noticed coming down the hill, when we first saw the Hive. CT's can garden. Leaning over, looking for the escape, sure, you could get down to all the metal spikes on the ground without too much trouble, rappelling from one to the next, as long as you didn't slip and shish-kebob. But then what? No towers on this side but I bet that's part of the final plan. I'm not going to argue about security on a beta release. This installation is more than impressive. Hitting a guy working slowly through punji stakes would be an easy shot. Those rainbow mirages around them are cool.

What a nice day! Low sixties now probably. All the noise from the construction seemed to be coming from overhead but there was a muffled stream from underneath. Deep blue sky and no clouds. A pleasant fall breeze.

The shadows of the mesas reminded me that it was getting into the afternoon. Wow. I hadn't noticed the time all day. 15:27. So they figure I'll be out of here at about 16:30, which looks to be about right to get another hunt in. Four thumbs of sun left. Oh yeah. Maybe I better get back after it or somebody is going to lose a bet.

Turning to go back in, I had to spend some time staring at the blue bands encircling the Hive. Standing next to the wall and looking through them, it seems obvious that they were just floating above the grating panels by an inch. Moving your head back and forth made their appearance change up. The nearest one was over my head. Staring at it, tossing my head back and forth was making me glad there were handrails. It was too high to reach. I could have taken my shirt off to dangle in the one below, probably, but it seemed a bit much when a bet was pending. I went back into the cell when I'd had enough.

Walking along the right side, the wall with the pages, I tapped a few as I thought about them and DAD. I didn't really read them. Who cares? This was all a very real thing, and whatever their motivation was just fine and dandy. Turning off from my tour of the wall back to the seat, one of the pages on the far left had pencil calculations on it. Oh, apparently the average prison cell is 6x8 and Henry David Thoreau's cabin at Walden was 10x15. I paced it to check. Three plus steps, so it probably is 10x10. Looks like they split the difference between Thoreau free and Texas Department of Corrections penned.

Now that I was alone, I could really inspect the exoskeleton. It was composed of something that I didn't recognize. If large rubber bands were wound really tight, then painted with a smooth coat of danger orange lacquer, it would come close. Only the long bones were represented on a frame with two backbones, one at each side. The joints were the size of a silver dollars, with the bones joining together at the center of one side. I looked at it closely, but I didn't *get* close. I'd already seen that some things around here could bite hard, and I didn't know if this was one. It definitely looked like it might bite.

Better get back to work. No sense making it

any longer than necessary.

Settled again at the work space, "Go".

The ten words reappeared and I waited the requisite seconds until *under* took the screen. When you're not counting, time sort of expands doesn't it?

"Under," she said.

I waited a beat before I repeated it back to her, then the ten words came up again. You know, if you can't read it, maybe it's not so tedious. If you can read, your brain is actually pondering the words, but faking wasting time is hard. Every.second.is.painful. Life is dripping out of you and you're watching seconds disappear that you can't ever get back. For nothing.

The ten words again with the first three dimmed, and I just had to get *the* out of the way so I didn't wait. As soon as I said it, it went dim, too.

Wait. One Mississippi. *No NO NO!* I'm not going to twist up my brain counting seconds. *American* became the center of the screen. Patiently I try to wait not thinking.

She said, "American."

It was very slightly different. Was it the tone? Inflection? Went by too fast.

"American," I said. The ten words reappeared with the first five dimmed out.

"Constitution is," I said and they dimmed.

What? A couple of minutes and you're tired of it already. There are too many thoughts that can bounce around. I heard once, that somebody said it was neutrinos shooting through us that made thoughts just appear on the surface of our brain. Real cosmically inspired thoughts. And, of course, since they come in different flavors, you get different thoughts. Not. Mine have always tended to gender so that simply can't be right: no variation in the exposure. Of course it would be something fast. Larisha sure is good looking, my goodness. Wranglers have never looked so good.

the filled up the screen.

Thoughts can consume time, too, you'd think. I repeated it immediately then the ten words returned.

Having a prison cell this big ... and why would I try to divert from Larisha? Mandy of course. Oh yeah, running wild, thinking about this and that. This and that, as seconds run off my life like water into sand.

"Greatest," she said.

There's something about that isn't there? The pacing maybe. Ok. I can't stand this any more.

"Greatest," I said. Some of my frustration

was entering into my speech.

political privilege that was ever accorded to the human race. -Calvin Coolidge.

I'm not stopping for a while. I read the phrase off. This really feels much freer. And I'm more into what it's saying, by actually reading, than stacking blocks of individual words.

"We the People of the United States, in Order to form a more perfect Union, establish Justice," I said.

I think maybe I'll test if with a delay on the multisyllabic words to slow it, then it won't be so painful.

"insure ... do ... mes ... tic tran ... quil ... i ... ty," I read. It didn't mind that at all. It just let me get right on like a slow reader.

"pro ... vide for the com ... mon de ... fense," I said. Ok, the crazy in the mind is coming back where the seconds are washing away, and I'm staring at them passing. This time, it's like I'm pre-counting syllables. Reading and critiquing at the same time, pacing without standing. Nope, not gonna do it.

Covered the preamble and started onward. It looks like the little circle in the bottom left of the monitor is a pie chart or something getting filled as I perform. Perhaps valid time not word volume. At this pace, it is filling my mind with the words, so I'm at least focused on a single task now.

"The Senate shall have the sole Power to try all Impeachments ... time out," I said.

Oh man, I need to pace myself. The circle at the bottom left is hitting the 1 o'clock so I'm just one twelfth done with this lesson. I guess. It is a lot more painful than I thought. I need to hit a steady pace, where I can read steadily without racing ahead. No points for speed reading, apparently. It hasn't corrected me stumbling over words as long as I could understand them myself. Oh. I should try some fake accents and see what it does.

A glass of water might help. Turning around to the sink, there was a small cup sitting in it. Filling it from the faucet showed the water was not really a pressurized system like I expected on the faucet turn. It drained out. Probably related to that plumbing fitting on the door. Whatever. It was wet. I know some had bet that I wouldn't finish the lesson so I've got to do that. Pretty cold water, too. And clean. Most of the stuff out here in West Texas is heavy with sulfur. You know, it might have been a bad idea to cut that plastic because it's definitely going to start cooling off and I'm noticing it. I think I need to shoot Mandy's gun at a hog and see how the .338 does. There's no reason that Bear ...

Oh, man. Got to get back to it. How long have I been day dreaming?

"Go," says I, "When sitting for that Purpose, they shall be on Oath or Affirmation." I forgot to do an accent.

"Win da predident," I say.

She says, "the." She caught that one I guess.

"Duh," I say.

She says *theee* again and I notice a real difference this time.

I say, "da."

She says "the."

I don't know how long she will let me recurse with this but I think she's a trans now. There's definitely something changing.

"President," she says.

Oh it is definite now. That's it. She/it is starting to sound like me. *Oh my God*! The robot is starting to mock me with myself.

"Pray ... de ... dent"

She says, "President." In my voice!

"President," I say, echoing myself. The ten words display.

of the United States is tried, the Chief Justice shall" spreads across the screen.

"of the," I say. I'm going to make it talk longer words.

After the quantum of seconds, it says, "United."

It couldn't be any clearer. It is mimicking my voice.

I repeat, "United." Saying it confirms it is definitely an echo of me.

"States," it says as me.

Oh man, this mule is stepping off sideways. This is so far past strange. We're into Terminator stuff.

"States," I echo. I am losing focus now. Dude. Hey. I guess trusting phone calls really is all gone.

Look how fast this sucker learned to talk like me. I look at the circle and it has barely moved. I've moved. Twilight zone. I can't let them beat me this early. I have to come up with a method. What does this mean about somebody calling my family? Get on up here now, dude. I'm starting to want to quit and talk about this crazy.

"Is tried," I say, exhaling. Slow inhale. Measured exhale.

"The Chief," I say. This might be something.

"Justice shall," I say. Yeah, breath reading, like meditation, focus the mind on breathing and two words or something.

Breathe. Read. Breathe. Read.

Oh, man, there's some relief, I think I'll be able to get past this. It's almost like sitting in an archery blind waiting surrounded by deer, but ... focus. Breathe. Read.

"Shall be convicted"

17.

Oh man Oh man Oh man. These last few minutes ... *brutal*! **Quiet desperation indeed.**

Inhale. "Be increased," I say evenly. Exhale.

Watching the circle on the left of the monitor fill slowly, out of the corner of my eye, has been actual torture. Moving like molasses. On a cold day. The only job I ever had like this was when I got a rent-maker job working the back office at a foster care agency, years ago in some tough times. That was when client-server computer networks were happening. The internet was spreading like fire through white brush. That company wanted to be able to document the mountains of paper foster parents were required to file. They had scores of foster parents under their corporate umbrella, and each foster parent had mountains of state requirements, reams of paper weekly.

They'd scan a drivers license. I'd get the file, right click, Oh it's a drivers license for Joe Blow expiration 11-2-95, right click 'rename', *19940723_DL_Joe Blow exp 19951102.jpg*.

Times six hundred per day.

Double Click. Oh, a weekly status report.

Right click rename. *19940723_SR1.jpg*.

Double Click. Oh, a discipline report. Right click rename. *19940723_DR9_Jesse Doe_19940325.jpg*

Oh, Lord Almighty, they had more kinds of paper in that job. We had a list of prefixes and proper descriptions that was four feet long, and taped to the wall by our desks, that we were using as they developed an automated system. But they had Jack, and Jack was meticulous. Nobody else was. Foster partial care mostly, if that's a surprise.

Exhale. "Nor diminished," I spoke at my alter.

Those were long days, too. At least this doesn't require actually typing stuff. Just talking to yourself. Talking to yourself in a very formalized routine. It is getting so close now.

Exhale. "during the Period."

The monitor abruptly stopped and repainted the display. After being unable to keep my eye off the circle, it completed while I wasn't watching.

Balance: -1 Ξ
Credit: 1 Ξ
Balance: 0 Ξ

It has been some time since I felt the kind of relief I felt on getting that affirmation. It's always nice to get credit even if you aren't exactly sure what Ξ is.

The sound of the lock mechanism in the door moving round was truly invigorating. I got up off the seat so the door could open.

Jam was the first face but was quickly surrounded by the others. They were standing just outside the door when Jam said, "Dude, you won that one hands down. Nobody thought you'd finish."

"Believe me when I say, sincerely," I said, practically panting, "that it is unanimous."

"Pretty tough isn't it?" said Mark. He stepped past Jam into the cell patting me on the back as he went by.

"Very. You've been doing this for a while?" I asked.

The rest of the group pushed by, smiled, and gave me a tender pat on the back as they went by. The others were taking their previous positions, I moved over to my chair, and Mark pulled the door closed and sat on the seat. A roll of duct tape appeared from somewhere and Kez and Sandy were fixing the exit I'd created to the balcony.

"Sorry about that," I said, as I looked over to them. Kez turned and smiled, shrugged, and went back to taping.

Jam leaned over from his folding chair and

grabbed my arm, shook it enthusiastically, and patted me on the back again. All of it with that giant smile of his.

"Hey, we brought this because we *always* need it," said Sandy. She didn't turn as she smoothed the tape on the plastic.

"Always, and I do mean always," said Mark, "on the first introduction people get sloppy and get shut down. Then we give them a little training about how to approach the system so they can make it through. How did you do it?"

"I tied it to a breathing pattern. Real regular. Inhale, exhale read a few words. Repeat for friggin ever."

"What we've learned is that once you get *your* pattern, it's a routine passage for the day."

"Yeah, routine, that's what I'd call it alright," said Kez, "As routine as chiggers."

"So how long have you been doing this?" I said again. I knew I was going to be impressed if it was more than a day.

"As a CT, I did 30 days," said Mark. "Now, I treat it just like a job. After my six hours are done, I free myself IF I complete the specs. I do stick to the diet, though, for research purposes."

"It was hard being away from him at the beginning," injected Larisha.

"But nothin'," said Mark. "It was cruel and

unusual to the limit." He smiled and blew a kiss to her which she faked catching it on her cheek and rubbed it in.

"Did you make it through the first time?" I said.

"Nope. *Nobody* has ever done that!" Mark declared.

Looking around the crowd validated it. Jam was nodding his head furiously and biting down his bottom lip demonstrating that extreme smile. Exultant celebration.

"It was a total sucker bet for these bozos," Jam said. "I told Larisha to make sure to tell you we were betting on you again because it'd make you crumble early. They were all betting on time till you quit. I was the only one betting on completion." He reached over and shook my shoulder again.

"I don't understand why you were so sure. You'd already been wrong the first time," Kez said to Jam. She then turned to me, "He didn't say anything, just bet on you finishing and shut up. No reason."

"Simple really," Jam said. "I've known this guy as softhearted but extremely, massively hard headed for a very long time. When we were young, arguing about who could shoot better, he'd spend time weighing each individual bullet. Measuring the volume capacity of each brass case, he'd trim them if they weren't exactly the 2.54ZERO inches defined in the standard for the .270 Winchester. He'd hand weigh each load to the hundredth grain. He even validated bullet seating depth with a micrometer on each and every one." He patted me on the back again.

"When you told him we were betting on him," Jam said laughing, "and told him how he might lose, there was no way in God's Texas that was going to happen. *No way!*"

We all laughed and I really enjoyed being special in this group of the super. It's been a while since I felt this much real warmth. When you make it, however you do it, you tend to pick up people that hang on to you. They worship you in an incomplete sort of way, just trying to find a place beside you. They're always in every crowd, once they know who you are, and what they think you can do for them. There's always someone that has been trained by marketing types that it's who you know. These people were reals.

Kez stood up from the bed and came over, rubbed my shoulder with feeling, and said, "It is so very wonderful to finally get to meet you. I'm so looking forward to working with you. Jeremy brought us to love you before we saw you."

After that, it was like the others were attracted to the huddle, too, and in seconds I was the puppy at the birthday party. They were all saying nice things, but I couldn't really pick it out. I just smiled and glanced over to Jam every now and then to see him wearing a knowing smile.

"I can feel it, I can feel it coming!" announced Mark.

"Oh man," said Larisha covering her ears.

The others were returning to sit on the bed with their ears covered, too. Jam had his fingers in his ears by this time, too. It was a solid clue I was sure, so I followed their lead.

"RRRRRREEEEEEE ha ha haaaaaa,", shouted Mark. After the humming in my ears stopped, I heard, "I just love it when a plan comes together!"

"Man, dude, that was a pretty big one for such a small space," I said. The smiles were brighter than before.

"But ... the plan ain't all together yet", said Jam. When he said that, the smiles smudged.

"It's Ok, It's Ok. We're good,", said Jam. He looked around the room at everyone except me. "Let's keep going." That turkey-like guest feeling returned from left field.

"Ok ... Well," Mark said to break the silence before it got grown, "So we consider the Constitution the most important thing that is read daily by every CT. The next thing is George Washington's book on manners[1]. And we ended up there because of ... ", he was waving his cane around pointing at the wall again, "Is it that one towards the top left?"

Jam got up again. I would have, could have since I was closer, but this show was for me. I was glad to be sitting without any need to act for a while.

Stepping behind me, Jam said, "This is Thoreau again ... 'Nations are possessed with an insane ambition to perpetuate the memory of themselves by the amount of hammered stone they leave. What if equal pains were taken to smooth and polish their manners? One piece of good sense would be more memorable than a monument as high as the moon'."[2] As he finished, he turned and smiled, "I say amen to that, and again ... I say AMEN."

Amen floated around the cell faster than the smiles.

"This is the thing today don't ya think?" asked Mark, "We got geeks like Kez-"

"Hey," said Kez sharply. She wasn't about to let it pass.

"That's spent all their time bit twiddling," said Mark, "and don't know how to talk with real people."

"Maybe not a great example," I said, as I smiled at Kez and eyes so blue, "but I've met geeks that fit that cut." Kind of weird how she attracted me so much now. Birds build nests in heads where they want I guess. Neutrino chaos. Muon and neuron collisions.

"That sounds like a great idea," I said. "Convicts coming out of prison with a standardized set of manners ... uh ... before we get too far," I said turning back to Kez, "What was that weird symbol on the screen when it was crediting me out?" I held up three fingers parallel to the concrete floor.

"That's the symbol for the Ether, a cryptocurrency from the Ethereum project," said Kez. She was owning this one. "Unlike Bitcoin, it allows smart contracts and that's what you're assigned to here. Instead of time behind bars as a 24 hour period, you get sentenced to training time behind bars that is completed in six hour blocks. So, thirty days is really 180 ether, and regardless of what an ether is trading for on the open market, your trade is one hour successful training for one Ether."

"So they know how good they're doing all the time, their balance and everything," I was guessing again, but it sounded pretty authoritative.

"Their balance and truly everything," Kez said. "Instead of getting good time for just hanging around and not killing anybody else, they have to earn good time. They can work more, earning an additional six hours overtime per day, which deducts another day. Of course, overtime is totally up to them. One to six per day. One day of the week is dead time by spec."

"Dead time?" I said.

Jam took this one, "Look, we enforce a day of rest. You get to pick the day. We figured when people get used to sentencing people to the panopticons ... Hives, this will be wrapped in. A person has to have a day off and we're going to force them to learn to enjoy doing nothing just like old time corrections." It seemed like he was a little testy about explaining this one.

"Aw righty, then," I agreed. Except when it was cotton harvest, sorghum, hay, or something equally weather sensitive, people seemed to just naturally follow God's suggestion on this one. Suggestion? When you come to believe that children are the heritage of the Lord[3] you start to see things like DNA memory all over the place.

"Mark, cover the last lessons," Jam said, "but don't touch the evening rewards. I think

Kez should cover that one." He turned to Kez, "And when you do, don't touch the dark net. I want to do that myself. Ok?"

She nodded with a pouty lip.

"Do you think y'all can do that in an hour, including Kez wrangling him through the exo?" Jam said. I been waiting for this.

"Not a problem at all," said Mark.

"Unless he can't take instruction," Kez said, smiling at me again, "I don't see a problem with that either, Jeremy."

"Ok, then, if you have time, try to cover the PPA," Jam said, "I'm going to go walk Bear and Aisley through some of the family compartments. Text me when you're done."

As he rose, Sandy went with him, slapping me on the knee as she passed.

Larisha walked to Mark for a kiss, then said, "Be easy on him, hon, he's something." She turned to smile at me before leaving.

18.

"**Now that all the distractions are gone,** we should be able to cover some ground here," said Mark. He went to the far corner and retrieved Jam's folding chair for Kez and formed us into a close circle under the monitor on the wall, right next to the exo.

"You got a clear idea about how the lessons work, right?" he said.

"Sure. The thing about talking in my own voice, now that was weird."

"That was my idea after about three weeks in," Mark said. He was clearly bragging here. "I'm really proud of that, too. I had it originally talking as Larisha to me. I realized I was emotionalizing that, so I figured that what we were supposed to be doing was forcing people to look into themselves and find the correct answers. You take away all contact with anyone but yourself, and you really are in isolation and willing to work harder to get out of it." Mark was moving his head in lazy crazy circles as he said that. "Oh yeah."

"I don't doubt that for a New York second."

"It is pretty shocking, though," said Kez,

"to hear a computer talking as You, to You, isn't it?"

"Oh yes," I said. I spoke it with affirmative energy, and little bit of a shudder.

"So basically, I'm just going to give you the synopsis of the rest of the day, if you have any questions you ask them. Ok?" Mark said nodding at me.

"You get to live the first hour of every day in the U.S. Constitution," Mark said, "the second hour is, as we mentioned, George Washington's Rules of Civility." Mark nodded at me sticking his chin out asking for acknowledgment.

I nodded, barely whispering, "Oh yeah."

"The third hour is math," said Mark. He spun back to the screen.

"That seems more difficult to handle this way," I said.

"Not really," Kez said swinging an imaginary rope over her head. "Math is the language of the universe. There are plenty of rote things you can learn, if that's all you want."

"Multiplication tables for an hour is pretty long, too!" said Mark smiling.

"That seems borderline cruel and unusual," I said with that tone that says I been whipped by math at least once. Oh Lord. Just reading with the computer was hard. Having to match the computer pushing math drills at me was almost unimaginable.

"Not really," said Kez. "They can advance to any level of mathematics they want. At the point where problems have to be worked, it just forces them to instruct the system what they want on the next line as they solve it. Unlike any other area, being wrong still counts for time on the first two attempts. Failure to get the right answer just backs them up. As long as they are participating, the time counts."

Mark then walked me through a *beginning* calculus problem. It all seemed so very logical as long as he was describing his work, writing the results down, and fitting the things into the derivative function. It seemed completely obvious as he consolidated thingies. The computer corrected him when he failed to account for exponents and backed him up two steps. It was as crazy listening to him talk back to himself as when it was me talking to me. Pretty much all of this lesson went straight on by me.

"Yeah, ok. I can see that," I said. I really wanted to move on here. There was absolutely nothing I cared enough about to question. Math is good. I do understand that, but the exo was right there.

"I think he just wants to move on," said Kez smiling at me.

"You got that right!" I said. "I have always understood that me and the universe ain't ever been on exactly the same wavelength when math is involved."

"Ok. Well. You can see that it moves forward," said Mark, "whereas the other two courses to this point were just meant to impart a base level of knowledge and continually reinforce it. Manners and civics are our foundation. Math enables everything. They can grow in math." He looked at me with a Mona Lisa smile.

I just stared at him, I guess. Honestly, I wasn't trying to be stubborn. I was just still numb after my first hour. Until a requisite number of seconds had passed on empty airspace, my brain didn't even recognize it. It was just waiting to be prodded again. They were quite happy to let the time pass staring at me.

"Ok, then, what's next?" I finally spoke into the silence. It was weird the way they would wait, apparently forever, to find out what my next desire might be.

"Well, that covers three hours of the day," Mark said, "From there we open it up more. The fourth hour allows them to have a little more choice. Sorta. The fourth hour is world geography minus any politics."

"No Politics," repeated Kez in a lower voice.

Mark hit the board on his lap, and a space-based view of the earth painted on the screen. Political boundaries began marking the countries. He moved a cursor over Texas, and as the county boundaries appeared, he noted Pecos and zoomed in to our location. He flew the cursor over to our position until we were right over where the Hive should have been. Based on the mesas and the draw, we were right overhead, but the ground was pixelated. Where there should have been buildings or construction equipment, there was only pixelated nothingness.

"How old is that image?" I said.

"A tad more than six months probably," Kez said. She looked into me with a wide smile, and turning to Mark, he mirrored the same broad smile. Both were clearly inviting questioning.

"Whatever," I said trying to avoid it. Investigating seemed tiring, plus the exo was right there. "But those political boundaries, I though you said no politics."

"We live in today," Mark said. "Today, these are the boundaries. We never allow discussion of how they got set." He started keying again.

"What is this county?" Mark's alter voice came from the monitor.

"Pecos," real Mark answered. He turned to me. "There are lots of things that have some political issues, but we only name the present. This mountain. This county. Whatever. Check this."

We turned back to the monitor as he flew over to the Indian subcontinent, drilling down to the heavily demarcated India-Pakistan border, one of the few man-made things visible from space. "This border, heavily engineered, obviously has some politics to it, but we don't cover that."

He hovered the cursor over the border, "Engage."

His alter voice said, "What border is this?"

Mark smiled at me and said, "Pakistan India." He started rocking his head from shoulder to shoulder, tick tock, at about the five second mark the display went all shades of yellow at which time he flew the cursor to the border again.

"Invalid repeat. Select again," the Mark alter voice said.

"Note that you have to select new things every time you get something correct. You can't just keep hanging on something you know in order to stall and run the clock out."

Mark flew the cursor over what could probably be a nearby city, based on the pixelization smear.

"The name of this city?" the *not* real Mark said.

I was starting to recognize that there was a very subtle difference in the computer voice. Something about it's modulation or trailing consonants, or just the feel of it on the ear. Very subtle. Skynet could lose. Maybe.

"Tando Alley high yall," Mark said.

Immediately, the computer said, "Tando Allahyar." *Not* Mark had an interesting accent now.

He rocked his head from side to side again marking the time. A short five seconds later, he got repeated to himself in the same accent, then the screen took on the yellow hue of the system warning.

"Tando Allahyar," Mark said, "Pause. See, it even teaches correct pronunciations."

"So it has the same timing requirements," I said.

"Sure," said Kez, "but this time the CT can pick whatever they want to investigate. They are required to investigate or they lose. You have to admit that this is almost a game."

"Oh yeah, I can see that, I know I could spend some time on it. I'm not sure I'd want some CT checking on my address, or the prosecutor's. Especially the judge's."

They both started shaking their heads in the negative.

"This only goes down to city and town boundaries," Mark said. "We thought of that right off." He flew the cursor closer to the town, and zoomed in to a pixelated mess. You were unable to discern anything about the area other than the boundaries. Streets, buildings, any man-made feature, was pixelated and smoothed into the background.

"It's another driven hour. This time they get to actually pick the things they're learning from anywhere on the earth. Every named prominence, coastal inlet, or whatever they want to look at. They are forced to be busy or they get turned off just like anything else. Screw around ... but purposefully."

"Generally," said Kez, "since they have to make decisions in fairly rapid time frames, they tend to investigate an area pretty thoroughly. The system gives you time, if you aren't moving too far afield. Spreading out from a starting location instead of hop scotching around is most common. Is that going to be a problem for you?"

Those are some blue eyes. She smiled as she sat back, and I really wondered if she knew the effect she had on men. She hooked her chin to me hinting a return to watching Mark. Of course she did.

I turned to Mark and said, "What about individual houses in the sticks or something?"

"Any residence, anything it deems to be man-made, is just blended into the image. As if it had never been there," he said. He relaxed back into his chair, too.

"Ready for the next one?" said Mark nodding in the affirmative.

I just nodded,too. I knew we were going to get to the exoskeleton within the hour so I was getting more eager every minute.

"Ok then," he said, "the next part is where they actually pick an educational field that they're interested in studying." He nodded towards Kez.

"This hour of the day is being laid out as we speak," she said. "We're gathering up knowledge from the world to enable people to share in our joint venture."

We all heard the door closure sliding, so Mark stood from his seat, and helped push the door open. Jam stepped into the cell and Mark closed the door behind him. He reclaimed his seat. Someone or something outside operated the closure. Jam took a seat on the bed.

"So where are we?" Jam said.

"Gosh, Jeremy, I was just getting to the part about our shared heritage and free knowledge, and then you bust in," said Kez, "Did someone tell you where we were at?"

The two of them laughed at that. I wasn't sure about that, but I wasn't laughing. It seemed to lean a little too close to spooky.

"Right," said Jam, and he clapped his hands together sharply, "We're almost to the really good part."

"Really good part? Exoskeleton?" I heard come out of my mouth. It's always a little surprising when your mouth operates without the brain in gear, but I have become accustomed to it.

"Oh Yeah!" Jam said, "Let me summarize this hour so we can get on. We have teams in all the major universities in the country archiving the lessons. MIT is very helpful, Harvard less so, but those are just examples. Two people from a project class are selected, we pay them $100 an hour to record the lesson they just heard in an off-site studio, and we can audit and QA every lesson since they aren't aware of the other person. We only pick the best so we get the best. They get their education paid. We get a full inventory of

Harvard Medical School, for example. Engineering schools, medicine, dentistry, chemistry, microbiology…everything that represents the advancement of human knowledge."

I knew why I was quiet, but the others were also. Jam waved his hands by them towards the heavens like he was scooping them up, and then, in unison, they said, "Our heritage." It had obviously been practiced a few times.

"I know I've heard that before," I said. "The whole 'knowledge is free' thing. It always seemed pretty empty to me. We've had libraries forever, but stupid is still incurable."

They all laughed.

"Look, unlike any other system," Jam said, "this one knows what you've covered, knows every answer you addressed, and because it's all retained in the Ethers ..." Jam stopped. My face must have shown some confusion, but I'm not sure how you could pick it out after all I'd layered on it lately.

"Y'all have talked about the Ethers, right?" said Jam, looking at the other two.

"We introduced it, but only as the ledger for the training lessons," said Kez. She exchanged a glance with Mark.

"Ok, Jack…eeee," Jam said, "Do you know anything about cryptocurrency and smart contracts?"

"They mentioned Bitcoin and it sounded familiar," I said.

"Exactly," said Jam, "so ..." he looked over at Kez, "Give him the elevator speech on smart contracts, please ma'am."

Kez took a deep breath looking at the ceiling, rolled her eyes to Mark, then focused those blue lasers on me and said, "Just like Bitcoin is a decentralized ledger for exchange," I blinked, "the Ether, from Ethereum has that functionality as well as smart contracts. We use smart contracts to measure the completion of a CT's criminal sentence, the file of their individual training during their lessons, and to enable civilians to store value for the CT's commissary if they are allowed into general population."

She paused for a breath and evaluation of my look. She obviously couldn't decide if I was wearing worse confusion, or not.

"We use it to track each CT in detail," said Jam, "monitor their training, and give them a real history of their performance when they get out. If they happened to study law, I think, maybe, we added something to civil society. Or maybe not."

"I think Jeremy is overly hopeful on this stuff," Mark said, "because CTs *ain't* here because they're on the top end of the ladder."

"But it is an opportunity. It is a project with a set and measurable goal. When we get it going, it will be for all, just like Jeremy always says," Kez was talking calmly at Mark. At Mark. You could tell this was a renewal of a previous discussion. Maybe it hadn't been completely resolved, but at least the waters looked to have been smoothed.

"Deuteronomy 29:29," said Jam, "The secret things belong to the Lord our God, but the things revealed belong to us and to our children forever."

He looked right into me, and said, "And that is what we're taking back from the Ivy League and the ivory towers. Our Heritage."

The atmosphere was a tad too dense right here, so I said, "I can see they might spend some serious time in the law angle. All prisoners everywhere beat on the law library, I think. I learned that somewhere. Might have been TV. Tell me about the canteen."

"People on the outside can buy things for prisoners," Jam said, "which they can receive. *If.* If they have finished a day successfully. They *must* successfully finish the day to get any privileges. The main difference, in this correctional setup, is that they have immediate rewards."

"Sure. Sure. Got it. But that still leaves another hour," I said.

Kez got up and went over to the exoskeleton hanging on the wall, shook it's limp limbs with a couple of fingers, and said, "Come on, time to try Baby on."

19.

When Kez touched the femur of Baby the entire exoskeleton only barely shivered. The very slightest quiver. The sound had an immediate emotional affect on me. When a rattlesnake is surprised, and they pull back into a coil, their scales scraping across the ground gives the same bare warning before the rattle.

That feeling ebbed, as an incident when I was bow hunting in the hill country lit on my consciousness. Corn was on the ground and several does were all over it, when a flock of turkeys came into the clearing. Two dozen turkeys came in, walking quickly in single file down the goat path. As soon as they reached the corn, two of the gobblers fanned their tails and spread their wings, their flight feathers dragging the ground. Then they approached the does, dancing sideways like bullfighters and stomping their feet rapidly. As they moved forward, they rattled their wing feathers against the ground for added affect.

The larger does immediately put their heads to the ground to face off with the newcomers, but were already backing up. The turkeys knew they had them. On the third charge the deer turned tail, and the turkeys owned the corn. They spent the rest of the morning, until the corn was gone, peeping happily amongst themselves.

The way Kez was looking at me, I knew I was about to enter some kind of new challenge. I was sensing the urge to back up, too. There were her blue eyes above that wonderful youthfulness, the orange skeleton, and the bright pink wall. What could be more jarring?

She knelt beside Baby and held on to it by the left ankle.

"Just put your heel in here and tap it against the ground three times," she said. This was the part that her bright smile showed she had been eager to begin, too.

The heels were really just little pieces the size of a shoe heel, the thickness of poster board. I stepped over, turned my back to it, and placed my heel. As it was touched, I had the odd sensation of the exo stiffening behind me, based on nothing more than a whisper of air brushing the wall.

"Normally, the CT's aren't going to be wearing boots with a riding heel," Kez said positioning my heel, "but this is still going to work fine I think."

Pulling her hands back, she said, "Ok, tap

it."

I looked down on her, our eyes meeting. The tension to keep from looking past those crystalline blue eyes and rushing down her blouse with them was a desire of it's own living energy. Turning to stare at my boot relieved the strain, and made me proud for Amanda. She married one strong man. Or I guess, she married a man that knew who to call on for strength in the flesh. What a fight! Thank you Jesus.

I tapped my heel three times and *slap*, a piece of kitchen plastic wrap topped my arch like a spur strap. I know it came from the inside part of the heel, but it was totally unexpected, so it left me feeling unsure. In the second after strapping me in, Baby tightened the strap to the point of being secure, but not uncomfortable.

I looked over to Jam.

"You're about to be controlled. Finally," he said, smiling that dangerous smile from our youth again.

"Uhmm," was all I could say before being drawn to look down. Kez was pulling Baby's left knee alongside mine with her hands gently holding my knee from behind, above and below.

As soon as she got our knee joints aligned, two more quick straps wrapped my lower thigh and upper calf, and snugged up. At that exact moment Baby came alive. Glancing over my shoulder I could see it extending the long bones to match my height. This operation seemed to be a kind of unwinding. The straws that made up the machine were twisting, as if they really were tightly wound rubber bands, needing to be unwound to allow for more length. The backbones, there was one running along each side of the body, were now stiffened upright. The arms were now extended downward at a 45 degree angle. I could tell without a serious glance, that it had matched my size. I was still standing inches away from the wall and even more suspicious.

"Ok now," Kez instructed, "At this point, all you have to do is place the other heel and move back into it and-"

I was already leaning in from the other heel. Imagine being one side of a Velcro pair. As I leaned back, Baby wrapped itself around me becoming a piece of me. It was no longer on the wall, and I was now standing alone with it. *Alone* and *with it* brought a chuckle.

"Ooooh man," I said, "this is ... uh ... uh ... something!"

"Yes it is," said Jam. "Take her for a walk."

I walked over to the end of the cell next to the now repaired plastic door. Other than me knowing I had a creature on my back, there was no noticeable change in my ability to move in any way. I stretched my arms and picked up my knees as freely as if I'd been dressed in the clothing of my birth.

At the window end, the light filtering in had a different feel. It was now coming in sideways as the day passed. The plastic covering lightly fluttering with the breezes. With the noticeable change in the lighting, it struck me how fast the day was going by. I'd already seen a lifetime of surprises, and now I had Baby riding piggyback.

I turned back to the group, Jam was standing with them now, and l said, "So what does this have to do with the last lesson?"

"The last lesson requires this as a base, in a couple of different ways," Jam said. He tapped Mark on the shoulder and he lifted his head towards me. "Tell him about the control part."

Mark waved me over to his seat and I skipped over. There was the slightest sense of skipping through ... puddles? ... but it did not affect my control. Kez and Jam took the open chairs.

"Wow. You can't even tell it's on you," I said to Jam.

"No you can't," said Mark. "This is a form of CT control, which was the first part of the project that Jeremy wanted us to work on. It is much smarter than it looks. It's part of the security infrastructure built into the panopticon ... Hive." He reached out and turned me around, inspecting the installation.

"Now, there are two types of CT in our system: the violent offender and the non-violent. The violent offender has to wear this over their clothes any time they're out of their cell. You can tell there is a little space allowed by wrinkles in your clothes. They're under system control and they're brightly designated for all to see."

He handed me a fancy stainless steel pen like the type I used to own. "Try to work this under a strap, bust it, and try to escape. Any bets?"

Sure, I say to self, I've had enough of that. Being ignorant and betting is the norm. It's only when you start calling it *losing* instead of *gamboling* that you start waking up. I'd been woke. My first thought was that surely I'd be able to pierce that kitchen wrap. On the other hand, there was the side where he armed me with a pen that looked like it was capable of being a serious weapon. Sandbagged for sure.

"Not this time," I said. Looking around the group, Mona Lisa smiles back at me.

"Come on. Let's see what you can do," said

Jam. He spun his index finger in the air.

They'd tested me pretty good up to this point, but I was on a roll. I was going to try my best. Unlike the lesson test, I could apply all my effort quickly for effect. These wimpy looking straps were practically invisible tightened around my clothes, except where the straps were on my bare wrists.

I supposed their invisibility belied their strength, just like kitchen wrap. The tension they maintained was surely a hint. My sister and a friend wrapped my toilet with Saran Wrap one time while I was out drinking. When I came back to take a leak, I lifted the lid and didn't notice anything. In the middle of a racehorse piss bouncing off the toilet bowl, the drunkenness hampered me peeling the wrap off the toilet before the entire pinched-off stream flooded the floor. There can be serious effort involved in fighting your way out of, or through, a plastic bag.

Analyzing this particular situation, I was thinking that attacking the wrist strap on one hand would be the way to go. I'd be able to use the strength of both arms and the fine control of my hands. I clicked the pen a few times while I thought. It's thin barrel was exactly what the doctor ordered for this task. With the point retracted, I pressed it against the base of my thumb in my left hand. It had a fairly sharp edge which I figured I could just fit under the edge of the strap by depressing the skin. If I go for the left wrist, forcing it under from the forearm side, I have the chance to dodge it if I slip. I've slipped many times to poor effect, so I'm aware. Coming back the other way, towards my forearm, and my heart, made me think I might be able to apply more pressure by bracing the pen against the wall. But, then I could slip it right into my arm, or heart, if I misjudged any part of it. No sense taking a chance on blood. Or death.

The vision became: the effort of getting it under the lip of the strap, then angling it outwards, perforating the thin strap forcing it to separate. It always worked with duct tape. I was gaining some confidence as the plan gelled.

"Well, I think a definite maybe," I said, "but I don't want to bet y'all. You've pretty much sandbagged me every step of the way."

I placed the pen against the strap on my left wrist. Looking around, just more non-committal smiles. And nods.

"Let's see it," said Jam.

I started trying to work the pen under the strap tenderly at first. I thought it was just the pen pressing through, initially, as I felt the tension increase. However, and this didn't take long for me to realize, fractions of a second really, the strap was tightening in a slightly greater proportion than I was applying pressure. It was overmatching my efforts smoothly, but I was forcing it, hoping to overcome. I turned, placing the subject hand to the wall, left palm on it facing outward, and tried to use my full body weight. It was at about the point I knew blood was no longer being delivered to my finger tips, that I surrendered, dropping the pen to the ground. Any further effort and I could have slipped into a potentially suicidal stab.

"Hey, am I going to be alright?" I whined. I held onto my wrist, and noticed that the bluish tinge to my fingers was already fading.

Jam giggled while the others just smiled.

"Jeremy really likes that part for some reason," said Kez. "I'm not really sure where that comes from, because his prayers are so heartfelt."

The pressure was reducing smoothly, the color was returning to my fingers, and I was breathing evenly again. That had been right up to the raw edge of freak out.

"I like it because it shows how far someone will try to push through a losing situation," said Jam. "There's a lesson in there. Maybe." He stepped over and slapped me on the back.

"That's just proof that the CT *will* be wrapped up in our world if they've ever been violent, and they won't be getting out. But that's just the beginning. Check this out."

With that, he stepped right up to my face, and said, "This is the part I'm really going to like. I'm going to slap you."

I looked around at the others, and they seemed as surprised as I felt. "Well, I'm going to punch you out," I said, matching his sing song tone.

"I'm going to slap you really hard. Okay?" said Jam.

"No okay to it. It you do, I'm going to frigging knock you out for sure," I said. I'm pretty sure I wasn't the only one that was unclear about where this was going.

Then, without any windup, he gave me a slap to the face that I know left a hand print.

"Holy crap! Are you crazy?" I yelled, rubbing my face.

"Somehow, I was really able enjoy that, and it was as good as I thought it would be," he said. He grinned to Kez, then, "Hit me. Punch me in the face. Do it. Do it now. Knock me out!"

"I'm going to, cabron," I said. There was a hidden well of emotion that was going to feed this particular punch.

"Ok. I'm ready. Give me everything you got. Don't hold back. Right here ... *cabron*!" he said turning his left cheek to me and tapping it with his index finger. He was leaning in towards me leading with his chin.

"Oh Lord," said Kez as she shook her head, her lips offering a raspberry. She leaned around to my face, "I think that's pretty clear license. I'd use it."

When we were kids, we'd played those hand slapping games. Although we were pretty even, I always ended up with the bright red hands because he could sucker me with a blink or quick breath. He always, and forever, beat me down on free slaps. This time, he asked for it, and it was going to arrive as a complete surprise.

"Nah, I'd feel bad," I said, "even though he deserves it." I started rubbing my cheek with my strong right hand, and I so enjoyed smiling at Kez on that.

"Dude, this is-" Mark said, and Jam started to glance in his direction.

I don't care what anybody says, there is a certain fullness of joy that comes from feeling bones crunch, and teeth clatter, in the face of someone that's been asking for it. This was one of those times that, even though he was a dear friend re-found, I was going to oblige him in every way. Why not? License.

My right hand was already at face level, he was starting to glance to Mark, I had him in my peripheral vision as I smiled at Kez. This straight punch to his face was going to be completely surprising. Completely devastating. I was completely sure. I was already contemplating the words of my apology inside the ER.

It was microseconds into the punch that I realized I had been had. It was going to be a great straight punch, with the added force of twisting my body into it like I'd been trained once upon a time, when I realized Baby was interfering. My fist had just started to fly, when it was slowing as quick and exactly like, the straps had defended themselves.

Jam turned back to me, stepped out of the way of a molasses-speed punch, and smiled as wide as I'd ever seen.

"Cowboy, what were you trying to do?" he said. "Sucker punch me?"

"Trying," said Mark.

"You guys and your pissing contests," said Kez as she sat down.

"So, you see," Mark said, "we can let even violent offenders loose in the general population without fearing for the safety of the other inmates. What kind of insane freak is going to get into a fight with someone when they can only fight through glue? Not a reasonable tactic."

"Plus, they *know*," said Kez circling her head like a drunk, "they're totally at the mercy of the crowd."

"And we believe that violent types do not get a second chance," said Jam looking around at the others to confirm it. "Once violent, always potentially capable of violence, and forever after accompanied by Baby in here. Only by successfully completing their training sentence do they get total freedom ... at their release."

All of us nodded our heads on that one.

"I really want to get out of this," I said. I smiled at Jam while rubbing my cheek.

"Oh sure, dude. They'll let you out after I go to drop the hunters off," Jam said. He was patting me on the back like burping a baby.

"Anyway," said Jam, "there's one more security feature I'd like to show you before we get back to the final lesson. General alarm."

"Whenever there is a general alarm, the rules state that every CT must hit the deck spread eagle. CTs accompanied by Baby are the same, but they are strongly encouraged with assists from Baby, if they are slow. Ten seconds after the alarm, the central tower guns are powered on, and any warm thing 24 inches above the deck, or moving laterally, is shaved off by those .50 cal rounds until it fits inside of those parameters. You've seen how accurate and fast they are.

"And you can imagine their empathy," said Mark, shaking his head while mouthing *no*.

"If you're interested in testing it," said Jam, "we'll set the alarm and you see if you can make it over onto the bed."

"It's not going to hurt me is it?" I said. It even sounded kind of whipped to me. I didn't want to find another slap I wasn't expecting.

"No, sugar, this one isn't going to hurt at all," said Kez smiling at me big. That kind of West Texas sugar is hard to judge sometimes. Does that really mean no, or is it a sucker's yes?

"Ok then," said Jam, "stand over here in the corner and when I say go, give it your best effort to get to the bed."

It was less than ten feet. It seemed an easy hop, skip, and jump, but recent experience hinted that thought was certainly wrong. Kez held her necklace bob near the corner of her mouth.

"Ready. Set. GO!" yelled Jam.

The instant he said go, Kez calmly stated,"Alert test 451." She said it quickly and clearly, like a practiced operator.

Two steps into my dash confirmed Baby had me again. I was headed to the floor. Every movement had a point where it could not be reversed. In no time, I was locked down, and getting more balled up as I struggled.

I stopped struggling, looked up at them, and said, "Uncle."

"Pretty neat, huh?" said Kez. "Every movement that takes you closer to being in the fetal position is allowed, all others are prevented. I took that from the constrictor snakes."

"She's one scary lady," Mark said, and smiled at her.

"If they assume the position immediately," said Kez, "they follow the rules, or they are forced into a ball." She was mimicking making a snowball with her hands. "It's perfect."

"Did I say uncle out loud, or was I just thinking that?" I said. I was smiling up at her, my eyebrows hiked up as high as they'd go.

"Sorry," Kez said. She canceled the alert. I was released and stood up.

"This Baby is a very impressive piece of equipment," I said. "I'm not sure why I had to learn that before the last lesson of the day."

"What makes her so strong?" I said rubbing the straps and shaking the kinks out of my body.

"It's all graphene[1] based," said Mark. "The straps are only three atoms thick, three layers, and you will *not* bust through. The bones of Baby are graphene, twisted up on a DNA core, which is what allows the changes in size. Baby fits all." He obviously had some ego on this part of development.

"Basically, Baby is the base of our security," said Jam, "along with the tower, and the foundation of our final lesson."

"What?" I said which sounded shrill again. I'd been slapped, slammed to the ground, and taunted by a computer, so of course, I was just a little uneasy.

At that, Mark reached above his head and opened the mirror, exposing several shelves of a cabinet. Inside, he retrieved two international orange gloves and a VR headset[2].

He tossed the gloves to me, and said, "Put these on."

I caught them, looked at Jam who was expressionless, but Kez was nodding affirmatively. Her tender smile was reassuring this time. I couldn't read the others.

I put on the gloves. Like the straps on Baby, the gloves immediately formed to my hands in every crease and knuckle. It was like they were every blob, in every old horror movie, enveloping my hands, only cuter and with less excess. In a long second, they were like orange skin.

"Now you have a choice," said Jam.

They all began that crazy patient waiting for me to speak again.

"Okaaaay," I said, finally, "lead on."

"You can either learn to play string instruments or learn to knit or crochet," said Jam.

There was a second there where the contrast between the two choices made me think maybe I'd misheard him. I looked around at all of them. Crazy, patient waiting again.

"Crochet or music? That's a pretty weird choice," I said.

"We've spent serious time on this. Having the system teach you to play the guitar, or whatever, was probably the easy part," Jam said, and they all nodded. "The hard part was what to do with CTs that say it's against their religion to do music."

"What *are* you talking about?" I said. Perhaps I said that with more disbelief than I could justify. This was obviously another area where I was completely ignorant. Again.

"You remember I told you I didn't have time to mess with Muslims earlier? We living off pig here. Well, there's another area where Muslims can be a pain in the ass and that is in regard to music[3]. I don't need to get into all the details, but basically there's a whole mess that believes it's sinful not to destroy musical instruments. Well, this is prison. We don't really do those kind of choices, but this is a hard one. If we only did music this last lesson, and allowed a religious opt out, we'd be making everybody else do 17% more to earn a good day credit."

They were all looking at me, unmoving.

"But ... crochet?" I said.

"Hey, we searched the net for it," said Kez, "and the only thing that really came up was the knitted kufi hat Muslims wear. Nothing about who made it."

"If they can wear it, they can make it," said Jam. "So that's where we are today."

"So what's *your* choice?" said Mark shifting on his seat. I got the impression we were all glad to be moving past that point based on the general uneasiness.

"Music, duh," I said.

"Of course, which instrument?" Mark said. He was leading this one. Jam and Kez went and sat on the bed and started chatting about something else. I was easily able to ignore them because I was really focused now.

"Guitar."

"Any special requests?" Mark said and

turned towards the monitor.

"How about Jimmy Page?" I said. I grew up with Led Zeppelin 4 and burned up three 8-track tapes. If I could learn any songs ... hail yes!

"Hey Jack, scroll through Jimmy Page guitars, please," Mark ordered. He turned to me and said, "Tell us when."

A guitar image would splash on the screen for a couple seconds with a paragraph of description in the bottom right corner. When that reddish Les Paul Deluxe No. 3 popped on the screen, I didn't need to wait for the description.

"That's *it!*" I almost shouted.

Mark handed me the VR headset and motioned for me to have a seat.

"The reason we wanted you to test the general alarm feature of Baby is because it is just like this training session. In the alarm, every motion you made that was not to fetal position was blocked and every one towards fetal position was allowed." He nodding towards me with eyebrows raised expecting a response.

"Yes," I nodded.

"So what we're going to do here is let you pick a song, the VR shows you how it's played by Jimmy, and you try to mimic it. As you move, the gloves nudge you into position. You will be impressed," he said, then "Go ahead, mount up."

I put the VR set on my head and positioned the headphones so they were comfortable on my ears. As the scene came into focus, I was obviously sitting in a small studio about the actual size of the cell. Looking around, I was alone.

"Where'd y'all go." I said, shaking my head and smiling in their direction.

"Oh we're here to watch the monkey," I think Jam said, but it could have been Mark, what with the headphones. I thought I heard him moving over there before things came to life.

Looking down, there was a guitar in my lap. As I put my hands on it, I could actually sense it. The smooth neck, the frets, even the tension in the strings was transmitted through the gloves. It was all there except for the weight of the guitar on my thigh.

"Oh my God, I can feel it!" I shouted. I'm sure I shouted.

"Pick a song," that I knew was Jam.

"Black Dog," I said. A pair of disembodied hands appeared on the guitar. As I moved around to match up with them, I had the sensation of falling into their synch, like I'd stepped into a pair of old shoes, or better, gardening gloves worn and sweated into the perfect shape.

"Just match up your hands with the images. You'll sense when you're together," said Jam "You can 'rewind', 'stop', and 'play' like any video, but you also have 'slow'. "Slow" will become your favorite. At your command, buck it out!"

"Play," I said, and the initial strumming entry to the song came over the headphones as the virtual hands moved away from my position.

"Rewind." I really was going to have to pay close attention to this. "Slow."

In this mode I was able to stay exactly synched with the ghost hands. The music itself was also slowed.

"Rewind."

"Slow." I was already starting to synch up.

"Rewind."

"Slow." As we melded, my mind was freer, not thinking about the moves. I was actually feeling it, the positioning, the strumming, the picking. I was beginning to think all the time spent playing air guitar to this song in my youth made a difference.

"Rewind."

"Play." I thought it sounded almost exactly

right this time. How would I know?

"Stop."

"Can I hear what I'm playing versus what the system is doing?" I shouted, not caring, to the empty virtual studio.

"You are track 2. You can alternate just by selecting the track," Mark said.

"Play."

"Track 2." I still pretty much sucked but not nearly as bad as one might think. It's close. Damn close for somebody who's never played a note on anything but an air guitar. Close enough to recognize the song.

"Rewind."

"Track 1."

"Play."

"Rewind.""Slow.""Rewind.""Slow.""Rewir ditto onward.

I wasn't exactly sure how long I'd been at this lesson but I was getting into the *Oh Yeah* of the song. My hands were becoming accustomed, almost nimble, to the parts that repeated. I was literally playing the guitar. I wasn't struggling with bleeding finger tips. When Jam touched me on the shoulder, I could have punched him out. Or slow tried. I didn't want to stop this one. Lucky for him that Baby was still babysitting me.

I raised the VR headset, and sat it on my

lap. "That was too good. I could do that all day." I could feel my smile stretching to my ears.

"Funny you should say that," Jam said, "The CTs only get one hour credit per day for music. They can play as much as they want, if they complete the credits for the day, but one hour credit per day. There is still one thing I want you to validate before we take off from this. Put the headset on, hit 'play' and then do not move your fingers or hands at all."

I put the Headset on. "Play". I did not move my fingers at all. I could feel very slight pressure but nothing more. The system was not strictly directing me, it was only guiding me[4]. After ten seconds or so, the visual yellowed out. It stayed yellow. Then it started blinking red. Then black.

I took the headset off and Jam was right there, "You just failed out for the day. So you see, you have to be a participant. You always have to be a participant. You can't choose to do guitar or crochet and not actually work it, and still get good credit for the day."

"I don't know what to say about this one," I said looking around. "That was a dream. Really."

They all smiled and nodded.

"So now, lets assume that you completed a

day," said Jam. "Six lessons, minimally six hours, completed between 8am and 5pm. Curfew is at 10pm. You can eat, pray, play music, read from the library of the world, and are released to the breezeway. If, but only if, you completed the day. Otherwise you're pacing until tomorrow, alone in your cell. Without access to anything. One hour on the deck at 6pm." Jam was saying this like a true warden, somebody that had instructed about rules numerous times. No nonsense.

He turned to the others and said, "Violent or no?"

Both Mark and Kez shook their heads no.

"But, I would caution you, Jeremy", said Mark puckering up his face and tapping his cheek, "He does owe you."

Jam looked at me, stuck out his lower lip, rocked his head side to side and said, "Nah, he's a good guy. Right?"

"Oh ... sure ... sure thing, buddy," I said smiling wide.

"Ok, just back up to the wall and push with the small of your back where it was hanging before."

I did as he said, noting that Kez was talking into the necklace again. As soon as I felt pressure on the small of my back from the wall, Baby let go. It fell off me like a leaf in winter, completely empty and without essence, clattering bones against the wall.

"Now we're going to exit to the general population," said Jam, "However, even though we've freed you from Baby, I want you to consider yourself as still a violent criminal wearing Baby. We're still demonstrating Hive details. Violent criminals are treated differently. Every culture." He could certainly put on that warden tone.

He motioned me to the door, and said, "This way convict."

I went over, heard the sliding of the lock being opened, but the door just released from the door jam slightly. I pushed and it yielded, confirming it was a heavy door. Applying a little more effort it began to swing on the hinges opening to something that wasn't there before.

Attached to the door was a cubicle like a man-sized rocket pod, blocking the exit. Inside it had a monitor facing me, and two extra large buttons, red and green, on either side of the monitor. Around the bottom of the pod was a waist-high stainless steel skirt.

I turned and looked at them with what I was sure was a pathetic look on my face. They were silent.

"Well, I give. What the heck is this?" I

finally said.

"Meet your victim, convict," they said in blank-faced unison.

20.

Jam stepped up beside me at the door and gently pushed me up to the door of the pod. "There's not room for both of us in there so I'll just instruct you from the door. *Do. Not. Touch. The. Buttons,*" he said with a smile. After a two second pause, "Just joking, it's only a demo." The device was positioned such that it completely blocked any exit from the cell. You entered the cubicle, or stayed in the cell.

I hadn't had any intention of touching the buttons, but as soon as someone tells you not to, the thought rises up in your consciousness. I know I wonder if the suggestion doesn't have its' own power, somehow influencing my leftover toddler. They were large plastic buttons the size of my fist, smooth and flush against the wall. It looked like ventilation slots around the green button to the left of the monitor. I was strongly drawn to at least feel the button's surface. Shiny objects. I resisted.

In the bullet-headed ceiling were four access ports for something. One was in the center with the other three slightly farther down because of the shape of the compartment, but symmetrically located around the center. In my Navy time, I might have called them battle covers.

"Come on convict, step in," said Jam. "This demo can't hurt you." I knew that particular smile. Whenever I'd seen it, I've always known to be especially alert, but I was intrigued again.

I leaned in and tapped around on the walls with my knuckle and confirmed it was a metal bullet. There are times you find yourself in close quarters and it makes you feel comfortable like you own the space. This void, with it's buttons and monitor, made me feel like a sardine, a product in production.

Jam applied a light pressure to my shoulder.

I stepped in with my right foot. As my left foot hit the floor the entrance swished shut like every science fiction space hatch. Who can't turn when something closes you into an unknown space? A quick spin. There in the porthole of a window were Kez and Jam, smiling.

"Can you hear us?" Kez said. I nodded.

"Every CT that has been convicted of harming a person," Jam said, "is required to pass through here weekly. Murderers *every* third day. This is what we call the PPA. It's purpose is to force you to face your victims. The most forgotten part of any crime, is now a recurring part of your sentence."

"PPA?" I said to the faces filling the porthole.

"POST Partum Abortion," said Kez, raising her eyebrows as she said it.

Locked into a metal bullet, with two buttons, and they tell you it's some kind of abortion. I leaned back against the doorway next to the porthole so I could see them over my left shoulder. What if I fainted or stumbled into one of the buttons that had seemed so attractive moments ago? What would I learn then?

"I'm not feeling loved," I said.

"It's a demo only," said Jam, "Relax."

As he said that, the monitor came alive with an older women leaning into the camera. At each corner of the screen were colored buttons: red and green in upper corners, blue and yellow in the bottom corners. As she started talking, I turned and looked to see Kez alone in the porthole.

"This is a victim statement. You are *required* to pay attention to this," Kez said.

The women started into a story about how she'd lost her only daughter to a drunken driver, whose role, I supposed, I was playing. There was no acting in her role, and I couldn't take my eyes off it as she described her broken life. Almost nonchalantly, she pointed up to the corner towards the red button and said, in a whisper, "Hit green," and then continued talking.

I immediately turned to look at Kez. She nodded towards the screen. I touched the green icon in the corner of the screen. The victim was now talking, amidst sobs, about missing the opportunity to love on grandkids. When she pointed to the red button again, she said in a whisper, "Hit red."

This time I decided to wait. Just like all the other parts of the system I'd been exposed to so far, at about the five second mark, the video went to yellow hues. Fearing something, but counting on it being a demo, I hit the green button on the monitor and the hatch swooshed open. Now Kez was just standing right next to me.

"You are forced to listen to the victim's statement by requiring that you keep up with the buttons they tell you to push. They do their best to fool you," she said.

I looked over to Jam now sitting on the bed in the cell. "The time when a convict could just go to jail and forget about their victims is over. Just like victims have to confront the results of the crime on a daily basis, the convict has to confront the victims and the consequences of their actions on a regular basis. The victims, or their family, can change the impact statement at any time."

"And when I miss a direction, then what?" I said.

"You just don't get to go to general population release that day," Kez said. "You don't get to this point unless you earned a good day, but if you fail here, your daily release to general population and commissary choices are curtailed for the day. It still counts as a good day regardless."

"Stay in your cell for as long as it takes you to complete a day and answer your victims to get more privileges," said Jam.

"So I'm guessing the buttons on the walls in here actually serve a purpose?" I said.

"Oh yeah!" Jam said, "PPA. If at any time a convict thinks they've had enough, they can choose the method of their destructor[2]. Green is nitrogen asphyxiation, two painless breaths and they fade out. Red is four shotguns with a mix of triple ought and four buck." He started slow nodding big motions with his head. "Red mist."

"Oh," I said. The vision of that much pointblank buckshot splattered across my mind.

"Pretty darn sure that mist don't have feelings," said Mark. He shook his head from side to side and curled his lower lip.

"And any prisoner can request a PPA visit. Choice, you know," said Kez. She was the first one to smile on this introduction.

"In fact, there is sort of a built in synchronicity between the PPA and the commissary," said Mark, "because this commissary lets them order up anything they want. Drugs, alcohol, everything except women or pornography."

"No. Really?" I said. In a barrel full of fascinating and shocking, this one really seemed to be far out in the field.

"We don't pay for it, but if someone puts Ethers in their account towards purchases, we purchase and hold it for them. Any type of liquor. Any type of drug, even pharmaceuticals," Mark said. He was waving his hands around the cell, "But of course, they have to do them alone in their cell. Imagine how much fun it could be! Buy a daily dose for the convict that destroyed some part of your family. OxyContin or 120 proof quality bourbon to get them started, then you quit buying it! *OH. Oh. Oh.* " Now he was smiling on that one.

"There was a song, 'Devil Lives in a Bag', that really says it to me," said Jam with a weak smile. "Whether dope, or drink, we always seem to pull it from a bag."

"You don't really think you'll be able to serve convicts drugs and alcohol," I said. I stepped past Kez and towards Jam on the bed.

"Think? Know. Look into Guantanamo," Jam said, and he nodded to Mark, now sitting in my chair.

As soon as I turned toward him, the large monitor on the screen was displaying an article that hinted that terrorists in prison were requesting and getting drugs.[1]

"But-" I started to say.

"Look, man," Jam said, "the current system keeps people locked up, and pretty much drug free, then lets them out into a world that is awash in drugs and alcohol. Then they're supposed to learn moderation? I know the devil in a bag, big time, and this system lets them use all they want, alone, in their cell. If they don't make it through the next day successfully, they added another day to their sentence. And, they are cut off from the commissary. It's training in the truest since. Truly effective discriminative stimuli."

Jam said that with a tone that let me know this had been contemplated and discussed in-depth. Any time there's eight syllables in a West Texan's description, it's been practiced more than once.

"Oxycontin?" I said, shrugging.

"Sure. Everything. They can experiment in here to their death if they want. Choice!" said Jam, "And the lesson shown to the world will be obvious, documented on the blockchain, and available for all to see. If drugs lead to depression and suicide, we'll pretty much be all over that, won't we?"

"We've got a team looking into whether nitrogen asphyxiation leaves transplantable organs," said Mark. "I'm betting we can even get an open market going, as long as some of the benefit goes to their own family."

"Oh," said Jam rising from the bed, "that's the one that still feels too-"

"*Crazy!*"[3] I finished the thought for him. I said it, but immediately I could see where someone facing 50 years of this might agree to a PPA if 25% of the money for selling their transplantable organs went to their wives or kids. They'd be doing something positive with their last gasp. Conceivably the only positive thing they'd ever done. It'd be practically irresistible without faith.

"I need some fresh air," said Jam, heading to the door.

As we got to the door, the PPA was zooming off to the left. I was glad to see it moving away. Although it hadn't been used, I could feel that magnetic attraction. I'd heard it described in France, **L'appel du vide,** the call of the void. Being totally canned up here, and offered that choice on a regular basis, would you listen to the *"Jump!"*?

We stepped into the remainder of the day, which was starting it's edge towards cold that happens quickly in deserts. The central tower of the Hive was a sun dial now, with it's long shadow falling on the east side of the Hive. It had been, if not warm, at least not uncomfortably cool during the day, but now the evening was coming. As the sun was sinking, it was pulling the temperature down with it.

The relief I felt getting out of the cell was real. Imagining the relief of someone living their life here was filling me. I turned to look at Mark.

"It's reeeeal good to be out, ain't it?" he said.

I nodded enthusiastically.

21.

The first few steps onto the freedom of the expansive balcony, after being confined in that roomy cell, made an impression. The cell had no air circulation except what was leaking through the plastic patches over the hatch. Re-breathing air with five partners is hard to describe. We were all presentable, so body odor wasn't the issue. The fresh, that makes air a joy to breathe, is gone after staying in a sealed cell for a couple of hours, even with friends.

This wasn't the first time I'd learned about air and fresh. I'd had my own drunk incident where taking a fresh breath had become precious, too.[S1]. It taught me that the body quickly learns to ignore the unpleasant in favor of the essential. I'd managed to pass a field sobriety test three times in a row beside the highway in San Antonio. But, based on the nose don't lie, the officer decided I needed to meet cell 13 at the Bexar County jail. I figured the breathalyzer would set me free once I got there, I'd passed the field test after all. I learned that an un-zeroed machine in a jail *never* reports low values. There is no way a person with the level of blood alcohol they reported could have stood on one foot, eyes closed, and counted off 30 seconds. THREE times.

Cell 13 was a hermetically sealed metal cell, originally meant for two prisoners. Bench for two, toilet and sink, the solid metal hatch dogged like on a warship. When they opened the door and pushed me in, the stench immediately stopped me from taking a full breath for several minutes. There were about a dozen prisoners in the cell, backs against the wall, legs intertwined like snakes, and they all knew what I was thinking. Collectively, they yelled, "You puke on me you collect a beat down," or words to that effect.

The air was thick with evidence that someone, fairly recently, had collected a beat down. It was dense atmosphere. Breathing it was like swallowing a fish bone. You know you can't do it in small increments, but you try. The common human instinct was recognized by everyone there, and all hands moved me over by the toilet in back, as the snake shifted toward the door. I was stepping between the legs and feet of a rough looking bunch, and all their hands were pushing and lifting towards the toilet in back. They'd all experienced that first moment, too.

I've heard say that since argon (AR) is an

element, and the third most abundant gas in the atmosphere, we've been re-breathing it for the entirety of human history. Being twenty-three times more abundant than carbon dioxide, we breathe a lot of it. A full history of it. Genghis Khan touched things we breathe. We re-breathe Jesus, too!

The minutes it took before I could take a regular breath again, passed slowly, but the time did come. Every prisoner removed to go for booking was replaced, and the routine was repeated. It really is amazing, how fast you can fall in to threatening violence if you're in the wrong crowd. Even while wearing a business suit. Maybe especially while wearing a suit.

There was no time in Cell 13 when I thought about Jesus having breathed the same air. There was no time in Cell 13 when I didn't look up to a newcomer and expect a shower. We all lifted them over to the space where we were safe. It was understandable, and all the rough strangers, and the businessman, worked as a team to move them away from us.

And now, this small group of pioneers in West Texas were going to be remembered as a specific time period. The argon that passed through these lungs would be remembered, too. This struck me as a very strange confluence of thoughts.

Jam was walking beside me as we moved to the edge of the balcony. The cranes alongside the hive were rapidly delivering groups of residents to our floor, and they were moving off to the next section on our left. All of them getting off at our section smiled and nodded at me as they passed. Some were wearing Baby, and carrying gloves like the ones I'd just removed. Many were also carrying musical instruments, whose shape was recognizable, but were of modern interpretation. There were shells of violins[1], guitars, every other type of stringed instrument. As we arrived at the metal railing, I turned to watch them mingling on the far section after they'd crossed the bridge between. As they mingled, and glanced towards us, I thought I could sense their eyes on me specifically.

"What's going on?" I said. Apparently, the entire resident population had been delivered by cranes along the Hive sections and were now slowly moving into a compartment on the next building. Stragglers were not rushing to catch up.

"Concert. Music is life, right?" Jam said.

"Sure," I said turning towards the tower in front of us, "Let's go over ... " but I was struck dumb as I reached the edge by the sight of the progress that had been made on the titanium tree.

The sun was low enough in the sky that the shadow from the leftmost section of the Hive was reaching into the central gun tower of the panopticon. The tower's shadow was piercing the rightmost section. What was mesmerizing was the trenches for the tree.

Each trench marking out the three branches of the titanium tree's roots were now bracketed with mounds of dirt, each as tall as a man where you knew the trenches would be deepest. The piles of dirt were all organized in triangular sections on alternating sides of the trench. Each triangular section was made of fifteen piles like dirt bowling pins. If you squinted you might imagine a snake skinned out on the ground due to the regularity and geometric sense of the piles.

Imagining it as a snake skin, gave space to imagine all the little bots marching to and fro as ants that had found a picnic on a snake carcass. There were lines of bots that were being fed by a shipping container off beside the Host. They would leave it holding a small bar of titanium straight up over their head as a flagstaff, deliver it to the trench, then return to get another.

The thing that really seized my attention was not the pattern of the dirt, the marching bots, or the awareness of how quickly things were progressing. The trenches, being uniformly in shadow now, were screens which displayed the welding going on below. There were scores of bright momentary flashes ricocheting along the trenches. As soon as I saw it, I thought of the early fall storms that rolled across these plains. You could see them coming for miles, with the lightening tracing along the edges of high clouds, long before you could hear thunder.

In that moment, faster than any of the photons generated by the welders, I completely conceived the storm this place was brewing. The amazement of all the things I'd seen no longer seemed bounded. I sensed it. I couldn't define it.

"Jam, this place ... this place it ... " I stammered.

"I know," Jam said, "it's very hard to believe that this is coming our way." He turned towards me. "From a Texas desert home. Who'd a guessed?"

He patted me on the back, and we took a step closer to the railing. As I did, I saw Larisha and Bear leading Aisley and Mandy over to the far left Hive section. They had stopped to look into the nearest root trench. Larisha was waving her arms around demonstrating something. I was going to step up and wave to them through the railing, and Jam was slow trying to stop me.

The instant my hand passed the plane of the railing, the real General Alarm went off. It is loud. Piercing. It reminded me of general quarters alarm on warships under threat. *Whoop. Whoop. Whoop. Whoop.*

I wasn't sure where they were in these systems, all I know was I had been told, and newly trained, to get down. I had been forced down. This time I dove at the floor and did not beat Jam there.

We were both spread eagle on the floor, face to face, and he was smiling so big. The sound of those collapsing to the ground that were wearing Baby I recognized. I was sure I heard some instruments break, too. The sound from the residents I'd heard many times before, when the network goes down in a city of office cubicles. *OOOOOOoooooooohhhhhh!*

"You're pretty fast," Jam said, looking over to me from the floor.

"Rarely miss the ground," I said, smiling back.

I looked over my left shoulder to see all those wearing Baby were on the ground. Those that weren't, were standing and starting to queue up at where the bridge between sections had been. The queues were perpendicular to the bridge for some reason. I looked back at Jam.

"Sorry, Bro," I said.

"No prob. Something for you to see here, too."

Within seconds, a new sound emerged.*Thwap. Thwap. Thwap.* It was coming from the central tower, repeating two or three per second. I could tell it wasn't gunfire, but the sound was doing a good job imitating a solid bullet strike on a meat target.

"What's that?" I said. Jam was completely calm and I turned to check on the crowd at the bridge. They seemed to be fine, but holding the queue way more formally than I would expect. All their instruments were held in front of them in the queue giving the appearance of a human and stringed instrument Dagwood sandwich.

"Those are practice sounds for shots. We recorded an aluminum bat hitting a leather heavy bag. Pretty good, huh?" He rolled over on his back. He held up his arm, plane of his hand perpendicular to the tower, with his arm lined up with a baluster. Instantly a green laser dot appeared on the exposed part of his elbow. I then knew what one *thwap* was about.

"It's a kind of closed loop system," Jam said, "where if you're not on the ground, the system puts one bullet into everything outside defined limits before coming back around for cleanup shots. That's why they're all lined up over there. They look like some kind of fat target so it goofs the system on the trials. Live ammo would take them down in orders of penetration."

"Orders of penetration. That's a term I've never heard before," I said.

Jam looked over to the queued crew standing on the side, at least twenty, and said, "Four shots I think. Five max."

We looked at each other, and mouthed *whew*.

The fake bullet strikes stopped quickly. The tone of the alarm changed to a bell fifteen seconds after the last thwap, then it rang three times.

The stirring of people regaining their feet, retrieving things they'd dropped, and laughing, replaced the alarm. Jam and I were slower getting up, and he slapped me on the back when he did. I leaned over to the railing to see my group waving up to me as they proceeded over to the far left section. I did not touch the railing.

"Let's go on to the concert. The rest will join us there," Jam said. He headed over to where the queue of residents had been. As we approached I understood better what had happened.

Each section of the Hive was aligned as part of a hexagon. There were only four being constructed because two were taken up by the tree and the Host, but the design was clear. Each of the sections was separated by a bridge which dropped out on the alarm, hanging down like a banner between the buildings. One connector on each side just let go, and the remaining side connecting the buildings looked like a pipe wrapped in razor wire with the actual bridge hanging below it.

We were within twenty feet of it when the bridge reconnected itself and the residents continued across. It was an ample bridge, easily twenty feet wide, half as wide as the balcony. The residents all crossed over quickly. One girl, wearing Baby, was fitting together pieces of a viola as she crossed. She did not look up or smile at me.

Looking over the side, I said, "How far is that?" At the bottom was the field of spikes, those not in heavy shadow had sun-side halos. The mirage around those spikes was shaped like a fish scale now. It was breathtaking. It wavered in the blown dust like a living beast.

"Right at fifty feet," Jam said. He pushed me along.

"This is something I know you'll really appreciate. This is part of our worship," he said.

We walked along the balcony as the sounds of instruments tuning up came out of a compartment at the end section of the hive. When we reached the end, there were five compartments that had been combined. Columns replaced wall panels that had defined the cells. People were moving benches stored there out to the balcony. Other benches were being organized inside, and populated by musicians.

Jam led me to seating at the front. The crowd parted for us as we walked to the front, but as soon as we sat down, we were swamped. Young men and women all came up and patted me on the back, smiling, thanking me, saying how glad they were to see me finally.

Thanking me. That got me. The first time I tried to question that, Jam broke right in saying, "There's really no need for that right now." He repeated this more than once. "We're all working to build up a team and decisions still have to be finalized." When he said that one, every single time, they would just put their hand on my shoulder, stare into me smiling, and say, "We just love that you're here." Maybe they'd wink. Then they'd go find a seat. The eerie sound of all the instruments being tuned added to the strangeness.

I was so glad when the tuning was done. A significant portion of the musicians were wearing Baby and had her gloves on. It was a strange orchestra of people and half exoskeletons, including fluorescent bones and hands. When everyone was seated, I noticed a half dozen broken instruments in a pile against the wall.

"Oh man," I said looking at Jam, "Did I do that?"

The words were barely out of my mouth when a young lady sitting behind us, grabbed my shoulders with both hands and leaned into my ear, and said, "They are nothing. We so appreciate the opportunity."

I turned to look at her as she sat back, and there were rows of smiles facing me, every eye in the place, too. I smiled around, nodded, and turned back towards Jam, and said, "Uh-"

"I'm so glad you've taken it off me," he whispered, then jabbed me with his elbow and nodded to the front.

A beautiful young lady, dressed kicker like we all did when we were younger, came up to me. She had the Wranglers, the boots that showed signs of serious stirrup time, and a little bit of bow-legged from time on top. She also had a quirt in her hand wearing the wrist strap, but the falls were mostly gone.

"Jeremy tells us y'all wore out Led Zeppelin IV," she said, nodding to Jam.

"Led Zeppelin in strings?" I said. "No wonder your quirt looks beat."

"Hey, you know it mainly works to scare," she said, smiling to us both before turning to the musicians. She had the thickest black hair and French braid going down to her belt I've seen. Ever.

When she got to the middle of the musicians, she raised both hands, one with quirt, turned and looked right at me. She raised her eyebrows and waited. Jam elbowed me again and I nodded. She turned, and counted it down.

22.

The concert was an unbelievable interpretation of the complete Led Zeppelin IV album in a way that was unimaginable a few minutes previous. In other words, it shocked my reality. It stunned me in the same way it had been, continues to be, shocked every minute since my introduction to this community. The orchestra was an organism, many helped along by Baby, floating on the organized chaos of great rock. They captured the complete, driving spirit of one of the most cherished pieces of rock music from my youth. Dear to my heart, but very different.

After each song, the conductor made mention of some flaws, perhaps even pointing out the person responsible. To my ear, most times, it was an insignificant hitch. The laughing and joking associated with being spotlighted for errors was extremely surprising. Each time the person responsible stepped forward and played the section again, perhaps several times, until it was passable. In almost every case, it was a Baby host. Their mention of time they'd been playing, was obviously to spotlight the rapid advancement of each student's talent for my enlightenment. Each attempt was celebrated with the rowdiest encouraging embrace from the crowd. There was never any embarrassment.

Bear, Aisley, and Mandy were led in by Larisha. Seats were quickly vacated next to us. They were just in time for the start of Stairway to Heaven. That song has always caused an emotional surge underneath whatever I was doing at the time, whether sober or not entirely conscious of my surroundings. How many 8-tracks did I burn up on that album? This time, like my time with Baby and the truest air guitar, there was enjoyment of the music that was attempting to weep out. I caught my breath a couple of times. Each time the waves of warm, quivering goose bumps rose to the back of my neck.

After the concert and the sustained standing ovation, the crowd surged up to me. Jam stepped aside, and the smiles and outstretched hands covered me completely. I now understand how a true rock star might feel. There is some anxiety about a mob of strangers reaching out to touch you, but in this case there was none. It was a tender expression. There were lots of thanks for my being there, pats on the back, and hands laid on me. The crowd was swirling around, enabling each one to share a moment of my space. When I caught Mandy's eye, she was looking as surprised as I felt. On the other hand, Aisley and Bear were standing back smiling like the others. It was all I could do to just keep repeating "Thank you" and "It's so nice to be here." There has never been a time in my life, until this couple of days, where I was so short of words, meaningful or not.

"Ok y'all, we got some things to do," Jam said. "I'm taking them back to some of my best home cooking."

"That's something Jeremy doesn't do for just anybody," said one of the young ladies as she moved aside with the crowd. Moses didn't part the Red Sea any faster. The path exiting the concert compartment cleared quickly as we all moved outside. Then, we were dropped off the Hive in the elevator cage like stones.

We stopped for a moment on our way to the Host to watch the digging and welding bots in the tree's trenches. Larisha gave me a short talk about how they were like mantis shrimp. They were pounding the rocks and soil with their little claws which, in this case, were enhanced with slivers of diamond circle saw blades. Watching the bots work, the dirt being vacuumed as it accumulated, titanium rod pieces delivered and welded all at the same time, seemed other worldly. Tiny bits and pieces, aggregating to something large, was akin to watching ants once more. Thousands of bits were being delivered, which seemed insignificant at any point in time, but the piles, depths, and structure were ever growing. The ditches were deeper, the titanium tree was growing, and it was happening without any obvious human management. Consistently. Precisely. Cohesively.

This was the only time anybody seemed to be in a hurry. Getting back, and into Martin, they encouraged us on in a way that was obviously goal directed. They all wanted us to get out of there with Jam. Nobody would do anything to delay us, unless we asked a question which they answered quickly, while walking with us, and without the patient waiting. Except for the smiling faces, it was the only time in the visit where we'd been rushed in a focused way.

We were aboard Martin quickly, and underway, without even passing out any rifles.

"I know we kind of used up today's hunts," said Jam, "but we might see something going back." Jam was looking around at us. Aisley was leaning up against the rear door wrapped in Bear's arms. Bear and Jam looked to Aisley and she just shook her head.

Mandy was riding next to Jam and she said, "Are you going to clean it for me?"

"I'm betting your man needs practice, lady," he said, with a laugh.

She turned to look at me.

"If you just gotta, I'm sort of not in the mood to get all bloody before dinner."

"Yeah," she said, "and I'd make you take a shower before sitting at the table with us." All the rifles stayed in the overhead.

The trip back was preceded by the rabbit bow wave around the truck, of course. Bear and Aisley weren't even looking out the window. They were involved in a whispered and nuzzled conversation. I was looking out the window, but my mind was not in the truck or on the landscape. All the things I'd seen on this single day were flooding across my mind's eye so that my awareness of the surroundings washed-out. The soundtrack for the musings was the concert, especially Stairway. Mandy and Jam talked a little about the concert but the two of them seemed to be just enjoying the ride, too.

"What time do you need to get away tomorrow?" Jam said finally.

Aisley whispered something into Bear's ear and Mandy turned to look at me. I could tell from her expression she was open to anything I had to say. Normally, she'd have already planned the packing and start time of the return trip. This time, it was different. Totally different.

"I just want to play it by ear I think," I said. "I know Mandy and I aren't in a real hurry, but the kids?" I turned to look at the huddle.

"Mom can watch the kids through tomorrow night," said Bear, "so I guess we only really have to be back before noon, day after tomorrow." He was looking into Aisley's eyes to be sure he didn't misspeak.

"Good. Maybe three more hunts then!" said Jam.

"Jeremy, I'd just rather go back tomorrow and look around some more," said Aisley.

This definitely caught me off guard. Aisley had always been the one that clocked the most time in the blind or on the trail. To have her turn down a hunt was as rare as hen's teeth. Except when she was about to bring on the grandkids, nothing got between her and another hunt. When she was growing up, she about wore me out cleaning her game until she was big enough. She could dress her own, but now it was on Bear because she liked being prissy if she could get away with it. He was a big man and he indulged her, but she was a big hunter. And this time, she was skunked. Bear didn't look as surprised as I thought he might.

"Me, too, Jeremy," said Mandy.

Jam turned to look at me and I just shrugged my shoulders.

"Well then, we can make a night of it and not worry about an early wake up," Jam said. He turned back and leaned against the door looking out. The conversation in the truck completely died. Except for the low throb of the diesel and the hum of the hydraulics, there was dead air for the first time since we arrived.

We were within sight of the fence and road when Jam sat up and said excitedly, "Stop, Martin." Two of the legs were frozen in the air. The diesel idled down immediately.

Without moving, other than to sit up straight, he said, "400 yards, ten o'clock, behind a big creosote bush. Just horns right now."

All of us turned to look, Aisley and Jam pulled up their binoculars.

Aisley was the first to speak, *"Holy Crap!"*

Aisley has seen, and taken, some big deer so that was a serious vote. I knew I'd agree, because when you can make out antlers at that range by visual alone, it meant something good.

"Lemme see," I demanded. When I got the binoculars focused, the buck had stepped into the open. I had to agree. A huge muley buck, a perfectly symmetrical 6x6, with the heaviest horn I'd ever seen. It was standing broadside, perfect shot, and then just dropped it's head and started browsing again. A heavy, healthy West Texas buck in it's prime.

"Oh man, that would be something there," I said. I dropped the binoculars and looked around the cab. Mandy shrugged at me.

"I got mine. I'm done," she said.

"Me neither," said Bear smiling.

I looked around him to Aisley. She looked back at me with an unhurried look I'd never seen when a trophy was within touching. She said, "I'll have another chance."

"Deer like that don't just wander around every day, Lady," said Jam. He turned in his seat to look at Aisley. "They don't get that size being stupid."

Aisley winked at him, and said "I'll get another chance."

Jam didn't even seem surprised. He looked at me for a bare second, then said, "Continue."

Martin came alive again, stepping out towards the road. The buck looked at us, but then put his head right back down.

"Yeah, right. I don't get a say?" I said.

"That's not the one I got tied up for you," Jam said, turning to smile at me. He turned back to watching his side. "I hope you'll get another chance, too."

The buck didn't look up again. They can sense when there are shooters, or happenings, on the ether.

23.

When Martin stepped up to the Trading Post and settled, Aisley and Bear were the first out.

"Do I have time for a shower before we eat?" Aisley said.

"Since we don't have to worry about staying up late," said Jam, "I'll just get it organized and wait till you give me the word. Baked sweet potatoes, salad, and the fattest, dry-aged ribeye." He was nodding in anticipation. "I like mine Pittsburg rare."

"Oh, we're every one of us bloody steak eaters," Bear said. He slapped Jam on the back as he turned towards their tipi.

Jam started to get the rifles out, but Mandy said, "If you think it's ok, we'll just leave them. I'm going to change my mind about that buck by tomorrow I bet." Mandy headed to our tipi, too.

She was looking back to see if I was going to follow, when Jam said, "Jack, why don't you help me in getting the steaks and prep work done, please."

"Sure," I said. I puckered up and smacked a kiss at Mandy and she and caught it in her back pocket wtih a slap and a hip twitch.

Jam led us to the side of Martin's home. There was a double door on the last quarter of the building and a patio with tables and chairs. The wall at the far right separated it so that you didn't have to watch the cleaning processes even if you wanted to. This side was neat and professional. Relaxing by a big fire was the design, set up with some rustic to it. Deer mounts, horns, and some beer signs served as decoration. Of course there was also a wet bar. The huge fire pit was already loaded with heavy mesquite logs.

We entered the building and the change was dramatic. The entire floor was in white ceramic tile. The commercial drain grate running down the center put the proof to all the stainless steel tables, racks, electric meat saws, grinders, and rows of knives in the space.

"If you're going to have meat processing for clients, you have to be FDA approved," said Jam as he headed to the corner. There were two doors, one a heavier door for a meat locker. The other was a glass door, frosted with condensation. He went in the glass door, waving me to follow.

Inside it was all stainless wire racks, 10x20, a cool 35 degrees by the thermometer hanging by the door. The back wall was covered in what I assumed were Himalayan salt blocks. I'd seen this kind of setup at a place in London. They aged meat there for 50 days, and the same smell of old meaty parmesan was thick in the air. I was already starting to drool.

Although the space could have held hundreds of pounds of beef, there were only three large pieces on the racks. They were crusty with rind. As he stopped, he lifted the tag on the first piece.

"About six weeks, ribeye roll," he said. "This one started out around twenty pounds. It's down to about twelve I'd guess."

"I'm in for sure," I said.

He lifted that hunk of meat and put it in my hands, and said, "That's what I need to talk to you about. I've been practicing my pitch to you in my mind for weeks, but now that you're here with your family, I feel just a little uncomfortable."

With a slab of aged beef, stinking beautifully in my hands, the look on my face must have let him know that I was really out of words.

"I need your help. I can see that there could be some potential risk, but I'd like for you to hear me out to the end. Is that something that we can do with all of them here?"

"I can't imagine that they wouldn't be in for another Jeremy adventure at this point," I said smiling. I could feel my head cocked over to the side, hard, I certainly had to have done it, but it was odd because it seemed flamboyantly excessive considering the discussion.

He made that tisk sound you use to drive a horse, walked past me, and we were back to the kitchen.

Over the course of the next hour, Mandy worked on the salad and the sweet potatoes went to bake (she always pokes, oils, AND foil wraps). Jeremy and I trimmed the rind off the beef, making some really nice two inch thick slabs of beef. We laid them out to reach room temperature while we waited for the kids.

Like any group of hunters sitting around a table, stories were being told. Most times, there are lies, too. Jeremy had some good ones about people from the far east, and we had some from the Hill Country and Mexico. There was lots of poking about the best shot, and Mandy was insistent that none of us, except Bear, had shown anything on this trip. She voted herself queen. Since Bear wasn't at the table, he couldn't campaign for himself.

Probably the funniest story was the one Jeremy had about the Japanese group that came down during mule deer season. He'd given them a map, put some way points on their GPS designating their hunting area on the map, and spent some time making sure they could hit what they were aiming at. On the morning of the hunt he sent them out in a jeep on their own. Of course, they'd been getting YouTube degrees in mule deer hunting and knew exactly what to do.

Now, I've spent some time out in the cold looking for the big muley. I've driven around slow all day, hoping for one to jump out of a bush for me, and shot them at 30 yards. Some especially rare ones at 400 yards. I've slow walked miles in full camo, skunk scent, with my .44 mag, and brought some down that I could have taken with a spear. I feel like I have the hunter's eye and can generally see them where others can't. I know how to plan a stalk.

These guys apparently thought they could herd them. Jam said they spent the day driving around their part of the ranch so fast that Jeremy could hear them from the Post. For hours, the four of them harried something over the four sections they'd been assigned. Over the course of the day, he'd heard them shooting intermittently. You can't have guns in Japan, and the selection Jam had for them to select from covered all bases. Those guys were going for the belted magnums only: 7mm, .300, .338. Each one more than enough gun for anything you'd ever see in Texas. Of course, each had booms that carry for miles in open country.

Anyway, towards the late side of the afternoon, one of them walked up back at the Post. He was looking sheepish. They had found a large flock of mountain goats and had shot some. They didn't have licenses for mountain goat, but there were so many they figured they could just buy the license now, and nobody would notice.

As soon as Jeremy said mountain goats, we knew something was coming. He apparently gave them a little scolding. Then he told them that he was friends with the game warden and they'd probably be able to work something out. The messenger went back out, and they came driving into camp with five Spanish goats splayed across the hood. Hardly a one hadn't been seriously tenderized to pieces by those belted mags. Their accuracy had obviously suffered in all the excitement.

I would have paid good money to see the game warden's face, when Jeremy called him up asking what the going rate for Spanish mountain goat was? Somehow, they determined that at two hundred dollars, for each goat, they could let it go.

The meat was packed up and shipped with the explanation that you really can't have a head and hide mounted if you don't have a tag.

For the same reason, you can't be taking pictures of game that was *poached*. Seriously. What would the law say? The Japanese are excellent chefs. But when you start off with an old, desert-raised, Spanish goat buck, there's some tough and rank in there that nobody on this side of the Pacific has ever been able to amend.

I really didn't have any story to beat that. I decided to start telling my old 500 yard bragger anyway, when Bear and Aisley came in. They were freshly showered, changed, and their hair was still wet.

"Your Dad was just starting on some lies," said Jam, "so I'm sure glad you got here when you did."

"Oh yeah, well," Aisley said smiling, "if you give him a chance to get his mouth moving ... " Aisley crinkled up her face. It was the signature look for the woman. From the time she was three till now, we had hundreds of pictures of it, in various stages of maturity. It was the look we all loved.

The table was set and the salad and sweet potatoes delivered.

"I'm thinking we should just gather round and bless the meal before the steaks get on," said Jam. "Since we're all just passing them over the grill, we can start on them as they come off."

"Sounds right as rain," I said. The rest circled up and we held hands.

"Dear Lord," Jeremy began, "We thank you so much for this opportunity to be with friends. Old friends found and new friends welcomed. Thank you for the sacrifice you made on the cross for us. Strengthen our faith as we enter each day anew. Teach us from your word. Guide ... (he shook our hands) ... our(again) steps (again) in *your* ... (he lifted our hands) ways. Bless this feast. In Christ's name."

In unison, "Amen."

The steaks hit the scorching grill, were flipped, and we were all to the table in five minutes. For the first few minutes, there were only animal sounds as the steaks were started. There are meals that are memorable, that can fill dreams for years. This was one of them. With only salt and cracked pepper on them, these aged hunks of meat were exquisite. They were full flavored and tender in a way that the English language cannot fully express. Hence, moans of approval.

As the conversation started coming back, Jam drove it. He was probing deep about our lives, families, and interests. If someone tried to veer it to the hive, something we'd seen, or an unanswered question, he'd deflect it back towards our lives. Before the steaks were done we'd covered generations of Bear and Mandy's families, and many grandchild stories.

"Now, I want to share something with y'all," Jam said. He wasn't wearing the smile that so routinely decorates his face. He looked slowly at each of us in turn.

"You've seen things in the last couple of days, that are, by anybody's definition, world changing. Unbelievable things. Examples of a completely different world and society." He ever so slowly moved his head from side to side. "The one thing that bubbles to the top, when you think about it, is what is man's role *now*? Where do we fit? Do we fit? Is there a place for us when automation is so thoroughly capable?"

The quiet in the room was such that you could hear the light breeze of the evening, humming against the Post on the northwest corner. At the same time, the last lights of the day were filtering in through the shades, with a strong orange and gold hue that gave the room a magical feel. It wouldn't be reaching far to say, at this point, that we all knew something significant was about to happen.

"Up until this moment," Jam said, "there are few people that know what I'm about to tell you." He barely smiled. "My given name is

Jeremiah."

We all laughed out loud. It didn't fit the expectation.

"What? I've known you all my life and nobody called you Jeremiah," I said.

"I know. Crazy, right? I had a relative that was called Johnny all his life when his real name was Milton. In his eighties, he got his name legally changed because it was causing problems," he said. This time the smile was much bigger. "I just didn't like it. Never ever used it. It kind of felt like Jemimah to me, a weird black name, until I learned it. Like Keziah, Jemimah was one of the daughters of Job, one of the only women noted for their beauty in the Bible. Maybe meaning Lady Daylight. And Jeremiah, a great prophet in a disruptive time. Over the last months ..." he let his voice fade out as he looked down and slowly nodded his head.

When he said that, I remembered when a friend's son, probably seven or eight, had said that he wanted to be baptized and claim Jesus as his savior. The scheduling began to make sure the grandparents, aunts and uncles, interested churchy friends, whoever, could be there at the scheduled celebration. Weeks passed with the schedule slipping.

Eventually, Evan finally looked at his

mother and said, "Are you ready for me to be baptized? I am." And that was it. Babes speaking truth. Things happen not on our time.

"That's nice," said Bear. "The prophet involved in great cultural and religious upheaval. I think it definitely fits. As if we'd have a say."

"Thanks for that, I think," said Jeremiah, "You can believe it, right? The cultural upheaval part at least."

There was low murmuring of agreement.

"Now I don't want you to think God spoke into my ear," said Jeremiah, "or that he put words into my mouth like the real Jeremiah, but I feel like we're all supposed to be here today. I know ... know for certain, that choices coming this way are your choices to make." He stood up and went to a lounger in front of the big television. "Come on. Let me draw you some pictures."

As we were settling, the television flashed on to a browser of some type. He controlled it by swiping and tapping his finger on the arm of his chair. He scrolled across pages, most of them discernible maps of the southern United States border areas. The scrolling stopped over the panopticon at buzzard height.

"Some of this stuff," said Jeremiah, "is ... Well, you'll see."

"We have been renting digital microwave capacity that fiber optic common carriers reserve in case they have 'backhoe fade' on their fiber systems. They're paying for it anyway, and we pay them after signing a contract that if they have to cut us off at any time, fine, we just quit paying. We get it at a very cut rate, they pay less for backup capacity."

The map zoomed out showing the entire U.S.-Mexico border but there were heavy black lines trending along the the border, taking dives down towards small towns at the border.

"This is what we call our dark microwave," Jeremiah said. "It's kind of a takeoff on the dark fiber that some of the tech giants have installed around the world. In this case, we're really dark. Nobody counts us because our traffic is on totally non-public routers." He moved the cursor. "These little legs go to small forgotten towns on the border. The guys we're renting capacity from think we're making some pointless broadband push into the boonies."

"We saw that earlier," said Aisley. "I wondered what that was about."

"Your clustered systems seemed way out of proportion for the kind of telecom we thought you could get out here," said Bear.

"Ok. You got me there. I'm glad somebody

understands it. The point is that these small towns are our jumping off point," Jeremiah said. He looked around to us all again with his serious face.

"In just the little amount of time that you've been here, you've seen the quality of the work we can do with the bots and the non-stop speed. Every one of these little towns is already forgotten by their states. When we applied for batch concrete plant permits, or microwave tower permits, or any of the other things that make it look like we're investing in small rural America, nobody thought anything about it. They just wished us well.

"Now, we're just about ready. Let's take a gander at the range south of Sanderson here. That's just about forty miles from here ... this yellow wash is the microwave path from our tower over on the hill."

In the next few minutes he spilled microwave yellow over to the Mexican border and across into vacant spaces on the other side. As it washed into the desolate areas, the shadows caused by intervening hills making fingers, his excitement grew as he pointed out the high points and hills they already had leased for towers on the Texas side. Potential sites had already been designated on the Mexican side. After penetrating deep into desolate areas of Mexico from Texas, he showed us the plans for small town launches all along the Texas, New Mexico, and Arizona borders. There was no time in our visit where he had been spurring the conversation so hard. He was driving direct to a vision.

In every case, the selection of towns was apparently predicated on avoiding the large population centers and focusing on small towns and villages. Sometimes they were just collections of huts on the Mexican side. The fewer roads the better it seemed.

As he talked, the story my father told me about his tour of duty during WWII in France came bubbling up in my conscious. It snuck in slowly. I was aware it was there when Jeremiah first noted that they were avoiding population centers. As he carried his plan all along the border and deeper into Mexico, avoiding the cities, it started pressing on me.

"For some reason," I said, "this reminds me of a story my father told me about his tour in the Army in WWII." They all turned to me and froze. "He landed on Normandy July 6, 1944, one month after D Day, and he was in hard fighting. I know, not because he told me about it, but because Mom pointed out the grenade tattoos on his back one time. It was only after he passed that I decided to get his service record. I found that he had a Silver Star with cluster, Bronze star with V for valor, and of course, the Purple Heart for the grenade near miss. I never saw him without a T shirt, and I forgot that time. Ignorant youth."

I glanced over to Aisley and saw her starting to well up. Her Dondod was the one that learned her hunting. He was a sweet guy, and very spiritual.

"The only two things he ever told me about the war was to avoid being in the infantry because *they really catch it*. The other thing, which struck me weird at the time, was because he shared this just weeks before his passing, out of the blue. He said they would come up against snipers, as they moved through the hedgerows in France, and they would just put flags out so other troops would know there was a guy with a gun in a tree or something. Then they'd just give them a wide berth *if* nobody had been hurt."[S1]

"That's why you're here, I think," Jeremiah practically shouted. "You're going to help us go around. I've been keeping track of you over time with all your deer hunting packages you put together in rural Mexico. You speak the language. You understand the politics and who to grease over there. You're the one that is going to help us grow to the people, and bypass the city corruption. Well ... it's a pretty definite feeling. God don't give us golden tickets with specific directions exactly."

"I just don't really think the market for prison space is all that high," I said, "especially in a foreign country, even if Mexico needs some."

"Oh Daddy," said Aisley. She hadn't called me that in years. She got out of her chair and walked over to put her hand on my shoulder. "They aren't spreading prisons, they're spreading a new vision of life. Our future."

"My fault," said Jeremiah, "I was just so eager to have this particular conversation that I didn't make time to show him the regular housing." He looked at me and shrugged his shoulders. "When I knew your family would be here I figured I'd have them cover that side."

"It's out there now," said Bear, "So we might was well address it. Aisley and I are going to be coming back as soon as we pick up the kids."

"I sort of figured you were fixing to go that way," said Mandy, then she turned to me, and fixed me with the decision-made stare, "And I'm kind of leaning over that way, too. You could tip me over with a feather."

"Uh-oh, what have you done, J ... J ... Jeremiah?" I said. Looking around at their faces it was obvious things were changing, had changed, in my family.

Now it was Aisley's turn to grab a hold of the reins. "They have it worked out so simple, Dad, but so old. This is all a gift which a person can accept or go their own way. Living in other's apartments, or backpacking across the world, even working for the man is still some kind of choice. If a family does decide to walk into this garden, each person in a family is allotted 400 square feet, four times the CTs. Imagine a large family of nine kids. How much easier is that going to be inside 4400 square feet? The only hard and fast rule is that each person, upon joining or upon reaching the age of 13, must do 90 days on the Constitution and Washington's manners, or they have to give that 400 square foot compartment back to the community."

"Foundational training just like a Bar Mitzva," said Jeremiah smiling. "I actually think I may have thought that one up. Maybe?" He smiled at us with puckered up face shaking 'no' rapidly.

"Go on now!" said Bear. "Kick it."

Now Jeremiah was really reining and talking to the team like six in hand.[2] Probes were scheduled at different state crossings, each tower position enabled different microwave penetration across the land. Each time he noted a tower position, he pulled that location over and added it to *my list*. There were fall back positions. There were forward leaning rushes if there was less resistance in a state. Painting the screen with the black lines of tower to tower access, the yellow ponds of their microwave reach, and the green dots of the communities engulfed, the team was taking off with Bear and Jeremiah in leaders, Aisley a springer, and Mandy and I as wheelers. Of course, the oldsters would be wheelers.

Watching him outline the plan, and the others enthusiastic input, reminded me of other times where his proposals were just as intricate. A loud and energetic review, with vivid graphics, and yet my brain could still be distracted. When we were in grade school, almost every day we'd go off hunting with our Daisy BB guns. Imagine, two young boys walking down the streets with working rifles today. In those days, nobody said anything to us. One of us carried our Boy Scout pack with the sandwiches, BBs, and mouse traps.

Most people don't know you can buy packs of mouse traps, and few used them as much as we did. That was the largest expense of our safaris on those days. Six to a pack, we'd buy as many as we could afford. Thirty was barely enough. It was always an expense, because you never can find them all after spreading them over acres.

There were large vacant lots near our houses. They were old farm fields waiting to be made into subdivisions. Now they were overgrown with prickly pear cactus and mesquite, and the borders were thoroughly hemmed by hackberry trees. Acres of cactus. We'd get to the field and Jam ... Jeremiah ... would start laying out the assault plans. He never waited to take charge. You had to keep the mice out of the tree lines or they were home free in the knotty hollows. Those are the paths that would be mined in depth. Going to the other side of the field, the runways they traveled would be mined with traps so that survivors would be channeled to a large cactus mass near the center of the field. That Kings X had to be bigger than several pickups to keep them localized.

When all the mining traps had been placed, we'd start slowly creeping through the cactus, starting from the tree line. Stepping slowly over, between, and through their cactus spine-protected homes. Wild animals don't like it when you're slow. They think you've spotted them, and they'll leave their hide. Back and forth across the fields we'd push them. We'd be resetting the traps, until we were exhausted or we weren't shooting much. At each pass, we'd gather up the carcasses for a brag line. On a good hunt, maybe three hours, there might be two hundred laying out.

"Hey, Jeremiah, you remember those mouse hunts?" I said, interrupting his flow again. He turned and looked directly into me.

"Hmm ... yeah," Jeremiah said, "I kind of wish you hadn't reminded me of that one."

Again in unison, "What?"

"The simple fact is that we will draw serious opposition," said Jeremiah. "If not from the Mexican or American governments, or other countries as we expand, then from organized groups." He was pursing his lips nodding at us. "That's why I warned you, Jack. We'll be sheep. Or mice. "

"But, it sounds like all the good, right? We've seen it!" Mandy said, looking around the room.

"You all know, now,", said Jeremiah, "that we have an unbelievable potential here. We're literally bulging at the seams, ready to get to work. We can feed people, clothe them, and house them faster and more efficiently than at any time in history."

He looked around at each of us not smiling, just nodding slowly.

"At the same time, no matter how poor an area is, there is always some house on the hill. Some entity that skims something from the people down below. The population may survive on two dollars a day, but the house on the hill might have air conditioning. Graft is the gravy that makes so many of these pathetic countries work today. We are going to go around them. We are going to use the blockchain Ethereum to anonymously go directly to suppliers and workers to finance and sustain this project. This *will* generate strong opposition. That's why we're working at the fringes.

"On top of all that, there are those places in the world where the fact of just being different can cause vicious, murderous attacks. Heck, there are places where glad songs of thanksgiving at a wedding can lead to being assaulted with grenades."

I looked around to my family. Each of them had raised eyebrows and cocked their heads to me. Mandy's lips were pursed.

"Jesus' command to Peter," said Jeremiah, "was to feed his sheep.[1] Remember how that worked out for him?" That froze the group. "Are you in? ... Or out?"

I looked across my smiling family, took a deep breath, then I winked at Jeremiah, and said, "Praise Jesus."

They swarmed around me like bees, but they were consumed as quickly as burning thorns; in the name of the LORD I cut them down.

Psalms 118:12

Epilogue

Someone painting a future can cause distress, especially when written by the wolves of the left, but it exercises us. There is a choice at every fork in the road, and one is the more narrow way. People writing about what they see coming allows us to ponder how we'd react. It is exactly like practicing Kung Fu. We train our bodies, and our minds, by exposing them to potentialities.

The changes coming at us, quicker every single day, demand we consider the place we will occupy when much of what we spend our day doing will seem pointless. Do you wake up to work at improving your mind when the entire world has the knowledge of ages within a keyboard click or phone swipe? Do you slump into drugs and waste away the potential that is your God-given strength?

Every person reading this will very soon know the answer, or they're already living it. Having noted that B.F. Skinner was once singing the praises of a Communist country, I think it's important to remind you of his thoughts. There are thousands that think of him as one of the leaders of the 20th century. A reminder of his thoughts, as pronounced via his main character:

"I have little interest in conclusions drawn from history," said Frasier
    Skinner, B.F.. Walden Two (p. 115). Hackett Publishing. Kindle Edition.

Sweet Lord Jesus, keep us from learning those lessons again!

Perhaps the most valuable result of all education is the ability to make yourself do the thing you have to do, when it ought to be done, whether you like it or not; it is the first lesson that ought to be learned; and however early a man's training begins, it is probably the last lesson that he learns thoroughly.

Thomas H. Huxley

Copyright Notice

Endnotes

This is fiction. There aren't any cases that I know of where a work of fiction offers footnotes and endnotes. They were included because everything in this book is constructed around bleeding edge technology existing in 2017. While Uniform Resource Locators (URL) are magnificent in the Kindle version, listing all the URLs in the paperback is unreadable gibberish, almost impossible to accurately transcribe, and so the actual URLs are not included. For example, URLS http://en.wikipedia.org/wiki/URL, but a more exhausting example is the one for the World's Fastest Deer Cleaning http://www.youtube.com/watch?v=XF2kKqjvG08

Hopefully, your interest in specific references will lead you to the internet if you're reading the paperback. I did my best to give a text description that would search the net and get you near your goal.

Chapter 2

Chapter 3

Chapter 4

Chapter 5

Chapter 6

Chapter 7

Chapter 8

Chapter 9

9-1:   Psalms 111:2 "Great are the works of the LORD; They are studied by all who delight in them."

9-2:   Jewish Cowboys

Chapter 10

10-1:   Sixth Sense gestural computing
10-2:   Laser tag fruit
10-3:   Hyacinth bean
10-4:   Corn field in a room

ear of corn 2.5"x 8" = 20 sqin of hanging space needed/ear

35,000 heavy field planting/acre x 20 sqin = 700,000 sqin

700,000 sqin = 4861 sqft

assuming vertical garden on 4'x8' panels, three stories high

4 - 4'x8' panels = 128 sqft per 3 story panel (32' high)

4861/128= ~ 38 panels 3 story high

7 panels in a row=28 feet will fit in one room (30' deep x 15' rooms)

therefore, ~= 6 rows, in a room 12" apart is perfect

Chapter 11

11-1:   Thoreau quote from Walden "I dug my cellar in the side of a hill sloping to the south, where a woodchuck had formerly dug his burrow, down through sumach and blackberry roots, and the lowest strain of vegetation, six feet square by seven deep, to a fine sand where potatoes would not freeze in any winter."

Chapter 12

12-1:   Skinner, B.F.. Walden Two (p. 17). Hackett Publishing. Kindle Edition.

12-2:   CRISPR genetic editing

12-3:   "Your members work only four hours a day?" Skinner, B.F.. Walden Two (p. 45). Hackett Publishing. Kindle Edition

12-4:   " The profit system is bad even when the worker gets the profits, because the strain of overwork isn't relieved by even a large reward." Skinner, B.F.. Walden Two (p. 45). Hackett Publishing. Kindle Edition

Chapter 13

13-1:   When everything we associate with agriculture can be a mimic grown in production quantities…imagine the possibilities!

13-2:   Chicken strips from a lab

Chapter 14

Chapter 15

by Senator Eugene McCarthy (D-Minnesota 1959-1971), ran for the Democrat U.S. Presidential nomination five times on a peace platform. In his book he argues that America has been reduced to a colonial position due to self-inflicted policies and a leading cause of the entropy in our culture is multicultural multilingualism. The subhead for the book failed to warn us then, when it said "America's senior statesman warns his countrymen."

He quotes William Torrey Harris on page 104 to great effect: "The full protection of one class of the population from another cannot be secured, unless all speak the same language."

Therefore, the future belongs to a language. What do YOU think the One World Government is going to use to communicate?

Zephaniah 3:9

15-3:   "Age is no better, hardly so well, qualified for an instructor as youth, for it has not profited so much as it has lost. One may almost doubt if the wisest man has learned anything of absolute value by living. Practically, the old have no very important advice to give the young, their own experience has been so partial, and their lives have been such miserable failures, for private reasons, as they must believe; at it may be that they have some faith left which belies that experience, and they are only less young than they were. I have lived some thirty years on this planet, and I have yet to hear the first syllable of valuable or even earnest advice from my seniors.

Thoreau,   Henry   David.   Walden (Annotated) (p. 5)

Chapter 17

17-1:   George Washington's Rules of Civility and Decent Behavior

17-2:   Thoreau, Henry David. Walden (Annotated) (p. 40). DB Publishing House. Kindle Edition.

Chapter 19

All the Mujtahids are unanimous in their opinion that the manufacture, sale and purchase of musical instruments is Harām and the income derived from musical activity is also Harām. The transactions involving these (instruments) are invalid. It is Harām even to keep instruments of music in one's possession. It is obligatory to destroy them. This is revealed in a lengthy tradition of Imam Ja'far as-Sadiq (a.s.) as recorded in the book "Tohafful Uqūl".

For a more modern Islamic take on music see "The Music Made me do it" by Dr. Gohar Mushtaq

Chapter 20

20-1: Prisons and Drugs

20-2: Death Penalty

20-3: from www.ocregister.com/articles/tissue-731858-fetal-research.html

The Orange County District Attorney's Office is suing two related Yorba Linda medical companies, saying they're illegally profiting off the sale of fetal tissue donated by abortion providers.

Chapter 21

21-1: PROD: Silent Violin

Chapter 23

23-1: John 21:17

Author Inspiration

I know you've had the feeling at times, that you've been presented with something that you just can't ignore, it's not any of your business. But, it weighs on you, bending your world and your very physical existence into granting it a hearing. You can only take so many sleepless nights, loud internal conversations, and bowls of ice cream before it forces action.

I've had this happen to me a few times in life and I can now recognize the signs. Nevertheless, every time, I try to talk myself into being calm. Ignore it. *You're taking this way too serious.* But, like this time, it causes so much tension in my daily existence that I have to get it *OUT*! It's exactly like the insomniac lusting for a good night.

I want that peace again, thought Jonah.

He tried to get peace by running away, but you can't really do that if you're called to something.

But Jonah got up and went in the opposite direction to get away from the LORD. He went down to the port of Joppa, where he found a ship leaving for Tarshish. He bought a ticket and went on board, hoping to escape from the LORD by sailing to Tarshish."

Jonah 1:3

I know what fired this one up. I can't remember when it first started worrying me, but I can remember the exact moment it burst into flame. Some writer had been discussing "Walden Two" by B.F. Skinner and something caught my interest. I'd been exposed to it in high school but I didn't remember a word of it, or have more than a vague memory that the famous psychologist author believed people were as trainable as dogs.

I downloaded "Walden Two" from Amazon onto my phone and immediately noticed that B.F., as I will forever after refer to him, had written a new introduction in 1976 entitled "Walden Two Revisited". Since this was decades after he originally published the book in 1948, I thought I'd check there first. He might have learned something important in the intervening years.

As I read B.F.'s new review, I started marking phrases that made me squirm. " ... control of human behavior had emerged as a central topic."

That one makes you look for the red flag, literally. Seeing the same leftist rants about "the exhaustion of resources, the pollution of the environment, over-population", etc. just informs me that they have been missing the true path for decades.

Scientists with political agendas which allows them to say with pride "Communism was no longer a threat" will always be with us I guess. Tens of millions of people are looking down on that statement, standing next to the Lord. It seems that scientists, the ones that should know about the ingenuity of man, are forever betting against the ingenuity of man. And God.

"Great are the works of the Lord, studied by all who delight in them."

Psalms 111:2

As I read, I was taking so much time highlighting text and taking notes of the leftist cant, that it was starting to make me angry. As an example of B.F.'s arrogance, I noted he said " ... contraception could keep the population within bounds." How many of those people alive today are outside his bounds? There were approximately 2 billion people in 1945, and in 2016 estimates are about 7.5 billion. Do you want a Communist apologist making those culling decisions?

No doubt, I'm sure, that his academic

friends would be happy to erase some of us based on their educated guestimates.

The line that actually lit the fuse was "China may be closer to the solutions I have been talking about" and it made me shudder. Here was B.F., an educated, well-respected researcher that was able to overlook the bloody disaster of the Chinese **Great Proletarian Cultural Revolution (1966-1976).**

Does it make you feel comfortable that leaders in our elite universities could look past millions of wrongs? It's not like the party had just started and we didn't know yet where it was going. For ten years, there had been every sort of abuse of human beings in the name of communism, but the goal was obviously worth the cost to Mao. And accepted, apparently, by B.F.

When I think of small groups of academics sitting around pondering things like, "Behavior could be changed by changing its consequences–that was operant conditioning– but it could be changed because other kinds of consequences ... " and at the same time praising the wisdom of Mao ... ?

I'm more convinced than ever that the founders were divinely inspired to include the Second Amendment in our Bill of Rights. Having B.F. and his friends deciding how to manipulate free United States citizens is something I hope we can still be enthusiastic about fighting. This is what gave spiritual fire to this endeavor.

Instead of trying to manipulate free men, the goal should be the rehabilitation of those that refuse to live peaceably with their fellow man. B.F. admitted that the world was a large and intricate balance of human beings that really couldn't be modeled well in his utopian society of only a thousand people.

B.F. Skinner, in Walden Two, tried to model a small utopian society, after World War II, using his behavioral engineering ideas. He also didn't feel there was any need to be fearful of communism any more. Among many of his ideas, the idea that babies should be removed from the parents in favor of the commune (state?) didn't strike him as strange at all.

When B.F. took another stab at reviewing his book twenty five years later, he still held no fear of communism. By that time, millions had died and he still thought that communist China was a respectable country. In his behaviorist speak, he wondered about how to induce the proper think in America.

Walden Shock is a book telling an American story about how a utopian society will be modeled. We're entering very interesting times where Artifical Intelligence and robots are challenging every part of society. The majority of our population now worry about their jobs being automated. The founding principles of individual freedom, as stated in the United States Constitution, are worshiped in this story, not thrown away in favor of inducing behaviors in the citizens.

Because the characters of Walden Shock are Texans of faith, there are callbacks to their religion, just as B.F. makes calls to operant conditioning or behavior engineering in his book. There are experiences and beliefs that infuse each of us, color our decision making, and inform our interactions with our environment. B.F. agrees with that.

In his book, B.F. notes, "Offenders are seldom improved by being sent to prison."

A goal of this book is to mark that statement as passe. A large part of this story is imagining what a prison of the future will be like. Offenders will be improved, and operant conditioning may actually be a part of it. However, unlike Walden Two, no part of this vision suggests removing children from their parents.

We are standing at the edge of a new universe. Whether it is a precipice, or an elevator to unimaginable heights, is not a sure prediction; there are people imagining both sides. The point, surely coming, when our machines become more capable and knowledgeable than the great majority of mankind will turn us into something new.

This technological singularity, this explosive advancement in knowledge and capability, is predicted to occur (it is now Spring 2017) as early as 2040. There are people saying that within a few years the typical radiologist is going to be a computer application. There have already been incidents of artificial intelligence systems generating their own language to communicate, which led the developers to shut them down.

If your self-worth is determined by your job, by your intricate skill set, or deep knowledge about any particular field, that capability is being supplanted faster than you can possibly imagine.

Without looking at Artificial Intelligence and its advances into self-discovery of Newton's Laws of Physics, or the power of quantum computing to harness processing power unimagined even theoretically a decade ago, I think we can know when the Singularity is imminent: a robot cracking an egg and serving it to you over easy. When you see that, what are you going to fall back to?

And the Lord answered me: "Write the vision, make it plain on tablets, so he may run who reads it."

Habakkuk 2:2

www.ingramcontent.com/pod-product-compliance
Lightning Source LLC
Chambersburg PA
CBHW071635260626
47170CB00001B/110